Fort Worth Cops

The Inside Stories

Fort Worth Cops

The Inside Stories

by Kevin Foster,

J.C. Williams Jr.

& Kathy Sanders

Published by Fedora, LLC, 2024

The names and characters in this book are often fictitious but the events in this book are based on real events from the history of the FWPD.

"Fort Worth Cops – The Inside Stories
First edition. November 2024

Dedication

Law enforcement officers are often referred to as "sheepdogs" because they stand guard against society's wolves – the nefarious, criminal and oft times, evil, among us. I disagree.

The best officers I've ever known lived to hunt the wolves, not wait for them to strike. They sought out, captured, and dealt with these predators to protect all of us.

This book is for them.

- Kevin Foster

Acknowledgements

The stories in this book are the product of oral histories; the telling and retelling, passing from one generation to the next. Committing these stories to paper required the help of many retired law enforcement officers. As time passes, memories fade and events are remembered differently by the participants. Some of our sources and key characters in our stories have passed away, but nonetheless, these stories have been captured to the best of our memories and abilities. It would be almost impossible to recall the source of every story that contributed to this effort, but we will do our best.

First, we wish to thank our readers and advisors for their insights and suggestions on how to assemble this book. A very special thanks goes to Professor Richard Selcer, Benita Falls Harper, and my oldest and dearest friend, John Marshall. This book could not have been completed without them and their input. Also, Special thanks to retired Lieutenant L.E. "Spider" Webb for his many stories and for sharing his memories with us, both in oral and written form.

From the Major Case and Homicide sections, we wish to thank Joe Wallace, David Thornton, Dana Miller, Danny LaRue, Ray Sharp, Larry Steffler, Larry Taylor, and Paul Kratz.

From Special Investigations - Vice & Narcotics unit, we wish to thank J.C. Williams Sr., Dub Bransom, Charlie Hogue, Ray Fisher, Bob Shaw, Ray Armand, Larry Alphin, Ronnie Gouyton, Hondo Porter, Nick Bradford, Garry Darby, Mike Miller, and Bob Bishop.

The Patrol Division of the police department has always been and always will be the backbone of the Fort Worth Police Department. Without exception, EVERY officer contributing stories spent time sitting in patrol cars and answering calls for service.

Some of these officers have chosen not to be identified in the stories they contributed, but we wish to thank every officer for their contribution. Among the many officers we wish to thank include are B.J. Erby, Eddie Pricer, David Marshall, Leonard Schilling, Phil South, Paul Strittmatter, Horace Phillips, Curtis Chesser, Doug Moss, Tammy Waxman, Lynn Bellar, Cliff Hankins, and Jimmy McCarthy. There are others, but far too many to list.

We also wish to thank every officer who was assigned to Weed and Seed. They made great contributions with their oral histories and have our enduring gratitude.

Table of Contents

Chapter 3 - Vice Intelligence and Enforcement

Chapter 9 – Leadership

FOREWORD

"It turns out that a book is more durable than a stone, more durable than a castle and more durable than an empire."

Jordan Peterson

"Then I heard the voice of the Lord saying "whom shall I send? And who will go for us?" And I said, " Here am I send me!"

- Isaiah 6:8

Law enforcement officers often stand witness to the worst of society. Killings, torture, child abuse, vicious sex crimes, stabbings comprise just another day at the office. They also witness incredible events, often bordering on the absurd, improbable and hilarious. But the stories have largely been kept in the family – those involved told other officers, their friends and sometimes, their families.

These accounts serve as an oral history of crime, criminals and cops in Fort Worth, Texas, and need to be preserved.

As such, several years ago, we created a social media group for retired officers as a platform to tell their stories. We hoped to preserve these stories for future generations - a legacy of these officers, their experiences and their reactions.

We also wanted an outlet for numerous officers who, not surprisingly, suffer from Post-Traumatic Stress Disorder (PTSD). It is cathartic for these cops – who experience agitation, anxiety, depression, flashbacks, headaches, memory issues, nightmares, suicidal thoughts, alcohol or drug abuse and mood swings from this disorder – to talk and write about what they encountered.

Officers witness hundreds of traumatic experiences during their career, while most people may have a few in their lifetime. How many mangled bodies from car wrecks does John Doe see? How many people have seen a body outside a funeral home? How many have found the bludgeoned, bug-infested body of a missing 10-year-old in a trash-strewn creek bed?

Writing down their experiences and talking with others who understand, helps these men and women cope with these tragedies – a constructive way to reduce the impact on their lives.

The group we started enjoyed wild success, resulting in hundreds of astonishing stories, heart-wrenching scenarios and hilarious memories. Amazingly, the overwhelming response - even from non-cops who followed along - was simple, "You should write a book."

We agree. This is the result.

We culled through the stories and chose what we believed to be the most entertaining, poignant and interesting experiences. Unless otherwise noted, we are withholding the names of people central to these accounts. As the Dragnet television series taught us, the names have been changed to protect the innocent. In some instances, we have attached a fictitious name to a victim or criminal to lessen confusion within the story. It is noted.

In most cases, accuracy is measured by the storyteller's memory. Since memory is a funny thing, some details may be sketchy or missing, particularly when the incident occurred decades ago. Please remember, not every murder is deemed newsworthy. Some murders are not sensational in scope, the victim not "sympathetic" or it might just be a busy news day. Some stories just don't make the cut at your local newspaper.

Most, if not all these accounts, are based in Fort Worth, Texas, and range throughout the city. We have tried to generalize the locations for you from a geographical perspective.

Most of the stories are recounted by Kevin Foster and J.C. Williams, Jr., both veteran cops.

Foster retired as a sergeant from the Fort Worth Police Department and a lieutenant from the Texas Christian University Police Department in Fort Worth. He has been a law enforcement officer for 45 years.

Williams retired as a highly respected FWPD commander and as the assistant police chief with the TCU police department. His family is a FWPD dynasty, beginning with his uncle and father (a wild, colorful Fort Worth cop). His son recently retired as a Fort Worth police detective.

We hope you enjoy our book

Chapter 1

Tragedies, Terrors and Killers

"People sleep peaceably in their beds at night only because rough men stand ready to do violence on their behalf."

— George Orwell

Facing the Devil

Told by Kevin Foster
with Kathy Sanders

Police officers encounter crime scenes so hellish, scars become embedded into their souls. Time may soften the jagged edges, but it cannot dull the gut-wrenching pain those memories cause.

Often, these tragedies involve kids who fall victim to diabolical violence

For me, it happened on July 30, 1995.

It had been a typical Sunday morning until the shooting calls came in from Les Jardins Apartments near Travis Avenue Baptist Church on the city's south side. Before it ended, three small children were dead, their mother was riddled with bullets, a responding police officer was critically injured, and two others had been shot.

It happened after an apartment resident snapped upon being accused of molesting a six-year-old girl he'd been babysitting. He grabbed his arsenal of guns and began his deadly spree.

That morning, Angie Anderson, a single mother of three kids, confronted her occasional babysitter, John Leslie Wheat. Her oldest daughter complained about the assault and the incensed mother wrote Wheat a scathing note, including her plan to call police.

After talking with a friend, Anderson headed to a public phone to make the call when she saw an armed Wheat running after her, firing. Screaming that he was crazy, Anderson ran into a neighbor's apartment and hid in a closet. Wheat charged after her, shooting until he thought she was dead. Wheat had only begun.

He moved around the upstairs sidewalk to the apartment of the on-site security guard. The guard, awakened by the gunfire, went to his window and looked out. Wheat shot him through the window, shattering the femur in one of his legs.

Then the 51-year-old church maintenance worker walked out and headed to Apartment 39, where Anderson had left her children.

He chased the children into their bedroom, screams and gunshots sounded, then he left, closing the door, neighbors said. Wheat was on the hunt for more victims. Another resident was shot through his door.

Wheat moved back upstairs to the second-floor walkway where he had an eagle-eye view of the courtyard and the front of the complex. He repeatedly shot at passersby but missed.

Nearby officers rushed to the scene, summoned by the gunfire and dispatchers.

A resident waved his arms and shouted to arriving officers in a vain attempt to warn them. He was shot in the chest, the bullet exiting his back.

Two of my officers, Angela Jay and Woody Holman, were immediately ambushed – Holman had already entered the apartments when shots were fired. He sought cover, while Jay, who was still outside the complex, was shot repeatedly before she could follow.

I arrived in time to see Jay seeking cover at the entrance while the sound of gunfire filled the air. Covered in blood, Jay was still at the entrance to the apartments where she had been shot. I couldn't find Holman and he didn't respond when I yelled for him. Finally, he answered, and I knew he was alive.

You could hear screams from inside the complex punctuated by rifle fire. Wheat wasn't spraying random gunfire. His firing was slow and steady. He had targets and he was aiming.

Other cops began surrounding the complex. Holman had unknowingly found cover underneath Wheat's position; the critically injured Jay was with me at the entrance to the apartments. Officers Jimmy McCarthy and Matt Smith were working at the nearby church when they heard the gunfire. They came running and joined the two of us at the entrance.

Wheat, a warped failure of a man, realized he was surrounded and outgunned. He gave up and asked us not to hurt him. The four of us took him into custody.

"When he realized he was overpowered and that he himself might get killed, Wheat took the cowardly way out,'' said Homicide Sgt. Paul Kratz.

The critically injured Jay was rushed to the hospital by another officer. Jimmy McCarthy and I quickly found Anderson curled up in the neighbor's closet, alive but barely breathing. McCarthy stayed with her, and I went back outside, unaware there were more victims.

Other residents who'd witnessed the gunfire were screaming and pointing to the security guard's apartment. I ran to the shattered window and saw him on the floor. I kicked open the door and found him alive and conscious. I briefly searched the apartment for more victims and told the guard help was on the way.

As I walked out his door, other residents pointed downstairs to Apartment 39. It belonged to Anderson, Wheat's first victim. I went inside and immediately was stunned at the sight of 20-month-old Lacey Anderson, lying on the floor, a gunshot wound to her forehead. Blood and brain matter covered the floor behind her head. I opened the door to the kids' bedroom and saw the bodies of two more children - Eddie Ochoa, aged 8; and Ashley Ochoa, aged 6.

Eddie was kneeling at the side of a twin bed, and he had been shot in the head. Ashley also had been shot in the forehead while she crouched in a corner of the room by a closet. All the children were shot with .45 caliber bullets.

I thought they were all dead. But one of the officers following me noticed the baby was still breathing – she died the next day at the hospital.[1]

The four others shot survived.

Jay returned to duty nine months later, though shrapnel and one bullet remained in her years later. Anderson remained hospitalized for several months and suffered brain damage from the shooting.

Nearly six years later, Wheat was dead, executed by the State of Texas for his crime.

His last words, "I deeply regret what happened. I did not intentionally or knowingly harm anyone. I did not do anything deliberately."[2]

Bullshit is all I have to say to that.

None of us involved were rookies. We all knew the score and still it affected us more than any other case I've ever seen. I was thinking of those children too often and hated the sight of those apartments, especially in the daytime. I eventually transferred back to the midnight shift. We had faced unspeakable evil. We all saw the face of the devil that day. The memories never die.

The Serial Killer

"Some people just need killing"

Told by J.C. Williams Jr.
With help from Paul Kratz
& Danny LaRue

Ricky Lee Green truly was the most evil, twisted, sadistic killer I've ever met. I'd been to more than 100 homicide scenes, spent 38 years in law enforcement dealing with criminals and their vicious, bloody handiwork yet Green overshadowed them all. I came away from a relatively brief conversation with the serial killer knowing he relished killing and convinced he was ridding the world of undesirables. When I asked why he'd killed his victims, he replied simply and coldly.

"Some people just need killing."

The State of Texas put Green to death in 1997 for one killing but he pleaded guilty to three other sexual mutilation slayings. One psychiatrist wrote that Green also told him, "He had killed 15 other people and that he believed that he was doing the country a favor by killing 'whores' and homosexuals," according to court records.

I was on the periphery of the investigation delving into the murders after Green, 28 at the time, confessed in April 1989 to killing four people – Jeffery Davis, 16; Betty Jo "Montana" Monroe, 28; Sandra Lorraine Bailey, 27; and Steven M. Fefferman, 28. All were viciously killed in less than two years, between 1985 and 1986.

Fefferman's death garnered the most media interest because he worked as a Fort Worth television advertising executive who died Dec. 27, 1986.

Fefferman, who was gay, encountered Green and the two eventually traveled to Fefferman's condo on the city's east side. Green convinced his host to be tied to the bed, saying they would switch places later.

Instead, Green stabbed Fefferman 47 times with a butcher knife from Fefferman's kitchen. He slashed his victim down the front of his body and then castrated Fefferman and shoved the appendage down the victim's throat.

With Fefferman mortally wounded, Green scavenged cash from the home, then fled in Fefferman's car. Fefferman's body was found two days later.

I talked with the lead homicide detective, Danny LaRue, at the time and went over the crime scene photos. We knew this disturbed psycho had done this before and would continue until police caught him.

In fact, Green had. Teenager Jeffrey Davis ended up dead after meeting Green, who disappeared in March 1985. The next month, his headless body was found at the Fort Worth Nature Center. Green told police he stabbed Davis to death, severed the teen's penis and tossed it away.

Six months later, Green encountered 28-year-old Betty Jo Monroe, who also referred to herself as Montana. She was a drifter from Amarillo who sometimes danced topless to earn money. Monroe accompanied Green to his mobile home in an adjacent county, where Green said he, Monroe and his wife, Sharon Dollar Green, had sex. Then Monroe was stabbed 17 times and struck in the head with a hammer. One breast was mutilated. Her body was found the next day, Oct. 13, 1985, dumped on the side of the road. Identification efforts failed – investigators referred to her as Mama Doe because she had a Cesarean section scar. In 1989, fingerprints from the Amarillo Police Department led to her identity.

A month later, on Nov. 23, 1985, Green met Sandra Lorraine Bailey at a bar in Fort Worth and took her home to the mobile home, where his wife was waiting. Bailey didn't want to participate in a threesome, but the Greens bound her and while Ricky Green raped her, she was stabbed 30 times. Bailey was also struck with a hammer and sexually mutilated. Her body was found Dec. 2, 1985.

Neither he nor his wife – who was convicted in the slayings of Monroe and Bailey – were charged in connection with any other slayings that occurred after Fefferman died. Nearly a year and a half passed with no new information.

Green's wife left him and while undergoing alcohol and drug rehabilitation, she told a counselor about the killings. She subsequently called Crimestoppers in April 1989 and offered details about the deaths.

Fort Worth homicide detectives, led by homicide Sergeant Paul Kratz, moved fast.

A large contingent of detectives swarmed Ricky Green's home in Azle, a Fort Worth suburb on April 27, 1989.

When they received no answer, they tried to repeatedly kick the door open. When they geared up for another kick of the steel door set in a steel frame, Green peeked out a curtain and finally opened the door. He told Kratz he held the pistol while trying to decide if he was going to give up or shoot it out with police.

In interviews with investigators, Green admitted to killing four people. When they finished talking with him, LaRue came to me in Major Case and asked if I could stay with Green in the interview room until they could arrange to get him to jail.

I was happy to help my friend. When we walked the hallway, we saw several people congregated outside the door. LaRue told everyone to leave because I was staying with Green.

Resources were strained on this crazy day and the others needed to get back to work. We walked into the interview room and LaRue turned to Green with a smirk and a short laugh.

"Green, you may think I am kidding, but if you try anything," he said, pointing at me. "He is going to pull your head off."

I smiled. LaRue was serious and knew firsthand arrested suspects could be dangerously unpredictable. An armed robbery suspect unexpectedly attacked him and fought for his gun in an elevator.
As I sat alone with Green, we didn't talk initially, and I began thinking of the Fefferman crime scene photos and the other killings he'd done. Green remained emotionless, just a cold-blooded, remorseless killer.

Knowing I wouldn't see him again, I asked him, "Do you have any thoughts, feelings or reasons for murdering these different victims?" That's when he said that some people needed to die.
That statement confirmed to me that he would kill again, if given the chance.

I spent time checking into Green's background as a capital murder case was prepared against him.

Family members and acquaintances described a brutal life Green endured at the hands of his abusive father, Bill Green, who by all accounts tortured his four children constantly.

A cousin told me that as children, he and Ricky Green were thrown into a geese pen to be "eaten by the geese." Instead, they were bitten repeatedly before they were released.

I learned Ricky, his brothers, Perry and Timothy, and a sister were physically abused by Bill Green. For example, he would apply electric shocks to their bodies, punch them in their stomachs and, on fishing trips, hold them underwater until they nearly drowned. His sister testified in court that she was sexually molested by her father. Ricky had a horrible, violent childhood, which may have helped him develop into the stone cold killer he became.

Sharon Dollar Green was convicted in the murders of Bailey and Monroe. But she received probation for two 10-year sentences.
A jury convicted Ricky Green of capital murder in Fefferman's killing and was sentenced to death. He pleaded guilty in the other three slayings and received life sentences in those cases.

After his appeals were exhausted, Green, then 38, was killed by lethal injection on Oct. 8, 1997. His last words included his religious awakening, thanks to his friends on death row and a backhanded apology to the victim's families, "I do want to tell the family that I am sorry, but killing me is not going to solve nothing," he said.
"I really do not believe that if Jesus were here tonight that he would execute me. … Thank you, Lord. I am finished."

I must admit, I was glad, knowing the community was safer with him dead.

Murder of the Professor

Told by J.C. Williams Jr.

With help from Paul Kratz
& Danny LaRue

My first homicide as commander of the Violent Personal Crimes unit took me back to my childhood.

Homicide Sgt. Paul Kratz called me about midnight on Nov. 8, 1994, telling me a burning body bound to a fence post had been found and I needed to be there. The media would be there in droves.[3]

While driving to the scene, a remote area on the far east side of Fort Worth, I was stunned to realize it was my childhood stomping grounds, next to the house where I'd grown up.

The house where just months earlier I cared for my cancer-stricken dad before he died. The house where my mom suffered and killed herself. The house where I learned that my mentor had been shot to death. A slew of other childhood memories washed over me.

When I arrived, the burned body lay in a field smoldering with the accompanying odor of burning flesh. The only recognizable feature of the man was his legs – they had not burned. To me, they resembled legs of an elderly man.

Kratz believed the killing may be gang or drug-related, similar to other recent slayings.

Our victim subsequently was identified as 77-year-old Lyle Williams, a World War II veteran and a popular history professor at Texas Wesleyan University. He'd been married for 41 years, but recently divorced.
He was living with an ex-convict recently released from prison. Williams had become prison pen pals with Lana Williams and allowed her and her three adult sons to move in with him.

As the investigation moved forward, one of Lana's sons was arrested during the Thanksgiving holiday. Ronald Stevens refused to cooperate or take a polygraph test to clear his name in the killing.
Even with her son jailed in the killing, Lana Williams refused to cooperate with police.

That forced Homicide Det. Curt Brannan to explore different tactics. Unknown hairs were found at the crime scene and we decided to pursue that, knowing the family had pets.

With Kratz on vacation, Sergeant Joe Wallace, Brannan and I coordinated to arrange the fur-plucking adventure. We went to the Williams' home to gather fur from the family cat. A match with the hairs from the crime scene would implicate someone in the home.
As crime scene officers took the feline to the garage to collect samples, Lana Williams and others sat nervously on the couch. All we heard was cat screams that got louder each time a hair was plucked. The screams completely unnerved Lana Williams. She began sweating and became more disturbed with each scream from her cat.

Eventually, the crime scene officer opened the door and asked permission to let the cat back into the house. I said yes and he let go. The cat jumped from his arms, flew through the air and bounced off the woman's chest.

She turned to us, completely broken, and said she would cooperate. And that was the turning point in the case.

I always found it interesting that Lana Williams was more concerned about the perceived torture of her cat than of her son sitting in jail accused of murder.

Detectives discovered that a woman named Lisa Witcher Stevens – who became friends with Lana Williams in a Louisiana prison – had moved in with the Williams' when she was released from prison.
Witcher got mad at Lyle Williams and strangled him with an electrical cord and hit him multiple times in the head with a hard object. She bound Williams' hands, tied him up and took him to my childhood neighborhood. Witcher hoped police would think

Williams had been killed after a robbery. She then set the gasoline-soaked body afire, hoping to incinerate any incriminating evidence. Though she acted alone, she told Lana Williams about killing the professor.

Cuban Exiles vs. Fort Worth Police

Told by J.C. Williams Jr
with help from Ray Fisher
&Larry Alphin

Recalling the 1980s summons memories of a vicious and deadly decade, fueled partially by the emergence and spread of crack cocaine, brutally terroristic drug rings and the popularity of criminal gangs.

One of Fort Worth's biggest challenges began in 1980 during the six months of the Mariel Boat Lift, where 125,000 Cubans immigrated to the United States in 1,700 fishing and shrimp boats. Most of these people just wanted a chance at a decent life. A few, however, were career criminals with no respect for authority.

Many of these criminal Marielitos bore tattoos between their fingers, certain ones for homicide, robbery, rape, and kidnapping. The violent ones who ended up in Fort Worth had all tattoos. Like this demon named Bobby Palomino.

Palomino and others like him terrorized local criminals and took over the narcotics and illegal operations in Fort Worth. They were extremely violent. Officers faced greater dangers from them as well – they had no respect for authority and no fear of reprisals.

As federal agencies began working cases involving these Marielitos across the nation, members of our Special Investigations unit heard a rallying cry from Fort Worth's Lt. Ray Fisher.

"This is Fort Worth, Texas, and we are NOT going to have this," he told us. Fisher directed us to target this group for the next few weeks. Narcotics officer Garry Darby, took over the preparations for search warrants.

Enter Palomino, who was leading the Fort Worth faction of Marielitos in drugs. One of our search warrants was at one of his houses.

More experienced officers said we could draw straws to see who would break down the front door and be the first inside. That was unnecessary, I said. I'm doing it.

We expected gunfire. Supervisors gave me a new, large, heavy shield to use for protection. At the time, there was no SWAT team or tactical unit to help.

When we arrived, I spotted Palomino and sprinted after him through the open front door, down a hallway and into a back bedroom where he was trying to get his .45-caliber automatic handgun. As he turned his head, I ran over him with my steel shield in front of me. The collision knocked us both to the floor. I hit Palomino with the shield to stop him from getting his gun and he kept fighting until my partner, Officer Larry Alphin, showed up to help. We promptly arrested him.

Palomino spent a few days in the hospital for his injuries afterward. No one would touch his civil rights complaint against us – neither the Federal Bureau of Investigation nor our Internal Affairs Unit found merit in his claim.

On August 31, 1985, after he was released, Palomino and some of his minions went back to one of his dope houses in the Stop Six neighborhood. He looked across the street, where a World War II veteran was mowing his yard. [4]

Palomino pointed his .45-caliber gun at the man, laughing as he threated the neighborhood veteran. Quietly, the veteran went into his house, retrieved his military rifle, casually walked outside and fired a shot at Palomino. That tough gangster dove behind his car, while the veteran fired through the driver's and passenger's doors, striking Palomino in the upper body.

The veteran called his neighbor across the street, asking if Palomino was moving.

"No, you got him," the neighbor said.

Homicide Detective Danny LaRue called our office, laughing, to relate the fate of Bobby Palomino. A grand juror later cleared the veteran of any wrongdoing.

We continued pressuring these Cuban criminals until they ultimately left Fort Worth. An FBI agent later called us to share some news.

Having obtained wiretaps in other cities where they were tracking the Marielito drug chain, they overhead talk about Fort Worth. "We are not doing anything in Fort Worth because of the police," one suspect was quoted as saying. It was good to know our enforcement had a lasting effect.

Cuban Castration

Told by J.C. Williams Jr
with help from Ronnie Gouyton

"Things don't always go according to plan."

I've been involved way too often in plans that went awry while making arrests, running search warrants and working undercover.

Once, while working Special Investigations early in my career, we targeted a house where officers made several drug buys. Search warrant in hand, leaders put a sledgehammer in my hand to break down the front door right after my friend, Officer Ronnie Gouyton fired tear gas rounds inside the house. At the time, these were standard tactics at the Fort Worth police department.

All Gouyton and I wanted was a quick, safe entry with all suspects rounded up. We also wanted narcotics officers to do all the work – collect evidence, haul the suspects to jail and fill out all the paperwork.

We didn't want surprises – a dead body inside, lots of stolen property or a gunfight – we'd have an easy time.

We should have known better.

To make sure I could jump out quickly, I held the car door slightly open as we pulled up in front of the house.

I'm not sure who drove – probably Officer Larry Alphin – but he screeched to halt so quickly, the momentum sent my flying out of the car holding that enormous new sledgehammer. I was in it now.

I plowed forward and hit the front door so fast, it immediately crashed open. Next thing I knew, I was by all five terrified suspects. They threw their hands in the air ready to do whatever I said because of my crazy, dynamic entry.

Step one, though not the graceful entry we'd planned, was done. Step two, however, was delayed, and that scared me.

Gouyton, the tear gas man, got snagged by the car door, slowing him down. Other officers were behind him. I knew hell was about to break loose any second. I yelled at the suspects to drop to the floor, and I ducked just before glass shattered and tear gas rounds blasted the room. Those cannisters flew in, nearly missing our heads.

When the chaos settled, I noticed that one of our suspects appeared to have a large wet, red spot on the front of his pants. It looked like blood. He was moaning and I knew I didn't fight him, and he wasn't hit by the tear gas rounds.

I asked about the bloody stain.

"They cut my "dick" off," he said.

"What did you say?" I asked him, certain I had misheard his answer.

Nope, I heard him right the first time.

He opened his pants, revealing a thick Kotex pad on his injury. It looked like a fresh wound. Now we had an injured suspect with a missing penis and I didn't know the location of said appendage or where to start looking.

Did another suspect have in their pocket or did the resident dogs find and carry it outside? Would we be working through the night on the "Dick Case?" Would we be known as the "Dick Squad" for weeks or months inside the department?

His horrible story unfolded, centered in Miami.

He worked for a local drug cartel but committed a big no-no when he started sleeping with the girlfriend of one of the leaders. When the cartel learned of the relationship, members held him down and sliced off his penis. This happened the day before our raid. He sought out help and spent the night on the bus coming to Fort Worth. He knew the people living in the drug house and hoped to re-start his life here.

At least the incident became Miami's investigation.

You just can't make this stuff up.

The Corpseless Head

Told by Kevin Foster
with Kathy Sanders

Dogs have long been experts at finding cadavers. They've also been known to scavenge bodies for food.

Local dogs did both on Jan. 7, 1982, at Fort Worth's Butler Housing Projects.

With mild temperatures, residents sat on porches, mingled with neighbors and enjoyed the day outside.

Several people saw two dogs fighting over a small object, but they thought nothing about it.

Until the larger dog, a Doberman Pinscher, won the fight and the dog's owner saw the object was a decomposing human head. [5]
The dog owner immediately called police.

Alerted to the incident, the police dispatch supervisor decided it would be best to dispatch officers but keep the details confined to a telephone call. News reporters, among others monitored police via the radio and the supervisor wanted to avoid a "media circus" at the crime scene. When the officer called the office, he was asked to try to keep the information off the radio. He headed to the scene, asking another officer to assist him.

Radio silence was broken soon, however, by the assisting officer who wasn't informed to keep it quiet. He called for homicide detectives, crime scene officers and a sergeant.

Officers seized the head from the dog, who was then captured by animal control officers.

A woman who watched the dogs fight over the head, recalled the gory details to police. She pointed out where the dogfight took place. Following her directions, officers found part of a jawbone and tufts of hair, but no body.

Investigators and supervisors arrived, as did the news media with many cameras. They were rolling when the medical examiner investigator put the head into a pillowcase and carried it to his car. Police continued searching in vain for the body. Supervisors planned on forming a large search party in hopes of uncovering the body. It would be a lengthy and tedious process.

But Officer David Ellis, the first cop on the scene, had a different idea – let the dog go and it would lead them to corpse.

Finally, officials in charge agreed, though none thought it would succeed. Freed, the dog immediately trotted to a nearby field of tall grass on a path strewn with pieces of flesh, bone and hair. At the end of the trail, they found the decomposing corpse of a 21-year-old woman. She wore only a blouse.

The sergeant on the scene said the entire body appeared to have been "chewed on all over by dogs."

Homicide investigators took over. She eventually was identified as a local woman and died of respiratory failure – she stopped breathing. Coroners could not determine how she died.

"Of course, we suspect foul play," said Deputy Medical Examiner Marc Krouse told a newspaper reporter, "This girl is 21 and in good health, supposedly, and you just don't go out and lay down in a field and die when you're 21 in November and the temperature is in the 60s."[6]

During the next two months, two other women were found dead within two miles of the initial case. All were decomposed and no cause of death could be determined. [7]

"We have exhausted every lead that we have on each of the three cases," said Homicide Lieutenant T.C. Swan. "The combination of the factors tend to indicate that there is some connection," between the three deaths."

None of the three deaths were added to the cold case files.

Murder occurred in the area. People died of drug overdoses. And alcohol-related deaths were frequent. And often, people just died from natural causes. Unless someone, somewhere confesses to killing these women, it's likely we'll never know what happened.

Unknown Dangers

Told by Kevin Foster
with Kathy Sanders

Dealing with individuals on the streets, who often used to be labeled as bums, transients, or winos, comes with an inherent unknown factor. These people are individuals, each with their own past and stories. Several have dark sides that led them to commit extreme violence, sex crimes, robberies and a host of other crimes.

A surprising number of registered sex offenders find themselves on the streets when they can't find a home or a job – they're rejected because owners don't want a registered sex offender in their apartments or at their job sites.

Back in the day, convicts also found themselves in similar situations, with few social programs to help reacclimate them to society.

The risks associated with these people become evident when others unwittingly help potential criminals by giving them money in well-meaning actions.

Take Tuley Begay, a Native American man who preyed on local winos when they were drunk and vulnerable. During the late 1980s, a disturbing series of crimes unfolded near downtown Fort Worth. Three men were beaten to death on separate occasions and locations. The cases shared a common thread – Begay, suspected of killing the men.[8]

Begay had lived on the streets for nearly three decades and spent two stints in Texas State mental hospitals. In 1990, Begay was finally charged with murder when he shot two people in separate incidents within a few days. [9]

One officer related; "I spent four years working in the city jail and I met many destitute alcoholic men. I listened to how their lives fell apart because of alcoholism and various other illnesses. One of my favorites was Whitey, a friendly man who, even when drunk, had a warm personality."

Whitey often was in Cell #7, a long-term cell for those serving extended misdemeanor sentences and I often visited with him there.

Begay ended that when he crawled under an abandoned building to beat Whitey to death for a few cents and the dregs inside a bottle of "Mad Dog."

In a different case, homicide detectives were summoned to Alabama to interview a man who claimed to have killed more than a dozen street people across the nation with his bare hands.

Prosecutors there said the convicted killer wanted to share his crimes with other law agencies to close the cases. His reason for doing so was simple and self-serving – he had lost his prison privileges and wanted them back, thinking that would happen if he talked about other people he had killed.

These cases serve as a stark reminder to never underestimate the homeless people encountered on the streets. Behind the disheveled appearances and struggles with addiction often lie untold stories of violence and criminality, highlighting the unpredictable nature of those navigating the shadows of society.[10]

The Murdered Woman

Told by Kevin Foster
with Kathy Sanders

One night when I was a midnight shift sergeant on the city's southside, we were called to a homeless encampment where someone had used a stick to severely beat a man in a sleeping bag.

A transient called 911 to report the assault and when we arrived, we found the injured man and arranged to get him to the hospital. I don't know if he survived, but it was one of the worst attacks I'd seen.

I watched as my officers interviewed the 911 caller – he didn't look like he belonged in the area. I walked up to the man, who we'll call Sam, and began a different series of questions – where he was from, what he did for a living and how long he'd been on the streets.

Sam replied it was his first day of being homeless - his wife told him to get out. I lectured him about the reality of living on the street and he needed to get home and fix his marriage. Sam said he couldn't call his wife because he didn't have a cell phone.

So, I drove him to a pay phone outside a 7-Eleven convenience store not far away. And gave him the 50 cents to make the call. Having done my duty, I left while Sam waited for his ride.

Two police officers combing through homeless camps in search of our assailant called me about an hour later, saying they needed me at a vacant lot. They didn't say why on the radio. When I arrived, they led me to the body of partially nude woman, killed and left on top of a fallen tree. She appeared to have been sexually assaulted and tortured before she died.

Investigators found a wallet in the middle of the crime scene. It belonged to Sam; the man I had helped get back to his home. Homicide detectives showed up on his doorstep and he easily admitted to killing the woman. Sam said he just wanted to experience what it was like to kill someone.

The stick-wielding assailant had seen the killing and believed the man in the sleeping bag was responsible. He meted out his own form of justice, but he got the wrong guy.

Catching a Cop Killer

Told by Kevin Foster
with Kathy Sanders

When a cop is killed on the job, nothing stands in the way of justice. Even if you must dupe the suspect. Or his attorney.

Such was the case when a drunk driver plowed into highly decorated Officer Alan Chick, striking and killing him in December 1993.

In the pre-dawn hours, the officer had finished helping a stranded motorist and her brother-in-law when a Cadillac careened towards them. The motorist saw the car's headlights reflected in Chick's eyes before the car slammed into him and their truck.

The impact catapulted Chick over the hood of his patrol car, inflicting fatal head injuries. Though rushed to the hospital, Chick - the father of two small children - died five days later, never regaining consciousness.

The Cadillac's driver, Eugene Lee Standerford, only stopped when his wrecked car quit running. He made no effort to help, witnesses said, just standing by his car, scratching his head.

Standerford smelled of alcohol and told police he'd had a "couple" of drinks. His blood alcohol level registered at .15, meaning he was drunk by Texas standards. This wasn't new for the 55-year-old Dallas County man.

His police record revealed 12 previous Driving While Intoxicated arrests, with eight convictions. He had served one three-year-prison sentence in 1984. He was promptly arrested in Fort Worth but made a $10,000 bond.

Minutes after Chick died on Dec. 27, a District Court Judge issued an involuntary manslaughter arrest warrant for Standerford. She set bond at $110,000.

It fell to me, as sergeant of the department's fugitive squad, and my officers to hunt down the cop killer and haul him to jail. We fanned out, hitting every Dallas County address we had, looking for the suspect.

We went home empty-handed the first day, a horrible feeling. The pressure to find Standerford was intense. Police Chief Thomas

Windham, the brass at headquarters, elected officials and every officer expected an immediate arrest.

It was early when I showed up to start the second day. I was determined to find this man. I scoured all the paperwork we had, then I had an incredible idea – one that might see me jailed or fired or both. But we would have Standerford.

I knew the name of the defense attorney. I knew the judge had signed the arrest warrant. All I needed to do was get Standerford to the courthouse. So, without the authority to do so, I set a hearing in in Criminal District Court.

I didn't ask for permission or advice. I called the attorney, informing them that judge had set a hearing for bond conditions at 1 p.m. that day. And Standerford had to be present.

The attorney was livid, asking about the conditions. I told him if he had questions, to call the judge. He sighed and said they would be there.

Truth be told, I was a little worried.

The judge had a reputation as being a fair, but tough judge. I was afraid she might find me in contempt for this stunt. But I was thinking outside of the box and I didn't think Chief Windham would fire me, but you never knew.

I went ahead and called the judge, told her what I'd done and waited for the thunder.

But she laughed. The judge said she had nothing in court then and would be happy to hold my hearing.

Now, we just needed Standerford to show.

All my officers were in plainclothes and covered every entrance to the courthouse. When they spotted him, they would follow him to the courtroom – never identifying themselves as police. If he made a break for it, they'd arrest him.

Reporters and cameramen showed up for the hearing, apparently tipped off that Standerford would be there.

By the time he showed up, I was on my third pot of coffee.

Standerford had his hearing. Then he went to jail.

Within a year, the cop killer was sentenced to life in prison. He'd have to wait 30 years for a chance at parole.

Death at the Paddock Viaduct

Told by Kevin Foster
with Kathy Sanders

Northside has always felt separated from the rest of the city, probably because it was founded as the city of North Fort Worth. That remains to this day.

The Northside was plagued with gang violence and drive-by shootings. Random violence could break out any given weekend.

One night during the Spring of 1990, a group of four teenage gang members, packed into a black car, spent the evening committing burglaries when they chose the wrong house.[11]

The intended victim saw what was happening in front of his house, grabbed his gun and stepped outside to confront the thieves. When he yelled at the teens, they shot at him. He fired back and one of gang members collapsed to the ground, shot in the head. The other burglars hauled him into their car and raced away.

I was a Northside midnight shift sergeant then and one of my newer officers, Duane Goings, saw a black car speeding down the road toward downtown, unaware a shooting had just occurred. He gave chase. I stopped what I was doing and headed toward the pursuit.

About a minute later, Goings radioed that the car was stopping at the top of the bridge near the Tarrant County Courthouse, known as the Paddock Viaduct. In fact, the car stopped at the driveway to the Fort Worth Jail. Then the officer announced he had a shooting.

Other police units and I raced to Goings, concerned he might have been injured or shot someone in the car.

When I arrived, a strange scene greeted me. Goings was performing CPR on a teenager, while three others, dressed all in black, stood in the road watching. His patrol car was parked behind the black car he'd been pursuing.

The teen was the kid shot earlier in the foiled burglary and had a large X-shaped wound on the side of his head. He lay on his back, his head downhill and a 15-foot river of blood and brain matter flowed down the street.

Each time Goings did a chest compression more brain matter exited – it was a horribly gory scene.

Goings saw me and yelled, "Sarge, I need you to blow," meaning air into the victim, referring to his CPR efforts. The teen was dead. The downhill flow of blood had stopped. Likewise, the flow of brain material had also stopped. His eyes were fixed in a hollow, lifeless stare.

I stood back a few feet from Goings and said, in a not-so-encouraging way, that the officer was "making a mess."

Going stopped the chest compressions and, for the first time, looked at the scene. He turned his head, looked at the body and the bloody street. He stood, wiped his hands, turned to the other three teens and simply said, "Your friend's dead."

Wails and screams cut through the night. It was one of the coldest things I have ever heard an officer said at a shooting. I looked at Goings, wondering if we would be fired – him for saying it and me for being there when he said it. As it was, the subject never came up.

The shot teen was pronounced dead at the scene when the ambulance arrived.

A grand jury declined to indict the homeowner who fired the fatal shot.

Murder on North Main

Told by Kevin Foster
with Kathy Sanders

Revitalization marks the stretch of land between downtown Fort Worth and the storied Stockyards nowadays. But back in the early 1990s, rundown bars, tattoo parlors and a few small stores ruled that same area.

It had its share of violence as well.

I was called to one of these bars one night because someone had been shot to death.

A man's upper torso and his head lay inside the doorway of this bar, while his legs and feet were outside the doorway. When I arrived, I saw a gaping wound in his chest with a growing pool of blood – his heart was no longer pumping so the blood was merely draining from his body.

A few feet down the sidewalk, I saw a 12-gauge shotgun in two pieces, it's stock broken off. It undoubtedly was the murder weapon.

As sirens announced other officers and an ambulance, I saw the bar was still open. To say it was a dive bar would be an insult to rundown bars everywhere. It was nothing more than a room with bare concrete floors, smoke-stained walls and a battered old wooden bar. A couple of tables and chairs sat on the floor. I didn't see a restroom, but the back door opened up to an alley – that likely was their solution.

The bar owner scurried around, trying to mop up the pool of blood. He probably thought it was bad for business. But two men walked up the sidewalk, glanced down at the dead man, stepped over him and went to have a beer.

I walked inside looking for the killer, then I interviewed the beer drinkers and ordered the owner to stop mopping the floor.

The owner ignored me and the other two said in broken English that they'd seen nothing. I sent them outside to other officers.

I again ordered the owner to stop mopping and go to the back of the bar. He angrily refused until I took a step toward him. He backed away and I told him there would be no more customers because his bar was now closed for the night.

He told me his brother was a Tarrant County Justice of the Peace and he would have me fired. He didn't.

Suicide by Cop (Nearly)

Told by Kevin Foster
with Kathy Sanders

Shortly after I became a police officer, I worked the near east side of the city, including an area frequented by the homeless, the mentally ill and transients with a criminal background. They preyed on everyone in the area. I learned about the plights of this segment of society but there was little we could do for them.

The homeless congregated around the Union Gospel Mission, one of the few places provided food and shelter to as many people possible. But with limited resources, many more homeless were without either.

On many nights, the best outcome for someone was to sleep outside near the shelter to be in line for a meal the next day.

Others slept in abandoned cars that had, unbeknownst to them, been stolen. They would end up in jail for auto theft if officers found them inside.

But that was a viable alternative for many homeless – a broken window would see them arrested and put in jail where they had a bed and food. Danger was everywhere for this population, and a few more killed for the spare change in their pockets. Others found way to kill themselves.

They would lay their necks across railroad tracks in train yards, jump off tall bridges or into oncoming traffic. Some tried to get shot by police officers, a phenomenon referred to as suicide by cop.

One day as a young officer, I drove close to the Union Gospel Mission where it was mealtime and at least a dozen men stood in front on the sidewalk.

Suddenly, one the men ran into the street heading straight for my car. I hit the brakes hard just as he launched himself into the path of my car.

He connected with the front part of my car and suffered slight injuries. I called for help and jumped out, angry and confused about what had happened.

I yelled at him while I handcuffed him, asking why he'd jumped in front of the car.

He wanted to kill himself, he told me and thought that would be the fastest way. He also said he thought it would be better for a police officer to kill him than a "regular" person.

I was shocked and angry.

An ambulance came and took the man to the hospital, where he was treated for the minor injuries and admitted for mental issues.

The car had very minor damage, just a little blood on the front end. A Crime Scene Search Unit came by and took a couple of photos, I wrote a quick report and went on with my shift.

I didn't think of this for many years. When I did recall it, I minimized it to myself, thinking this was no more than the actions of a "crazy bum." I still have trouble reconciling the man's actions that night.

He had tried to use me as a weapon to kill himself. Fortunately for both of us that night, he failed.

The Murder of a Drug Dealer

Told by Kevin Foster
with Kathy Sanders

Fortunately, most people will never experience a homicide crime scene. Police officers undoubtedly will. Encountering death is part of the job.

For the more experienced officer, it is often given no more consideration than where you plan to have lunch. It's self-protection.

Sometimes, however, you just can't unsee the incident.

I was with several officers sometime in the late 1990s outside a southside problem bar. Violent crimes had increased in and around the bar and parking lot, so we were giving the area extra attention in the freezing cold.

Suddenly, we heard a gunshot about a block away and sought out where exactly it had originated. Luck was with us, and we found the house in less than a minute and the front door stood open.

Cautiously, we entered looking for victims. We found one man and he was alone. Dead and alone. We knew him by name and reputation. Our victim was a known drug dealer who contributed heavily to the neighborhood problems.

Someone showed up at his house, intent on robbing him and then killed him. The bullet tore open his throat, exposing the inside tissues. Death came so quickly, there was no blood flowing from the injury, best described as "inconsistent with life." A 7.62 casing lay on the floor, leading us to believe the killer used a rifle.

The cold air caused steam to rise from the wound where cockroaches were already scurrying, looking for a meal.

The Home Invasion

Told by Kevin Foster
with Kathy Sanders

The worst weather makes routine calls difficult. But it complicates and hinders intense calls for help. As the lone midnight shift sergeant in the North Division one Sunday in 1989 or 1990, we got word about 3:00 a.m. of a possible home invasion along the shoreline of Lake Worth.

Heavy fog and mist covered our area this cold night, with visibility near zero. The location of this call couldn't have been worse – it took a long time for us to get to this lakeshore mobile home. Once we arrived and confirmed the house, we parked away from it and walked back, trying our best to be quiet. The thickness of the fog hid us well. A quick look at the home showed the door open with lights inside. It was silent. As other officers arrived, I began arranging for a perimeter around the property and setting up a makeshift entry team. I didn't believe we could wait for our Special Weapons And Tactics (SWAT) team because of the fog and remote location.

Just as I made the assignments, a man appeared in the doorway, drenched in sweat and acting too calm for what police he could see. Somebody, maybe it was me, grabbed the man and threw him on the ground before handcuffing him. We pulled a pistol from his boot.

A middle-aged woman then hopped into the doorway, duct tape around her wrists, ankles and mouth. As we were helping her, her daughter showed up in the doorway, trussed the same way except she was holding a baby.

The women said a second attacker had fled when we approached – we must have missed him in the fog.

We found his footprints in the wet grass leading to the lake front. Then he disappeared, probably walking in the water to a spot where he could escape.

The women told me the men burst into their trailer, demanding money and drugs, neither of which they had, the women told us. Apparently, a neighbor was a methamphetamine dealer and the robbers stumbled into the wrong home. It was fortunate we arrived when we did, preventing any more violence against the women or the baby. As for the crook who got away from us - we identified him but before he could be caught, he committed at least two killings in Oklahoma, including one during a bank robbery. I don't remember his name, but last I heard, he was sitting on the state's death row. Our success, of course, apparently annoyed a few people.

At roll call the next night, I received a note directing me to notify Lakeside Police Department whenever we worked a similar call in that area.

Their police officials apparently got mad because we didn't notify them about the home invasion while it was happening. I responded that the crime was in the City of Fort Worth and thus our jurisdiction. The small agency also neither had the equipment nor staff to help. I never heard another word about it.

The Body and the Medic

Told by Kevin Foster
with Kathy Sanders

When death comes to a person, decay begins almost immediately. While we learn what we can in the police academy, many of the details of decomposition are learned through experience.

Early in my career, I received a call about a young woman found dead in her apartment on East Lancaster. At one time, this area was high-end with exclusive apartment complexes for the wealthy with grocery stores, movie theaters and other amenities suited to the clientele. That time passed not that long ago and left in its wake rundown apartments, used car lots, dive bars and prostitutes walking "the stroll".

This woman lived by herself in a small apartment and on this day, a passerby glanced in and saw her dead on the floor.

When I arrived, I looked in the window and saw the unresponsive woman beside the bed. On top of the bed was a small amount of cash, counted and put into individual stacks. I thought death had found her after she cashed her paycheck and she had been separating the money for specific bills. Still, she was dead, the window was raised and there was money and we needed to know what happened.

I went inside and found no signs of forced entry, weapons or injuries that explained her death. I approached the body and smelled a slight odor of decomposition and blisters had appeared on her skin.

Blisters show up after gas in the body builds up and seeks an outlet for release. Large blisters and the smell proved to me she'd been dead for a couple of days.

At the same time I was dispatched on the call, an ambulance also was called to the scene in case the woman was not yet dead and needed medical help.

In those days, very few paramedics or police officers used latex gloves to protect their hands at crime scenes. Neither of the medics who showed up wore gloves.

One of the medics walked into the apartment and I quickly told him they woman had been dead a couple of days.

"I have to check for a pulse," he said.

Before I could issue a warning, he reached down and took hold of a hand and wrist. There was no pulse. As he gently laid the hand back down, much of the arm's skin attached itself to his hands from a huge blister.

I was a little disgusted. I had to force myself not to say, "I told you so," as he walked back outside to find something to clean his hands.

An autopsy concluded the young woman died of natural causes.

Killer at the Riverside Village

Told by Kevin Foster
with Kathy Sanders
Welcome to hell.

Also known as the Riverside Village in Fort Worth, it was a sprawling low-income apartment complex dangerous to anyone at any time on any day. Particularly for residents and police officers.

Nothing was sacred to the throngs of predators who preyed daily on the Village apartments. Daylight hours usually promised more restrained violence, but when the sun went down, it became like "the valley of the shadow of death." Decent residents, forced to live there, locked and barricaded their doors and windows.

A boisterous swarming mass of humanity congregated on the parking lot of an adjacent dead Montgomery Ward shopping mall on Friday and Saturday nights. Assaults, shootings and stabbings were common there. Due to the hostility towards police officers, no one went in The Village without at least two assisting police units.

The Village's most infamous resident was Kenneth Granviel, a 24-year-old machinist who massacred three sisters and two of their children inside their apartment. He'd been cruising and got a sudden urge to have sex with the 21-year-old sister, Laura McClendon. Granviel walked in the open apartment door, armed with a bone-handled steak knife. The date was Oct. 8, 1974.

Before Granviel left, he'd slaughtered five people inside – Laura McClendon; her 3-year-old son Steven; Laura's 19-year-old sister; Laura's 24-year-old sister Martha McClendon; and Martha's two-year-old daughter, Natasha.

He told police he couldn't control himself after the urge hit.

Another sexual urge struck him four months later when Betty Williams, 24, came to his apartment to make phone calls and bum some cigarettes, he said in his confession.

"The next thing I knew, I had my hand around her waist and it was the same thing all over again," Granviel said. He raped her and stabbed her repeatedly.

About then, another neighbor, 21-year-old Vera Hill, came to his door. He grabbed a knife and stabbed her in the chest, stomach and back. He left intent on leaving town, but went to another friend's house, where he raped the woman's mother. He kidnapped his friend, picked up his minister and headed to the police department to confess. He told his preacher he "wanted to be taken out of society and that he didn't want to kill any more innocent people."[12]

Convicted of capital murder for killing 2-year-old Natasha McClendon, Granviel was executed Feb. 27, 1996. He never had a visitor during the 21 years he was on death row, [13]

While he was an extreme case, many people at The Village were die-hard criminals, heartless, vicious and cold. And some weren't very bright.

Tasked with working a burglary at a nearby business, I followed a trail of beer cans and cigarette cartons from the business to an apartment in the Village. We knocked on the door and when it opened, we saw five young men dividing up the goods from the burglary. They went to jail. These were daily occurrences.

There always seemed to be problems among residents and fights were common. Officers went in swept up the injured losers and then hoped we'd be able to leave unscathed. We were not popular in the Village.

The complex at one point was broken up in smaller, fenced complexes, but danger remained.

Many officers reported they felt like weapons were pointed at them as soon as they entered the property. Over the years, no one could keep track of the number of assaults, shootings and stabbings there.

A few innovative young officers decided to fight back. They collected expended handgun rounds from the academy shooting range and brought them to work. They sat on a hill across the Village and when the crowds gathered, they'd use slingshots to fire the metal casings into the crowd. Eventually, after several broken car windows and skinned appendages, the crowds dispersed.

Bulldozers finally ended the Village. Single-family homes replaced the complex.

Every time I hear the phrase, "It takes a village," I think of that place.

Chapter 2

The Williams Way

When facing death, the perception of what others think does not matter. As my father was dying of cancer, he had many regrets and believed he had not been the best father or husband. He did, however, believe and say to me and his close partners, "I was a good cop!"

My father, J.C. Williams Sr. - A fearless cop needed at the time for gangsters and violent criminals in Fort Worth. – J.C. Williams Jr.

Cold Beer, Trucks and Parking Etiquette

Told by J.C. Williams Jr
with help from J.C. Williams Sr.

My Dad J.C. Williams Sr. was a lot of things—an army veteran, a cop, a bricklayer.

He was also a force. A force of what, I can't say. A force of nature? Maybe. A force for good or evil? Neither. But a force, nonetheless. He had very clear ideas about how he wanted to be treated, not just by his son, but by anyone he met. Now, he never said such things outright, but kids catch on. All I had to do was pay attention—not even a lot, mind you. I just had to watch him go about his everyday life to understand one of his biggest unspoken rules.

He didn't like to repeat himself. When he asked for something, big or small, he'd ask real nice. One time. If he had to ask a second time, he got more direct. And if you made him ask a third time? Well, at that point, something bad was going to happen.

It's nineteen seventy something. I'm about 10 or 11. We live on the east side of Fort Worth, and there's a Mr. M's convenience store nearby that my Dad and I routinely visit for beer and whatnot after work.

On this day, we've been working on a house, and we're covered in mortar and all the grime that comes with laying brick. It's the end of our workday, and we're in Dad's old Ford pickup truck, which looks as dirty and dinged up as we do. Covered top to bottom in dried mortar patches, with a welded front bumper, a giant pipe rack around the bed to carry scaffolding, and a broken passenger door handle, that old truck is everything we need it to be. Especially that day.

Dad pulls into Mr. M's to get a 12-pack of beer, like he's done many times before, and he parks that beast right out front. I'm sitting in the passenger seat, planning to stay put while he heads inside. I can't open my door anyway, because that damn broken handle. Someone has to open it from the outside to let me in or out. The passenger window doesn't roll down, either.

So he goes in, gets what he came for, and just as he's coming out, a Corvette pulls in next to us on my side. Was flashy as hell. A man gets out of the driver's side, dressed to the hilt—fancy suit, shiny shoes, not paying a lick of attention.

I guess the man's in a hurry because he hops out and goes to close his door but decides it's not worth the extra effort. So he leaves it open a hair, leaning butt up against my passenger door.

Remember, I can't roll down the window to ask this asshole to close his door. I can't really do anything. Of course my Dad knows this, sees the whole thing unfold. He stays calm, calls out to the guy before he reaches the doorway, "Excuse me, sir, you know your door's against my truck and I need to go."

"Yeah, yeah," the mystery man hollers back. "Just wait, and I'll be..." He's rushing, this busy and important fellow, in his expensive new Corvette. Maybe he thinks it's not too much to ask, having us hanging out while he handles his business inside the store.

And there I sit, watching this man's carelessness with the wide-eyed amusement of a kid who already senses what's brewing under my Dad's calm demeanor. So my Dad repeats himself, "Uh, hey! You need to close your door so I can drive."
I barely breathe, counting to myself.
That's two.

By this time, the man's already slipping inside, all polished shoes and bad manners. He manages a brief wave in our direction before the door closes behind him, both an acknowledgment and shooing away of the second ask.

Dad growls, "Sir—" one last time as the door squeaks shut, you know, to make the requests an even three.

As I sit helpless, I start imagining scenarios. Because I know my Dad, and that's strike three. God help him.

Will Dad follow him inside? Grab him by the hair on his head and drag him back out? Or hit him in the store in front of God and everybody?

I can't do a thing. So I sit there and wait.

I watch as Dad shuffles to the driver's side and gets in. I barely move my head trying to read each of his movements the best I can out the side of my face. But I can't sense any anger. He seems strangely unbothered.

He sets the beer down between us and starts the truck. His breathing stays steady. The engine starts to rev up but we're strangely not moving. Then it happens.

He throws it into reverse and I hear the crunch of metal before I see, in slow motion, that shiny corvette door give way against the welded bumper of our filthy pickup. Like a loose tooth hanging onto gums by a bloody tether, I'll be damned if that door doesn't somehow stay connected.

I lean to the right, stretching just enough to see how our bumper looks. Not that it matters. That old truck's full of battle scars.

Next thing I know, Dad inches the truck forward again, lining everything up at the perfect angle. He revs the engine, throws it back into reverse, and hits the gas a second time. Well, that's all it takes. That door rips and takes wing, like a glorious beacon of justice. Our eyes follow its trajectory as it sputters across dust and gravel, at last settling flat on the road, sad and bent and ugly.

I suppose the man finished his shopping, or maybe he heard his Corvette's death rattle, but he comes flying through the front door of Mr. M's, mouth hanging open, arms flying. He's screaming, too, spit going everywhere. But with both windows up, we can't make out his words.

I lean back in my seat, and maybe these events should bother me, but I feel better, actually. See, the anticipation was the hard part, not knowing what Dad might do when that man ignored him a third time. Feeling the air shift under the weight of my father's need to realign this man's expectations.

Still, I say nothing. No point. I'm just going anywhere he goes, like a passenger.

As he drives away, slow and steady without a care in the world, he reaches down and grabs a beer. He pops the tab one-handed and takes a sip. A few beats pass before he looks at me and smiles. Then he says, "I bet the motherfucker shuts his door next time."

My grin breaks into a cackle because I'm used to his savage responses by this point, and no tension or distress messes with the mood as we drive home.

Even at my young age, I recognize the situation for what it is—another lesson about the way he looks at life. He is who he is and he does what he does. No apologies given. And in that moment, I'm Happy with all of it.

World War II Machine Guns

Told by J.C. Williams Jr
with help from J.C. Williams Sr.

Battling organized crime, drugs and other illicit enterprise in the 1950s and 1960s was a brutal undertaking, particularly with minimal resources. Undercover police officers, like my dad, fought the battle hard, improvising when they ran out of options.

Even if it meant robbing the bad guys.

My father and his partner, Texas Agent Bob Richards, had arranged to buy drugs from this one group of criminals. When they met to complete the deal, the crooks showed them several rare World War II German and Italian machine guns they were willing to sell.

Richards and my dad desperately wanted those guns, primarily to stop them from getting to the streets and endangering other officers. Naturally, they didn't say that. The men negotiated a price, but the undercover officers didn't have enough money for both the guns and drugs.

They reasoned they had one option – rob the crooks of the goods. They simply pulled out their guns, took the drugs and machine guns and convinced the group to stay out of Fort Worth. Forever.

Dad and Richards never announced they were cops, so they could protect ongoing undercover operations.

Unconventional. That's how they survived these challenging decades. My dad finally convinced officials that undercover police needed to blend in with the those they infiltrated. Drinking at bars, wearing long hair and beards, using unmarked vehicles were their tools to effectively succeed in operations.

Before he died, I promised my dad to share his experience to show how policing was and how his generation changed it.

Undercover Narcotic Operations Change Forever

Told by J,C, Williams Jr,
With help from Dub Bransom
& J.C. Williams Sr.

During the 1960's, police supervisors recruited Police Officer D.W. "Dub" Bransom Jr. to work vice, but quickly tapped him to work narcotics.

In their first meeting, Capt. Robert E. Pinckard changed Bransom's life – he assigned the young officer as a partner with my father, J.C. Williams Sr.

If Bransom had issues with Williams, he was to contact the Captain and not their supervisor because Williams was close friends with the supervisor.

While others worked in the office during the day, "J.C. worked by himself as a lone wolf at night," Bransom said.

All excited, Bransom showed up for work at 6 p.m. the next day. He reviewed the narcotics complaints and waited for Williams. When my dad arrived, he walked past Bransom, said nothing and then left. This went on for a week. Williams came in irritated, looked at Bransom and greeted him.

"Who in the hell said you could be my partner?" he demanded to know.

"I was told I would be your partner by the captain." Bransom said. Williams paused, before asking "Do you really think you can be my partner?" "Yes, I think so."

"Ok, so follow me."

Bransom got in Williams' car and later recalled that he had never seen such a crazy driver. Williams flew through intersections and streets at such a high rate of speed that Bransom thought they for sure were dead.

He said nothing, pulled his seat belt tighter and held on with both hands. Williams skidded to a stop, turned to Bransom and said, "You still want to be my partner?"

"Yes!" came the reply.

Satisfied, Williams looked at drug house addresses Bransom had brought.

They headed to the city's southside. Williams got out with Bransom following, then he kicked in the front door.

About a dozen "hippies" were inside and Williams proceeded to knock everyone to the floor.

He ordered Bransom to look around for drugs. All the newbie found was residue.

"I'm not going to arrest all of you this time. BUT, you all owe me if I need something in the future," Williams told the group.

A two-story house was their next stop. They kicked in the door, found people upstairs and Williams commenced pistol-whipping them all to the floor. One bold young man started cussing.

"I knew that was a huge mistake," Bransom said.

Williams responded violently. He grabbed the man, threw him up in the air and over the upstairs balcony. Bransom said the others sat quietly while they searched for drugs. Returning to the car, Williams asked, "Do you still want to be my partner?"

The young officer was too smart not to say "yes" immediately.
"Okay, then you understand I run everything. You do exactly as I tell you and don't talk to anyone about what we do until you talk to me first," Williams lectured.

A few weeks later, Williams stopped by to see Bransom, who was at home on vacation.

Williams wanted Bransom to grow a beard and let his hair get longer. He was going to arrange their schedule so they'd only work nights. They were focused on buying directly from drug dealers.

So Bransom made the undercover buys and Williams took the cases to friendly district attorneys.

At that time, possession of narcotics was 2 years to 10 years, and selling narcotics was 5 years to life, a much stiffer sentence. Williams wanted all the dealers to go down at one time, so they kept quiet about their investigation, even when the captain demanded answers.
A reckoning was coming, Bransom knew.

He'd been nominated as Officer of the Year and the captain demanded the officer attend the annual banquet where they would discuss the pair's activities.

The department forbade officers from having long hair and beards and Bransom had both. He knew other officers had been fired for violating that rule. But he would compromise the undercover case by getting a haircut or shaving. Bransom was stuck.

Williams reassured him.

"Dub, you're not going to shave or change your appearance and I will take care of it," he said.

"You're going to get me fired," Bransom said.
"Partner, you know I can take care of it because I'm close with the chief," Williams said.

The night of the Police Awards Foundation Dinner, Bransom showed up with his undercover look. Standing outside the building, Bransom saw Police Chief Cato Hightower, Deputy Chief W.T. McWhorter and his captain, Pinckard.

"Is that the officer that used to work at the Fort Worth Police Department?" Hightower asked Pinckard while pointing at Bransom. Sternly, Pinckard told Bransom he wasn't going to the banquet.

"You need to go home and then report to Chief Hightower's office in the morning at 9 a.m.," he told his officer.

Bransom said he obviously didn't get the award that night: "It went to an officer that was nice to the drunks downtown." He spent the night trying to call Williams.

The next morning saw Bransom at police headquarters. The deputy chief wanted him fired without bothering Hightower. The captain was nervous and had no idea what was coming. All of them assembled in the chief's office with Bransom thinking his career was over.

Then Williams sauntered in, "wearing a Town Pump Club t-shirt which was a wild club in Fort Worth, holding a box of folders. He told the chief , 'You better know about what the situation is about narcotics and what we have to do.' "

Bransom said he'd never heard anyone talk like that to Hightower. Williams informed the brass that they'd made 40 cases against drug dealers working directly with prosecutors and judges. He had sealed indictments. The charges called for up to life in prison sentences instead of a handful of years, Williams said.

With narcotics traffic soaring, something had to be done.
"We have to change everything now about how we operate narcotics enforcement," he told the chief.

Hightower wanted Williams' ideas for change.

"Undercover officers have to be able to drink in bars, have long hair and beards," he said. The department needed "buy money" and undercover cars, using local car dealers so they could be switched out as needed.

Immediately, Hightower started things in motion, calling the city manager to get funding. He sat with Williams to draft new narcotics procedures.

Gangster Killing in Fort Worth

Told by J.C. Williams Jr
with help from J.C. Williams Sr. &
Wayne Boggus

While working narcotics, my dad arrested some young men. It wasn't unusual except that the father of one of the suspects was present. That dad, who we'll call Scott, tried to interfere with the arrest. Predictably, that didn't go well for him.

Now Scott was a well-heeled businessman on the west side of Fort Worth and boasted connections to influential city leaders.

It was no secret that Police Chief Cato Hightower worked closely with my dad on crime issues, so Scott realized the futility of complaining to Hightower.

Instead, he approached Tarrant County Sheriff Lon Evans to file an assault complaint against my dad.

Investigator Wayne Boggus worked for Evans, and he'd also worked on some narcotic cases with my dad. The sheriff summoned Boggus to the room when Scott made the complaint. Boggus was as nervous as a cat on a hot tin roof – he didn't know what would happen, he said.

Scott carefully explained the altercation and claimed J.C. Williams Sr. whipped his ass. He wanted to file charges against my dad.

He came to the sheriff, he explained, because he didn't think the police department would act on his complaint.

Evans leaned forward after listening to Scott, Boggus said.
"If J.C. Williams whipped your ass, then you had it coming," he said. "If you do not get out of my office, then I am going to whip your ass."

Boggus later told me this while he stayed with us during his divorce. He said he never knew Evans and my dad were so close until that moment. Scott's son was shot later and paralyzed for life while attempting to buy heroin on the east side of Fort Worth. Years later, Scott apologized to my father for trying to make a complaint on him.

Boggus told me another "J.C." story during another stay with us.
He and my father went drinking at a west side bar and this new, huge man came in and walked up behind my dad. Boggus didn't know this guy, except he was connected to many local gangsters, including Danny McComb.

This hulk tried to start a fight, calling my father vile names. At first, my dad ignored him. Boggus was shocked that my father didn't take immediate action.

The big guy turned to the crowd and shouted that Williams was a "narc." With that, my dad grabbed the wooden bar stool he'd been perched on and broke it over the mouthy guy's head. Boggus said blood splattered everywhere and the man went down, unconscious.
Dad looked down at the lump on the barroom floor, finished his drink and left.

Shortly after this, McComb died in a drive-by shotgun shooting. Many people believed another local gangster, Harry Kirk, had killed

McComb or arranged for it to happen. People also whispered that Kirk snitched on other crooks to Fort Worth police.

He did. Kirk was an informant for my dad and frequently stayed at our house. And Kirk was extremely loyal to my dad. That resulted in an unspoken rule that protected my dad from other gangsters.

Body in the Trunk

Told by J.C. Williams Jr
with help from J.C. Williams Sr.
& Hondo Porter

Hondo Porter said every day was an adventure with my dad. You never knew what danger, shenanigans, brilliance of just plain weird shit would go down.

Early in their partnership, Williams announced the two were grabbing food. This in itself wasn't unusual, even though only an hour had passed into their shift.

Williams tossed the keys to his take-home car to Porter. "You drive," he announced.

Porter pulled into a quiet alley behind a café and Williams hopped out to fetch the hamburgers. In a few minutes, he was back with food.

"Give me the keys. I'll drive now," Williams said and the two waltzed around the car to change places. Williams stopped at the trunk and popped the lid. Porter looked and had one thought.

Well, shit.

Inside the trunk was a 30-something man. Williams handed the guy a burger and a drink then slammed the trunk quickly.

Porter was shocked silent, through questions swirled in his head.

How long had that guy been in there? This morning? Last night? All weekend?

Did I witness the guy getting his last meal?

Just before Waco, Williams pulled off Interstate 35W and found a remote area and got the guy out of the trunk.

Though he couldn't hear the words, he heard Williams' firm, direct tone as he addressed the trunk man.

Williams walked back, told Porter to drive and sat stoically in the car.

The only mention of the guy in the trunk was by Williams.

"Sometimes, it's better not to know all the details."

Test of a New Narcotics Partner

Told by J.C. Williams Jr
with help from Hondo Porter

Revenge, it's said, is a dish best served cold. In my dad's world, however, it was best served immediately and with a gun.

Just ask Hondo Porter, who's introduction to J.C. Williams Sr. involved robbing a con man.

"There was the right way, the wrong way and the Williams' way," Porter said.

An eager Porter got his long-awaited chance to work narcotics in the department's Special Investigations Unit back in the 1970s. His boss soon hauled him into an office and let him know he would be partnering with Williams.

"I'm not doing you any favors. J.C. Williams has his own way of doing things," the captain said. "You will see as you begin working with him."

"I think you'll be able to handle it."

Williams was a force in the department, working directly for Police Chief Cato Hightower, solving "particular" problems for the chief. Hightower protected him, but warned him, "the only way you will be here 30 days after I retire is to take vacation days." My dad merely laughed because policing didn't pay the bills – his off-duty bricklaying paid more money.

Unbeknownst to Porter, Williams had traipsed to the Hungry I club that night, tossing back a few drinks with his friend Bo Yale. While there, a guy approached their table, saying he had a 25" television new in the box that he was trying to sell, the last one from a big shipment.

Looking the box over, Williams thought it looked like the original manufacturer shipping box and he handed over the money. The man even agreed to tie the box down to the trunk of Williams' car. Before the man left, Williams – ever the cop – wrote down the license plate number. Just in case.

At home, my dad opened the box to find nothing but heavy packing material and air. No television.

The next day, Williams put Porter behind the wheel of their unmarked car and told him to drive to a "known" drug hot spot.

He conveniently failed to tell his new partner about the television scam and that Williams was about to deliver a reckoning to the con artist – he'd found the man's address through the license number he'd scribbled down.

My dad spotted the scammer sitting all pretty in his car and told Porter to slowly pull their car behind him and wait.

The new guy watched as Williams angled out of the car, sauntered up to the hustler and pulled his gun. He took the man's wallet, counted out the cash and slung the wallet down the street.

"Let's get out of here," Williams told Porter when he got back in their car.

Porter sped away, stunned.

"Did you just do what I think you did?" he asked his new partner.

"Rob that guy back there? Yes, I sure did," Williams answered.

"Well, I thought you were a bricklayer and did that for money."

Williams' answer was to suggest they go see a movie, "to get off the street."

They emerged from the movie theater and thought they were in the clear. They headed out to work actual drug complaints. In a few minutes, flashing lights behind them caused Porter to pull over.

"Well, they got us," he told Williams, putting his hands on the dash, resigned to being arrested.

"I will handle it," my dad told him and got out to talk to the officer. They were stopped, he later reported, because of a broken taillight.

Porter still believed they would be caught for the robbery, particularly when they got back to headquarters and two of the department's best homicide/robbery detectives hustled him into another office.

"We are going to need your statement for the robbery you did with J.C. Williams," one of the detectives said. "We already have a confession from J.C. and now we just need yours."

Porter paused, frantic thoughts running though his head.

"I don't know what you're talking about," he said. "I was working narcotic complaints with J.C. and if he said anything different, he is lying."

The detectives waited a couple of minutes before they opened the door to two laughing men – Williams and the detectives' supervisor, Bud Fowler.

"You can trust him, J.C.," the investigators said.

"I knew I could,' my father retorted.

Porter then learned about the con man, who the detectives intended to serve with several arrest warrants.

"You know the only bad thing about this, Hondo," Dad said. "That guy was $10 short on what he owes me and I'm going to have to do this again."

Partner's Secrets

Told by J.C. Williams Jr
with help from J.C. Williams Sr.
& Hondo Porter

There are times, I believe, that God uses unlikely people to do his bidding.

My father, J.C. Williams Sr., was an unorthodox cop from a bygone era who befriended and caught bad guys and relied on heavy-handed policing to accomplish his goals. He was not anyone's idea of an angel.

And yet in the early 1970s, he acted like one.

Williams and his partner, Officer Hondo Porter , were assigned to the narcotics unit and set out to raid the east side home of a purported drug dealer whose business growth had caught their attention. Police carted the suspect to jail, leaving his girlfriend and their two young children – aged 1 and 3 - behind. They both noticed food and necessities were scarce. After a conversation with the woman, the officers went to the jail and before leaving, Williams gave the suspect his business card.

Williams dragged Porter to a grocery store, loading up several bags of food and other necessities. Porter didn't know why they were grocery shopping. He thought Williams was starting a weekly routine of buying groceries on duty. He didn't bother seeking clarification.

The next thing Porter knew, they were back at the suspect's home, where they delivered the groceries to the young family.

"You need to listen carefully," Williams told Porter. "If you tell anyone about this, I will kill you." Porter, warned by the glint in Williams' eyes, agreed.

My father's tough reputation scared gangsters, drug dealers and other criminals he encountered. He knew that fear was imperative to his job and didn't want anything "good" to tarnish it.

A couple of years later, Porter met Williams at one of his off-duty construction jobs. He pointed to a bricklayer working nearby.

"Do you recognize him," Williams asked.

When Porter said he looked familiar, my father responded, "That was the drug dealer with the girlfriend and kids that we helped out on the east side. He has been clean, supporting his family and is doing well."

Angel, indeed.

Everyone Loves a Parade

The Williams Family Parade

Told by J.C. Williams Jr
with help from J.C. Williams Sr.

As a kid, I loved professional wrestling in Fort Worth watching Fritz Von Erich, Wahoo McDaniel and Johnny Valentine.

My dad was best friends with Bo Yale, a man who owned numerous bars in Fort Worth.

Yale, his two boys, me and my dad spent every Monday night together at the Northside Coliseum to watch World Class Wrestling. Saturday nights, I watched the taped replay they had on television. I was seven years old.

I felt like a celebrity along with other kids at ringside, grabbing autographs from the wrestlers before each match.

About this time, Yale bought a 1925 red fire truck. Not only did we ride in it to the weekly wrestling matches, but we also rode in it around town.

Fort Worth in the 1960s was a different city then – better in some ways and worse in others. At night, downtown was a hot spot for darker, more adult activities with a mix of bars, porn outlets and theaters. More prominent people drank, gambled and bought sex.

In my father's opinion, everyone downtown was underserved for entertainment. They needed a night parade, he decided.

Dad convinced Yale to participate in his bright red fire truck. All the scantily clad waitresses and prostitutes that wanted to be in the parade were welcome to ride on the fire truck, my father said. He also thought throwing candy to everyone on the street was a splendid idea. Yale knew my police officer dad would prevent any of them from being arrested, so he signed on.

My dad wanted to do it immediately, so that night, he held the first parade. It crawled around city hall and the jail, then traveled to the other end of downtown and back. Everyone loved it, my father said, so he planned for a parade every week.

After the second or third night, however, it came to an end. I'm pretty sure the police chief encouraged my father to stop.

Cops, Criminals and Construction "A Williams Christmas Story"

Told by J.C. Williams Jr.
With help from J.C. Williams Sr.

I was six years old in 1965 and Christmas was a little more than a week away. That's when they started to appear, one by one.

They had two things in common, these men – my father knew them, and they were, at the time, homeless. All were invited with one condition; a mission that would test their previous experience in life along with their ability to work together. On Christmas Eve, these men were tasked with assembling one of the biggest toy racetracks I had ever seen in my life.

One was a Texas Department of Public Safety undercover officer who was separated from his wife and children. Another cop was a Tarrant County undercover officer who recently divorced. A convicted safe cracker newly paroled. And a recovering addict who worked construction rounded out the four guests.

Santa, my dad, donned a red elf cap with a large fur ball at the end and sat drinking beer throughout the night, periodically checking on the progress.

They worked in the game room, next to my bedroom. My door was shut, and I pretended to sleep when they first started. But I listened closely.

The lawmen in the group started separating parts to make the job easier. They had trouble finding a few parts.

Frustrated, the safe cracker popped off.

"Well, you two must really be good at your job when you can't even find toy racetrack parts," he said. They tried to ignore him.

The construction worker began putting the track together, but he ran into problems.

"No wonder you have a drug problem. You aren't worth a shit at construction," one of the undercover narcotics officers said.

Their sniping made me nervous and worried there would be no racetrack the next morning.

Suddenly, the safe cracker took control. He used his experience in burglaries and tedious work with safes to figure it out.

Santa Williams was getting tired and time was critical.

Santa leaned down and growled in his caring Christmas spirit, "You better get this fucking racetrack built before my son wakes up."

After several hours of quiet, curiosity got the better of me. I cracked open my door to peep out. Even with low light, I could see this amazing giant racetrack sitting there, waiting for me. That moment was burned in my memory forever.

I did not sleep for days as I continuously raced with my four homeless "uncles" who had assembled it.

Thinking back, I know it was not lodging nor the food my father provided for them that year – it was playing a part in creating a magical Christmas for me.

Drugs and a Hit

Told by J.C. Williams Jr
with help from J.C. Williams Sr.
& Hondo Porter

Desperate bad guys do desperate bad things. Like hiring hitmen to kill police officers.

In one case, however, an alert officer and a pair of close friends set in motion a series of events that saved the lives of several brothers in blue.

During the 1970s, a prominent Fort Worth physician gambled over his head and was in drastic financial trouble. The doctor, who we'll call Peter, turned to writing multiple false prescriptions to help cover his debts.

Peter, located in the wealthy and prestigious west side of Fort Worth, treated attorneys and local business owners. He was a longtime friend of Police Officer Bobby Whiteside, a great, popular officer with many friends affiliated with the doctor.

But one day, he learned Peter sought help from Benny Binion in Las Vegas, Nevada to find hitmen to kill Fort Worth police officers investigating his illegal prescription writing.

Whiteside raced to inform FWPD Capt. Charlie Hogue, an experienced hard-core cop.

During his tenure at the Fort Worth Police Department, Hogue worked his way up the ranks and dealt with many dangerous suspects. He became close friends with legendary Texas Ranger G.W. Burks when they worked on robberies together.

My father counted him among his friends and often introduced him to his partners, such as Hondo Porter, when they met for lunch.

Hogue listened intently to Whiteside describe the proposed hit. Peter gambled in Vegas in big money games and soon found himself overwhelmed with debt. Investigators had learned of the doctor filling out fake prescriptions to make money and had several cases pending against him. Peter had not yet been arrested or charged.

Hogue called his friend for help. He wanted Burks to verify whether the plot was real and gather whatever information Burks could get from Binion. He aimed to protect his officers and knew Peter had the means to pay for hitmen.

Word came back that Peter had offered $35,000 for each officer killed – the officers were those involved in the investigation, including Porter.

Burks informed Hogue that Benny Binion wasn't going to have anything to do with the plot and officers were safe from him.

Binion was a career criminal and native Texan. He killed at least three men in Dallas in the 1930s and 40s. "By the early 1940s he had become the reigning mob boss of Dallas and was seeking to take over the gambling rackets in Fort Worth. The local mob boss of (Fort Worth) was murdered shortly afterward," according to authors Reid, Ed and Ovid Demaris on page 158 in the "The Green Felt Jungle."

Still, Hogue worried the doctor would seek out other hitmen to kill his officers. Burks told him not to worry, he would take care of it.

Burks made an appointment with Peter – he didn't mention he was a Texas Ranger.

When he was alone with the doctor, he pulled out his .44 Magnum revolver and told Peter he knew the targeted officers well and if anything happened to them, he would come back and blow Peter's brains all over the white walls of his office.

"I have a message from Benny Binion," Burks continued. "He said to never contact him again."

Burks related the story to Hogue. He said the officers would be fine because of the way the doctor "pissed his pants." Burks knew for certain the doctor had gotten the message.

Subsequently, police arrested Peter, who was convicted and had his medical license revoked.

A Murder, A Witness & A Narcotics Officer

Told by J.C. Williams Jr
with help from J.C. Williams Sr.
& Dub Bransom

My father forged his own path, much of it during the 1960's alongside his partner, Dub Bransom. Both men, now deceased, remain legends within the department. Their loyalty to each other was legendary, based on exceptional and horrible experiences.

Bransom and dad, J.C. Williams Sr., worked in Special Investigations together – my father also did private, special projects for the police chief. They trusted each other until my father died.

My father never was popular with supervisors above him. And he didn't care. He never curried their favor.

One night, several police captains descended on Bransom in the Special Investigations office, where he was filling out paperwork. They were led by Garland Geeslin, captain of the department's Intelligence and Internal Affairs Unit.

They wanted to know how long Bransom had been in the office then demanded the whereabout of my dad. Bransom had just had a drink with Williams at an east side club, but he wasn't about to share that information.

"I'm not sure where he is. What do you need?" Bransom said. He knew something serious was up, because of the men's demeanor. The captains also never worked at night if they could help it.

Geeslin hauled Bransom into an interrogation room. "Can you get in touch with J.C.? We need to talk to him," the captain said. "We have a female witness right now, that saw him do a drive-by shooting, killing a bookmaker on the northside."

He ordered Bransom to call Williams.

"Just tell J.C. that you need him to come into the office and meet with the captain. DO NOT tell him anything about this," Geeslin said.
Bransom told me he didn't trust Geeslin or the other captains standing around him. He agreed to call dad, but he wasn't going to be part of an "ambush."

They set up a recorded line for the phone call. When my father answered his phone, Bransom quickly told him, "They want to talk to you about a murder and you need a lawyer."

"When and where are they saying this happened?" Williams asked.
"It just happened on the northside," Bransom said.

Dad agreed to come in.

The conversation infuriated the captains. Bransom said he wasn't sure if he'd be fired, but he was going to support his partner over Geeslin & Co.

The higher-ups always believed my dad was involved in everything such as shootings and conflicts with criminals, Bransom told Geeslin. He didn't believe my father was involved in this one.

Bransom knew Williams was involved in only 70 percent of what he was accused of. But not everything, he told me.

The captains were all over him when my father walked into the office, telling him he needed to confess to the killing because a woman saw the shooting and knew it was him.

Williams said he didn't have anything to do with the killing. He didn't tell them he knew the victim well. He said he wasn't giving them a statement until he talked to his attorney, Ward Casey.

Dad told Casey he was accused of killing a man, but he didn't do it, he said. He asked if it was okay to give investigators a statement.
"No, you are not going to give a statement or cooperate in any way with this investigation," Casey nearly yelled into the phone.

"I did not have anything to do with this and can quickly clear this up with a statement," my father said.

Twice more, the colorful Casey said they weren't giving the cops the time of day, let alone a statement.

Finally, after my father insisted that he didn't have anything to do with it, Casey fell silent.

"Really? You didn't have anything to do with this?" the lawyer asked. "I DID NOT do this or have anything to do with it," Dad said, rather intensely.

"Okay, we will cooperate and give a statement," Casey said. "But tell them I am going to sue every one of them for these bogus, trumped-up charges!" Turns out, it was a case of mistaken identity.

A Dallas hitman named J.C. Mize killed the local gambler. The woman at the scene knew Mize well, but when she said, "J.C." did it, Fort Worth cops assumed it was my father.

My dad, Casey and I laughed over the years about how hard it was for my father to convince his lawyer he was innocent.

Premonition of Death

"Gunfight & Death of Wayne Allen Nolley."

Told by J.C. Williams Jr.
with help from J.C. Williams Sr.

Gut instinct. Bad feelings. Premonitions. Strange dreams. Intuition.

Many police officers swear these intangible feelings saved their lives or lives of others for decades. It led them through successful missions or led them away from devastating catastrophe. Veteran law enforcement officers tell younger officers to just trust it.

My father, J.C. Williams Sr., had a premonition so strong that he spoke to other officers about it. Death was coming for someone involved in an upcoming undercover drug deal. Dad was convinced it would happen and nothing could shake him from that belief.

At the time, May 1974, Williams was assigned to the U.S. Drug Enforcement Administration task force in the area, working undercover.

He aimed to buy 10 pounds of heroin, 50 pounds of marijuana as well as other narcotics from a drug dealer. Five briefcases held $107,000 in cash, buy money from task force. The deal would go down in a central Arlington shopping center.

I was with my father when he called the supervisor, telling the man he'd had a dream and knew someone was going to die. Afterward, he assured me – a young teenager – that he would be okay. But the dream had my dad shaken, so much so that he called one of his longtime supervisors and asked the supervisor not to participate.

Williams left to have drinks with a longtime friend and federal agent, Jim Hunter.

Hunter knew something was amiss with Williams and wanted to know why.

Williams explained the drug operation he was working on and that he knew someone was going to die.

Hunter told him to trust his instincts and call the deal off. My father told him he couldn't because too many people were involved. He was going through with it.

"J.C. take this, it's my lucky coin and I want you to carry it on this operation to make sure you're okay," Hunter told him. Williams accepted the coin.

My father was very close to his father, who died when my dad was in his 20s. Whenever he felt stressed, worried or needed to think, Williams traveled to his dad's grave in Tioga Cemetery – usually with a bottle of booze. Sometimes he spent the night beside the grave.

After meeting Hunter, that's where my father headed.

May 3, 1974, dawned and with it the gears started turning for the drug deal. My father chose the busy shopping center in Arlington because it would be safer for him and the other officers, provide witnesses and decrease the chance for violence. It was far better than a rural or remote place.

Federal agents and Fort Worth police officers hid in a pickup camper and a nearby barber shop. The deal was on.

Williams sat in the driver's seat of his car, idling in the parking lot. When he saw the dealer, Wayne Allen Nolley, he had his gun drawn and pointed at the approaching man. He ordered Nolley to walk closer because he wanted to check him for weapons.

Nolley stepped closer and grabbed the cylinder of my father's gun – that prevented the gun from firing. Noley tried to take the gun.

My father had big hands and a strong grip and held on. He surprised the drug dealer by jerking him through the window into the car. Dad didn't want to get out of the car because he knew Nolley had at least one accomplice there. He just didn't know where or if the accomplice would start shooting.

In this life and death struggle, Williams put his gun against Nolley's chest, but it wouldn't fire as long as Nolley held the cylinder. Nolley grabbed a gun tucked in his waistband, shoved into Williams' side and ordered him to drop his weapon.

Acting quickly on instinct and experience, my father released his gun at the same time he lunged for the passenger door and dove headfirst out of his car that was slowly rolling through the parking lot. He started rolling on the pavement.

Nolley let loose a volley of gunshots targeting Williams and then other officers as they emerged from their hiding places. He missed everyone.

The task force agents returned fire with shotguns – they didn't miss. Nolley was dead.

The accomplice in the drug deal, identified as Federick Allen Thomas, lurked in the parking lot, but was arrested after the gun battle. During the arrest, one of the officers shoved a shotgun in Thomas' stomach and pulled the trigger. Nothing happened. After the shootout, the shotgun was empty.

I still don't know if that officer knew his gun was empty.

Crime scene officers counted 160 bullet holes in my father's undercover car. They impounded the car so they could continue examining it the next day. That bothered my dad.

As friends and old partners checked in on him, he asked one for an important favor.

"You have to go to the impound lot tonight and climb over the fence," Williams said.

Then get my sawed-off shotgun out from under my car seat."

Dad had used this gun several times and carried it as a back-up weapon – not really allowed by the department. He knew he had enemies in the police department who were gunning for him – they wanted him gone and looked for any reason to discipline or fire him.

His old partner got the shotgun.

Hunter met with my dad a few days later.

"J.C. you can keep my lucky coin," he said. "You deserve it!"

An Innocent Man

Told by J.C. Williams Jr
with help from Dub Bransom
& L.E. Schilling

Kenneth Leslie Miller spent a dozen years as a fugitive for a crime he didn't commit.

A 24-year-old Vietnam veteran, Miller returned home with healed battle wounds, haunting memories and a reputation as an efficient killer. By his account, he killed 32 enemy soldiers during his stint there.

So, when a neatly dressed young gunman attacked a Texas Christian University student in her garage apartment, Miller came up on police radar. When the young woman recovered enough to speak with investigators, she identified Miller from a photo spread as her attacker.

Before night fell on June 11, 1974, the attacker entered her apartment and tried to lock handcuffs on her wrists. She grabbed at his .22-caliber pistol and he, in turn, shot her five times in the face and head and left her for dead.

Meanwhile, Miller's fetish for guns drew the attention of one of his neighbors, who called police to say Miller was dealing in automatic weapons. Acting on the tip, police raided Miller's apartment in July but found only a small amount of marijuana. He was arrested for the pot and a homicide detective interviewed him about the Kirby attack.

A month later, my father was one of the narcotics officers working with federal agents that swarmed Miller's apartment again, searching for drugs and guns.[14]

"Two men yanked me out of bed and (threw) me up against a wall and they kept kicking my feet apart," Miller later testified. The narcotic officers "really worked him over," he said. Miller was beaten severely and at the hospital, surgeons had to remove his spleen.

Miller knew my father well and never accused him of hitting or kicking that day.

Officers insisted Miller had damaged his spleen in a motorcycle accident but Fort Worth Police Chief T.S. Walls didn't buy it. He ordered my father and Officer B. Ray Armand indefinitely suspended – tantamount to firing them. Sgt. H.L. "Curly" Wyatt, who headed the raid, received a reprimand. A civil service hearing was set for Sept. 30 to hear the officers' appeals.

My father told me he would take the punishment when he did something wrong, but he wasn't going to let administrators railroad him for something he didn't do.

During his internal affairs interview, officers accused him of hitting Miller. He told the investigators it was obvious he didn't beat Miller because Miller "looks too damn good."

My dad felt the chief and others wanted him gone, but he knew Miller respected him and was not going to help.

Homicide investigators had an attempted murder case ready to file against Miller but chose to postpone arresting him until the hearing. No one was sure why.

Tensions were flying high the day of the hearing. Before the hearing began, my father and Wyatt argued until my father held up a small black book.

"If needed, I have a lot of information to share about what has happened at the Fort Worth Police Department over the last 20 years," he told Wyatt. My father wanted the message heard by everyone trying to oust him – he had the dirt on all of them.

Wyatt stormed over to my father's one-time partner, Sgt. Dub Bransom.

"You were partners with J.C. Did he carry a black book and document things?" Wyatt asked.

"If J.C. tells you something, you can bet it's documented and it's right," Bransom retorted.

Miller testified at the hearing that my father didn't hurt him. When asked to identify Armand, Miller couldn't. Armand's attorney, Jerry Loftin, made Armand cut his hair, dress in a business suit, and hide his prominent teeth, according to a newspaper article.

Wyatt claimed that my dad oversaw the scene at the drug raid. My father rebutted that in his testimony saying he was surprised that officers were also supervising sergeants at the police department.

Before the hearing ended, two homicide detectives arrested Miller in the Kirby case. That ended the brutality case against my father and Armand, who were both reinstated.

Miller later was convicted of attempted murder. Before the jury could sentence him, he fled in a panic.[15]

The jury sentenced him to 70 years in prison, anyway.

Twelve years passed. Leonard Schilling – a colorful character in the department – became sergeant and headed the Crime Stoppers unit.

I worked with Schilling in patrol and he had earned three nominations for Officer of the Year and two certificates of merit for courage in dangerous situations. Schilling also had been suspended twice, fired three times and may have been the only police sergeant in Fort Worth history to have been jailed twice.

Schilling received a series of phone calls about Miller. One caller told him Miller had recently been back in Fort Worth and using the name Allen McGinnis. The sergeant was able to tie Miller to a traffic ticket and several pawn receipts. He knew then Miller was using his ex-roommate's name, Allen McGinnis.

On June 9, 1986, time ran out for Miller. He was arrested for shoplifting at a Las Vegas wholesale store by a clerk.[16]

With Miller's arrest, Schilling celebrated with many of his friends at the Albatross, a dive bar popular with off-duty cops, investigators, lawyers and reporters.

While there, Schilling received an upsetting call.

"You got the wrong guy" an unidentified caller said. "Miller didn't shoot Janelle Kirby."

Schilling conducted a new investigation with help from Miller's attorney, Bill Magnussen. The result? He found the guilty man, proving Miller was innocent.[17]

Application for Retirement

The Retirement of J.C. Williams Sr.

The True Story

Told by J.C. Williams Jr.
With help from J.C. Williams Sr. &
Dub Bransom

Bransom was a die-hard loyal friend, no matter what. He often did things my father asked. That included when Williams decided to retire.

"I have decided to retire," he announced to me one day. He didn't care that he wasn't yet eligible for retirement benefits. That wasn't going to stop him.

He had told the police chief and others that he wanted to leave with a bang.

"I think I'm going to drive my patrol car into the front doors of city hall and other wild things to get a reaction to start with," Williams had proclaimed.

His requirement request reached the retirement board and most of them didn't want to approve it. But Bransom happened to be one of the board members.

"Is he going to do this crazy stuff," the other members asked him. "J.C. was my partner and he always did exactly what he said he would do," Bransom said.

He proceeded to tell them that after the vote, Williams wanted the name of each board member and how they voted on his request.

Unsurprisingly, the board voted 9-0 to approve the retirement request.

The police chief was the first to call Bransom after the vote to say he was glad it passed.

Many still at the police department worried about any stories Williams would tell. They knew he had incriminating evidence against numerous people.

My father believed the Fort Worth Police Department needed him at one time to deal with the worst criminals in a way that was no longer acceptable or tolerated.

He was right. And he went out the way he wanted. He returned to construction as a bricklayer. He never changed.

A true leader, Bransom retired as a sergeant in 1983, several years after my father's retirement. He lost his election bid to become sheriff but took over as police chief in nearby River Oaks. Bransom was appointed as the United States Marshal of North Texas, serving seven years. After that, he won election three times as Constable of Tarrant County Precinct 4. He retired in December 2016 because of his deteriorating health. Dub died three years later. He was the best supervisor I ever had and he was my mentor my entire life. I still miss him.

Chapter 3

Vice Intelligence and Enforcement

"On the street there is no tomorrow. There is only here and now and nothing else. And yesterday is just another day you're trying to forget."

excerpt from: freefalling - Darlene Susan Girard

A Day in the Vice Unit

Told by J.C. Williams Jr
with help from Larry Alphin

Vice. A unit that addresses the sordid and sleazy – gambling, prostitution, some drugs and illegal sales of alcohol. And anything else that pops up.

6:00 p.m.

Start of shift.

I was talking with some fellow vice officers when my partner, Larry Alphin, walked in, carrying a box of candles to deliver to those who had kindly signed up to help Larry's daughter with her school fundraiser.

Eloy, a new officer to the unit, stared at his candles and shook his head. I asked why he had such a funny look on his face. "J.C., I'm glad to support Larry's daughter, but I just think $6 seems kind of high for these small candles," he said.

I laughed and told Eloy the candles only cost $3. "Always buy them from Larry's kids or his wife, never directly from Larry," I told him. Eloy got mad and confronted Alphin. Of course, in typical Alphin fashion, he said he had to add fees for his personal handling and transportation.

We all laughed hard.

7:30 p.m.

Another vice officer, Ronnie Gouyton, Alphin and I met with two Texas Rangers who were on the hunt for an escaped prisoner who'd been seen in Fort Worth. Texas Rangers Tom Arnold and Jack Morton wanted our help ferreting out Richard C. Franklin.

Franklin, three other men and a woman escaped from Austin County Jail in Bellville, Texas, six weeks earlier. The inmates overpowered a jailer and fled in a sheriff's patrol car. The group next carjacked a man for his pickup truck, using a shotgun they'd stolen from the patrol car. It was the first escape from that jail and the sheriff was furious. Four of the five inmates had been recaptured, but not Franklin.[18]

The Rangers told us Franklin planned the breakout and was dangerous.

8:30 p.m.

The three of us agreed to help and when we arrived at the 651 Club, we opted to go in undercover to find Franklin. Arnold and Morton, who had an informant inside the bar, and stayed outside. If we couldn't find the escapee, they would come in and ensure Franklin wasn't there.

More than 100 people packed the club. If Franklin's violent friends were inside with him, we knew we could get stabbed or shot at close range. We had to be cautious.

I spotted a guy that looked like Franklin, although he had a beard and longer hair from being on the run for six weeks. I moved behind the suspect and said, "Hey, Ricky!" to get his reaction.

Franklin turned quickly, reaching for a knife in his back pocket. Gouyton and I grabbed him, bounced him off the bar and shoved him out the exit. Alphin was on our heels.

We knew if anyone followed us out to help Franklin, the Texas Rangers would take care of them.

We threw Franklin in the back seat with him still flailing away. By the time we reached the jail, the fight was out of him, and we hauled him downstairs to the jail.

Alphin, being Alphin, wasn't about to miss an opportunity to have some fun.

"Sorry, wrong guy," he told the Texas Rangers.

"Definitely not your guy," I chimed in.

"J.C. that BETTER be the right guy!" they shot back.

We all knew what a catastrophe it would be if we'd arrested the wrong person. We cut the tension by laughing. We were just kidding.

A couple of weeks later, we received a commendation for the "outstanding" work from Austin County.

Arnold and Morton called later to tell us the only thing Franklin said on the drive back was that he would never return to Fort Worth for any reason.

10:00 p.m.

Alphin and I met a Fort Worth Police reserve officer, who was smart and wanted to help with some prostitution complaints.

The reserve officer that we'll call George drove one of the undercover cars and we took the other, driving on the southeast side of the city looking for working prostitutes.

When we noticed some, we pulled onto a side street and gave George instructions to stay put until we could park on a parallel street. We walked around the houses to be close to the prostitutes when George pulled up.

We noticed that the prostitutes were actually men in drag. We had received reports of really tall male prostitutes robbing men on the prowl. Most everybody believed they were women.

A few months earlier, one of our vice officers was in a life-or-death fight while working prostitution in this area and had to kill the suspect. We were understandably nervous for our reserve officer. He was small and had turned off his radio. We had no way to let George know who he was about to pick up.

As we looked on, one of these "working girls" jumped into the front seat of George's car. We were about 20 yards away and saw the two talking before George flashed his badge. We knew he'd made a case. Immediately, the suspect knocked the badge out of his hand and started slamming the officer against the car door and window.

I ran up to the car, opened the passenger door and jerked the man out of the car by his neck and wig. About the same time, Alphin performed a perfect knee strike to get the man under control. The prostitute's giant wig, gaudy hair ribbons and all, went flying – it looked like his head went sailing.

A shocked George started screaming, thinking we had just jerked a woman's head right off her shoulders. As we calmed everyone down, we took the man, still in drag, to jail.

1:00 a.m.

Back at the office to finish paperwork for the night.

Attack of the Catwoman

Told by J.C. Williams Jr
with help from Larry Alphin

Police work is funny. Not funny ha-ha but the other kind, weird. It's long stretches of nothing special interrupted by blasts of intensity, like lying on the couch watching daytime T.V. (that's some mind-numbing garbage, I tell you), except every so often—you never know when—you get a bucket of ice water dumped on your head.

The point is, spending your days (or nights) like that does something to a person. Training your body and mind to function under a very specific kind of stress, well, it's not a perfect science.

It's winter, early 1980s. I'm working Vice (undercover) with my partner, Larry Alphin. It's around 12 a.m., and our shift ends at 2. I'm not a rookie in so many words, but I'm not experienced, either. Worked patrol for a couple of years and been undercover about a year now. So, Larry's the veteran on this team, in more ways than one. He was in Vietnam, and nothing bothers him now. Like war set his crazy-shit bar so high, nothing else could ever reach it. Like death for breakfast, daily, made cop life a bowl of Fruit Loops.

It's either side of midnight, and we're cruising around Riverside Drive. There's a bar in that area that is set on an interesting spot on a slight hill. And we're doing okay, nothing out of the ordinary on our radar.

But that bar has a reputation for being frequented by pimps, prostitutes and drug dealers. Sometimes we get complaints from businesses and civilians in the area. Never a good thing. Now prostitution, no matter what side of the argument you sit on, isn't exactly in line with the law. So as cops, we have a solid amount of interaction with the unsavory business.

We're driving around but decide to pull off to the side and watch the bar more closely. After a bit, we see someone. She's trying to solicit different cars coming and going, you know, and she wears this long, black coat that goes all the way down to her ankles. We watch her for a bit, then decide we have enough to move in.

I tell Larry I'll get out and cross the street. We decide he'll head that way in the car, and splitting up will make it easier to pick her up. So I start walking across the street, and as I get closer to her, two things happen. One—I get an eye full of her, all of her, and I estimate her height at 5'11", about my same height. For some reason, the black coat makes her look taller, broader. And her eyes, when I get a good look at her face, her eyes tell me she's on something. Not sure what, but something. And it's late (or early, I guess), so the whole getup catches me off guard, makes me wary.

Two—as I'm performing the mental calculations necessary to assess the situation, I say, "You're under arrest for prostitution. We're going to have to take you downtown."

She looks at me, eyes big and bloodshot, trench coat flapping behind her in the cold wind like giant wings. Then, bam! She takes off running.

Shit.

As convenient as it would be to track a towering, winged, loaded sprinter on a sunny spring day, it's decidedly less so trying to spot one at winter's midnight in a parking lot on the east side of Fort Worth.

So, I start stepping in and out of cars, keeping my breathing steady, looking around. I see movement ahead and realize she's slowed to a jog. Well, that's something at least. Then I see her zigzagging around cars further ahead at an incline (the slight hill, remember?). It's a pretty big parking lot, but I can see her.

Until I can't.

I move forward, keeping my steps easy. Don't want to give away my location. I reason she must have stopped somewhere because I didn't see her exit the area. As I advance, I brace myself for an arrest. We make hundreds of these, and runners aren't necessarily unusual. A pain in the ass, though.

I expect her to be in one of the cars, so I start peering in, hands cupping the sides of my eyes.

At this point, I think I'm getting close. I round a corner, saying, "Okay, you're under arrest. I know you're here." I hear nothing, so I walk around another vehicle, glancing up at a few cars parked along the hill. Then I see her. Holy hell, she's crouched between two vehicles on top of the incline, perched like a panther.

Before I can register her distance and elevation, she rises, spreads her arms to an ungodly wingspan, and leaps—toward, not away from me. As she jumps, this sound comes out of her, high pitched and unsettling, like the battle cry of an injured animal.

Now, I don't know if the wind's direction and speed team up to create the perfect lift under that black ankle-length coat at approximately 12:30 a.m. on this chilly morning, but when she hits the air, she takes flight, that blood-curdling howl following in her wake.

And me? I'm cold and pissed off, not mildly shocked by the scene unfolding above my head. I can't fully register this odd act of aggression (or escape). I can't get my brain to do a damn thing except unpack the fact that Batman has just declared war.

So, something else takes over, because clear-minded thought has gone and left me. I do what my B-Team brain decides in that millisecond, freaked out by the Dark Knight's close proximity.

I think, I'm not going to fight this woman. It's a situation, so I'll deal with it.

I do the only thing that springs to this cold, tired mind. I use her momentum and position to aid her trajectory in a way that seems optimal in that moment. You know, I grab her and throw her, so she'll keep flying. Away from me. When we make contact, she gets a hold of my head and face, her nails digging into any flesh she finds.

I'm a fairly strong man, so I shake her off, and when she finishes her unholy arc through the air, aided by my panic, she lands on the concrete. Hard. Self-preservation is a mighty force. And she is a formidable human. I don't feel proud of myself for throwing her like I did, but God help me, I didn't know what else to do.

Of course, right around this time Larry pulls up, and he's chuckling, shaking his head. "Man, J.C., I've never seen anything like that in my life. Whoa boy, did she come flying!" So, he steps out of the police car and starts walking toward her, like it's as good a time as ever to make an arrest. As he walks he says, "you need to get up. You're under arrest for prostitution."

She doesn't move, so he says, "Okay, on your feet."

Nothing.

So, I'm thinking she must be faking it, and Larry's ahead of me, making his way closer to her. With each step, I get less sure of myself, for she has surprised me on more than one occasion. When we get to her, he grabs the huge coat and flips her over. We don't see blood or other visible signs of trauma, but her eyes are flickering. We take a moment to look her over, then Larry stands up, looks at me and says, "Welp, guess you killed her."

"Oh no," I say. My mind starts going in all directions.

This is crazy and now we are going to have to deal with this. What a long night this will be. Getting her checked out at the hospital and then waiting so she can be transported to jail.

I turn to Larry who says, "Nah, let's just go." I think he's kidding. But maybe he's not. But I think he must be kidding. He's grinning, kind of.

And Larry, his face doesn't always match what he's thinking, or what you think he's thinking. So, I have no real clue what he means. But I don't have much time to weigh the issue before a car drives up and a woman jumps out screaming, "My baby, my baby!"

Once again, the absurdity of the situation knocks me sideways, and I stand there slack jawed, unable to react with the God-given dignity of a grown ass man. Not yet 1 a.m. and we have a mostly unconscious prostitute laid out in the middle of a parking lot, her mother hunched over her crying, trying to get her daughter to wake up and respond. I look over at Larry for guidance, or hell, anything other than what I've got brewing, and before I can beg him to drive us far, far away from here, the mother starts trying to explain through sobs and half snorts, "I've been looking for her for weeks. She's been with a pimp, and he's held her hostage, I think. But she won't leave him, and with everything else, and…"

Larry steps up to her and says, "Well ma'am, okay, I understand. This one time, we'll let her go with you. We won't put her in jail, and if you can take care of her, we'll let you have her." I'm still thinking maybe we should call and have her checked out. See, I know I did what I had to do in the moment, but I'm feeling pretty terrible about the woman's less-than-lucid state and the crying mother at her side. But Larry gives me some serious side eye before lowering his voice and saying, "Listen, I got it. I got it."

He looks back at Mom and she's nodding, agreeing to do whatever it takes to keep her daughter from the clutches of pimps and jail cells. "Yeah, I'll take her. I'll take care of her." Then she plants both feet on either side of her daughter and grabs both her arms before dragging her over to the car and hefting her inside. Not wasting any time with formalities, she drives away.

Well, none of this is sitting well with me. So I can't let it lie. I keep pushing, "I'm not sure, Larry. Don't know what's going on with the drugs she's definitely on and everything else. Not sure this was the best way to end things."

But Larry's been on the force a lot longer than me, and I don't know how much I can question. It's a real dynamic with veteran officers. Anyway, he sticks to his guns, explaining how our shift's almost over, there was no arrest made, no paperwork to sign. "Besides," he says, "she attacked you. It's not a big deal, you know, so let's not say anything about it."

When we get back to the office I'm still thinking about it, about how I can't believe this night got this crazy and wild. The rest of the team is there, about 8 of us in all. It's late at this point, almost 2 in the morning.

I see Larry go to the front of the office and I'm wondering what he could possibly have to say at this point. And he says, "Hey, boys, you missed it tonight. This crazy prostitute attacked and leaped onto J.C. Wildest thing I've ever seen. It's okay, though he threw her about 15 feet in the air, killed her dead."

About a month later, and I haven't stopped thinking about what went down that night. I'm on a rotation, so I'm on day shift for a bit, and one afternoon I see her at the front desk. She's been arrested for prostitution again.

I stop and think about walking by, but I can't stand it. I've gotta say something. "Hey, do you by any chance remember me?" I ask.

It takes her a few seconds to respond, but when she looks up, her eyes are clear. "Yeah. Yeah, I remember you. I'd been on some drugs, and you were going to arrest me or whatever. But you didn't."

I release a breath I didn't know I'd been holding and walk away. She is not bothered by that night. I think about the world she is in, the wild streets of the eastside, and I think about how I'll probably see her out there again, though I don't want to. But that's just how it is sometimes.

Mamas and pimps and black trench coats.

Prostitute on the Loose at FWPD

As told by J.C. Williams Jr.
With help from Nick Bradford

When you work vice, you must enjoy yourself whenever possible. I excelled at that, even if it was occasionally at the expense of a fellow officer. Or supervisor.

Enter Fort Worth Police Lt. Bob Shaw, a popular supervisor named head of the Special Investigations' Vice unit in the mid-1980s.

I was working vice intelligence on long-term organized crime cases, but I volunteered to help train a new officer, Nick Bradford, on a routine prostitution complaint.

Driving out to the south side, I told Bradford to let me do all the talking and make the prostitution case.

We saw the woman, who we'll call Tiffany. We pulled alongside her, had a brief chat and she agreed to have sex with each of us for $20 a pop.

Before we identified ourselves as cops and arrested Tiffany, we saw a chance to have fun with our new supervisor.

I began weaving a story about us working for a financial service business, with a boss who would allow us use of the downtown office if Tiffany would service our boss, as well. She was all in.

"I know this is odd, but I need to stop at a pay phone first and make sure it's ok to use the office," I told Tiffany. "Can you get on the phone, talk dirty to my boss, and then make a deal with him on the payphone?"

Sure, came the reply.

Bradford waited with our prostitute in our car, while I got on the phone with Shaw.

"Lieutenant, you want to turn on your phone recorder because the prostitute on whom you received the complaint is going to get on the phone, talk dirty to you and solicit you," I told him.

Shaw laughed. "Come on J.C., don't joke with me. You can't be serious!"

I was. Tiffany got on the phone and propositioned the lieutenant.
We drove to police headquarters downtown and told her to duck because we needed to avoid her seeing police officers at our building. When we drove into the parking garage, there were at least 20 parked police cars. She was lying down in the back seat.

The next obstacle was the breezeway from the parking garage into the building. There are glass windows with police cars parked within view. We had her crouch down and run to the stairwell. Our office was on the third floor.

Bradford and Tiffany waited in the stairwell until I made sure the coast was clear.

Walking into our office, our working gal invited other men she believed to be businessmen, an assistant district attorney, plainclothes police officer John Whitener and some other detectives - to partake of her services. It was a miracle that they didn't respond. They probably were shocked Tiffany was soliciting them in a police station.[19]

When she made several deals, I arrested her. She paused.

"Okay, but exactly where are we?" Tiffany asked.

"We're in the Special Investigations Vice office in the downtown police facility," I informed her.

She started to laugh.

"You must be kidding! You are good," she said.
Caught in the act, she opted to help us identify others involved in prostitution at a higher level.

The report I submitted caused a little panic further up the chain.

"J.C., if your report on this prostitute is not true, then we're both going to be fired," said my new Deputy Chief Coy Martin after marching into the vice office shortly after I filed the report.

It became a front-page story when reporters caught wind of the arrest.

Calls flooded in. Initially, Chief Thomas Windham was mad, thinking it was a hoax. When he learned it was true, he relaxed.

Dynamic Entry on the Southside

Told by J.C. Williams Jr.

Sometimes, a "badass" just isn't much of a badass. Particularly when surprised, they scream like schoolgirls and soil themselves.

As a young officer in 1982, I knew about the infamous Bandidos motorcycle gang, but locally, the Texas outlaw gang suffered – one of their leaders had been killed and members suspected Fort Worth police officers were involved.

The United States Department of Justice branded four notorious outlaw motorcycle gangs as organized crime syndicates, responsible for drug dealing, arms trafficking, prostitution, extortion, money laundering and murder.[20]

Members were violent, hated cops and dealt in methamphetamines. That held true locally even with the reduced numbers.

We received information about a southside house in Fort Worth dealing meth with the dealers possibly connected to the Bandidos. Acting on that tip, one of our undercover officers bought drugs at the house. While there, the officer overheard the dealers talking about killing anyone that got in their way.

It was time for a bust.

Back then, Fort Worth had no SWAT (Special Weapons and Tactics) unit nor were officers trained in tactical approach and entries.

This is how we executed search warrants:

Everyone sprinted for the door and the "winner" – whoever got there first – earned the right to kick the door in and enter first, using a 12-gauge chrome double barrel, sawed-off shotgun. Then you knocked the suspects to the floor. Simple.

It had changed little in 1982. The winner was anointed ahead of time. When plans were made to hit the southside house, I volunteered to be the winner, as I usually did.

Styling the latest in gas mask attire to ward off tear gas rounds fired through the windows and brandishing the shotgun, I broke through that front door like it was nothing.

The open door revealed a four-foot mound of junk covering the entire floor in front of a 12-foot door. I knew the drugs and suspects were behind that door.

I scaled the top of the junk mountain and used my shoulder to crash into that door – it came off its hinges and exploded into pieces like a bomb had gone off.

Luckily, I landed on my feet in front of three of the four suspects. I don't know how I avoided landing on my head and breaking my neck. There I was, breathing hard in this huge gas mask, holding a double barrel shotgun a foot from the heads of two of the men. They promptly fell back on a mattress and shit their pants.

A third man shrieked like a little girl and fell flat on the floor.

I had my eyes on the fourth suspect, a big man who was standing by an open window. Suddenly, two very long and muscular arms reached in from outside and jerked the 6-foot-tall suspect right out of the room, taking most of the window glass and frame with him.

Those arms belonged to one of our giant officers we'll call Bubba. He had been tasked with keeping me safe.

Afterwards, we laughed when we realized these men were not the dangerous, badass killers they purported to be.

Operation P.E.S.T.

Told by J.C. Williams Jr
with help from Larry Alphin

In the era dominated by Fort Worth Police Chief Thomas Windham, a wave of change swept through the vice unit, bringing with it more extensive and covert investigations.

One of our prime targets was Rendezvous Adventures, a sophisticated prostitution ring catering to rich, out-of-town businessmen. The high-class operation raked in $2.5 million a year, with escort service fees ranging from $225 to $625 per meeting.

Rendezvous used more than 30 motels and hotels in the Dallas/Fort Worth area and accepted credit card payments on site. If we were going to break up the system, we needed to follow the money. Our investigation was dubbed Operation PEST (Prostitution Escort Service Termination) and included the Texas Department of Public Safety, the Tarrant County District Attorney's office, banking and credit card companies, and the Internal Revenue Service.

Our plan was simple – make appointments with Rendezvous, meet the prostitutes and pay for the services. Arrest and search warrants were in the works, and we were going to raid several locations involved in the organized crime.[21]

However, we needed that last case. I was a seasoned vice officer working undercover. I would meet the prostitute at a prestigious suburban hotel and would show that Rendezvous was still working when the raids occurred. It was crucial the credit card payment be made before stopping the meeting.

Surveillance equipment in my room was monitored by officers in a room next door.

Whenever I said, "Baby, you have a beautiful body," one of those officers would call me so I could end the meeting with some made-up excuse.

It all would have worked so well. Except for my partner, Larry Alphin. The surveillance equipment...He wouldn't make the call. By this point, the prostitute was now nude, jumping up and down on the bed saying, "Come on, we're going to have a good time". To keep from compromising this huge case, I had taken off my shirt and was slowly removing my shoes and socks, silently cussing Larry Alphin. I shouted my line one more time, "BABY, YOU HAVE A BEAUTIFUL BODY".

When I said my scripted line, the phone call didn't come. The prostitute started shedding her clothes and tension began rising, I repeated the phrase several times. Nothing.

The surveillance equipment was silent. Alphin had the telephone and wouldn't let anyone call. My friend and my partner had decided it would be funny. He wouldn't make the call.

After a several minute delay, the call finally came, and Larry said, "I had you sweating didn't I"?

I had to compose myself and continue with my story; that my wife had been injured in an accident and ending the encounter.

We arrested 12 people involved in Rendezvous. Then we temporarily took control of the business and used female undercover officers to arrest more people for solicitation.

Operation PEST remains etched in the annals of vice investigations.

The Cab and the Jumping Prostitute

Told by J.C. Williams Jr,
with help from Larry Alphin.

When someone hears, "You're under arrest," it's likely their fight or flight response is about to kick in. It's unknown where that will land them.

A perfect example happened when, once again, my partner Larry Alphin and I were working prostitution complaints in the 1980s. This time, we were focused on the New Lincoln Motel on the east side. Alphin had a brilliant idea.

"Why don't we just see if the local Yellow Checker Cab company will give us a cab to use," he said. We never bothered with getting permission beforehand and this time was no different.

Company officials were happy to loan us one of their taxis. Since I was still clean-shaven from an earlier case, I played the out-of-town businessman looking for some fun. Alphin was the cab driver.

When we pulled up in front of the motel, the first prostitute we saw was standing next to her pimp – Alphin "the cabbie" approached the pair and soon the woman, who we'll call Rose, jumped in the back seat and set a price for a specific sex act with me. I was in the front passenger seat.

As we drove away from the motel, I showed her my badge and said, "You're under arrest for prostitution."

Surprised, Rose looked at Alphin. He flipped open his wallet to display his badge. "We're everywhere," he told her.

Shocked, she looked out the window. I could tell she was thinking of leaping out, even with us going 20 m.p.h. Rose reached for the door handle.

"I think she's going to jump," I shouted to Alphin.

I reached back to stop her at the same time she opened the cab door. Alphin jerked the steering wheel to the right to scare her from jumping out. Unfortunately, this sent Rose flying out of the car headfirst. The rear tires ran over her.

"Well Larry, you got her," I said, shaking my head. We looked back and saw her sitting in the middle of the road. Alphin pulled the cab around to block traffic and stop other cars from hitting her.

When he got out the cab, Alphin told Rose, "Get up because you are going to jail."

She said she couldn't.

Alphin kept telling her to get up until I intervened.

"Why can't you get up," I calmly asked her.

"Because I'm paralyzed," Rose told me.

Alphin didn't miss a beat.

"Hey partner, if you'll say you were driving and take the heat on this one, I will catch the next one," he said. Alphin was not in good graces with our sergeant for some damage he'd done to other undercover vehicles.

I just shook my head and smiled. Typical Alphin. I called an ambulance for the injured woman.

As we waited, the night patrol commander, Captain Swift, who was about to retire, pulled up in his marked unit with the lights going. He got out of his vehicle, not knowing we were there and that the police were involved.

I walked back to his car and greeted him. Swift recognized us and realized the cab was ours. Rose still sat in the middle of the road. Swift didn't want any part of whatever this was. He got back in his car, turned off the lights and left without a word.

We followed the ambulance to the hospital, where doctors determined Rose had a broken leg, but wasn't paralyzed. Her cast reached from her ankle to her thigh.

We interviewed her in the hospital and became friendly. She offered information about her pimp and her life.

Rose wanted us to be the first to sign her cast, which we were happy to do. She was proud to show it off. Later we took her to jail for prostitution.

Dayshift vice officers told us when Rose came out of the jail on crutches, they saw both of our signatures and just laughed. They asked Rose if they could sign it, too.

The last thing we had to do was explain to Lt. Ray Fisher what had happened. He needed to prepare a statement for the media. Fisher was secretly happy with our initiative to use taxi cabs in the fight against prostitution.

Leaders, Prostitutes and Silence

Told by J.C. Williams Jr
with help from Larry Alphin

Pouring your heart and soul into a large, complicated investigation pays off. Unless it just disappears. Though not frequent, it happened in Fort Worth enough to raise police eyebrows.

Cops never worried about cases involving street prostitutes with their pimps, little escort services, male prostitutes and daily working girls at low-rent motels and hotels. But those involving more prominent people with more money rarely saw the light of day.

One case started with a tip from a judge friend of ours. My partner, Larry Alphin, and I were working in Special Investigations in the 1980's when the judge voiced concerns about a house in his upscale, westside neighborhood. He didn't believe it was a drug den, but many business-type men frequented the house where several young women were living.

The men always drove down a large driveway to a back garage, apparently so they wouldn't attract the attention of nosy neighbors.

With no other direction, we dug up the unlisted phone number to the house and called. Alphin talked with a woman who answered.

"I know this isn't how it usually works, but Robert gave me this number," he said.

"Depending on your schedule, can you or the other girls with you take care of my friend and I?"

They chit-chatted a couple of minutes until the woman became comfortable with him. There had been a cancelation, she said, and they'd be thrilled to take care of us both. Well then. Sometimes, the biggest cases start with trying different things and enjoying some luck.

We drove to the house and met with two women who were not street prostitutes or escort service women. We found the house immaculately clean with nothing out of place – much like a model home with no residents. It was furnished with red, blue and green bedrooms decorated with silk and satin fabric. A fully stocked bar beckoned.

Alphin and I had planned to make our agreements for sex and price individually, then we would insist we wanted to be in the same room. That way, we could file two prostitution cases.

Once inside, we went our different ways and made our deals. Alphin soon came knocking with his would-be sex partner. We talked a little, then arrested both women.

What we discovered was astonishing.

Several women rotated in and out of California to work the house, staying five days to a week before returning to California – this ensured they would never be connected to Fort Worth. I was impressed with tactics used by the organization, including that all clients had to be known and approved before they were able to partake.

We seized a ledger and a current client list we found in the house, as well as records connecting the organization to prostitution. All of this because we stumbled into the case and used a common name to talk our way inside.

I filed the police report and documented everything we'd found. I decided to make a copy of the ledger and all the information in case

it was lost before the case made its way through the courts. It was an unusual case.
The women were released immediately after posting bail. The prostitution house sold quickly.
The district attorney's office requested the case be turned over immediately. They took all our original files and casework from our office. We never saw it again.

I'm glad I kept copies of the information. It was obvious, later, why this was such a concern at the time. One or several people never wanted the information released.

Over the years, people who knew about the investigation and arrests questioned me about it. I never talked about the whole case.

The Shooting Bootlegger

Told by J.C. Williams Jr
with help from Larry Alphin
& Larry "Duck" Taylor

Crooks fall into distinct types.

They include the truly evil, dangerous, twisted, desperate, petty and harmless.

Occasionally, they cross into other types. Like our bootlegger, Frank Vaughn, a petty and relatively harmless regular on the city's southeast side.

See, Vaughn liked to sell booze out of house without a license, it didn't matter what kind and, after the local businesses closed, he didn't care who he sold to – minors, crack heads, winos, prostitutes and their pimps. Vaughn had been busted for illegal liquor sales many times. It didn't bother him, he just kept going.

We knew he also bought stolen liquor and had other sources of cheap booze that he sold. We had a few reports that Vaughn was selling marijuana and other drugs, but not enough to consider him a high-risk drug dealer.

Those of us who worked vice complaints in the 1980s ran hundreds of warrants on Cuban drug dealers, crack houses, methamphetamine operations and organized crime. Often times, it was difficult and always dangerous.

So when it was time to arrest Vaughn again, we thought it would be a piece of cake. My partner, Officer Larry Alphin, myself and two others - Officers Ronnie Gouyton and Larry "Duck" Taylor – headed out one day, expecting to just walk up, explain the warrant and be done with it. Taylor was there to help us. Gouyton, directed other officers to cover the perimeter and back of the house. Gouyton liked coming along and was our "expert" on the quality of alcohol Vaughn had.

The house looked like a well-illuminated convenience store when Alphin and I walked toward the front door. Vaughn sat in a chair on the covered front porch and when we called out to him and told him he was under arrest, he looked at us, stood and moved to the front door.

It wasn't going to be easy after all.

He'd seen our police jackets, heard us identify ourselves and still was going to barricade himself inside.

We immediately started running toward the door, which was solid wood with a large steel lock above the door handle.

We didn't make it in time. Alphin and I hit the door, trying to kick it open. It didn't work. Taylor joined in. We hadn't expected this, so we didn't have a battering ram or anything else to help us. With three of us kicking the door, it finally started to break.

Inside the house, Vaughn grabbed a handgun and started firing at us through the door. We didn't hear the shots at first, but Taylor looked inside and saw that Vaughn was armed.

When we crashed into the house, Vaughn threw the gun across the room and threw himself on a couch between an 8-year-old and a 12-year-old, both boys. That weasel had his hands up in the air as if he hadn't tried to kill us seconds ago.

Vaughn fired as many times as he could and three rounds were found lodged in a tree in front of the front door. Fortunately, the gunshots went in between us. But they were high enough that our small bullet-proof vests would have done no good in protecting us.

Routine warrants such as this are the ones that get officers killed. Though we laugh about it to this day, we're stunned no one got shot.

The Pornography Ring

THE MALLICK TOWER

Told by J.C. Williams Jr.
With help from Bob Shaw.

Fort Worth's Mallick Tower has been a fixture in the city since it opened in 1968, all 10 stories of it.

It carries a prestigious past and few could believe that nearly 20 years later, one of its tenants ran a highly profitable, national pornography operation inside those walls.[22]

Federal and state agencies investigated the company for months but couldn't make a case because of the way the business was organized. The business sold hardcore videos and other material, primarily shipping their goods through the United States Postal Service.

Advertising and other company business was conducted through ads and mail-outs. This allowed key executives to deny that they knew the content of what shipped out. This company also developed decoders to allow people to view hardcore pornography throughout the United States.

Federal Postal Inspector, Wayne Meyers, couldn't identify a way to prove the that president and national marketing director knew the content of their pornographic material. They had no informants.

That's when I entered in 1986.

"Wayne, has anyone with all the law enforcement agencies tried to just walk in the business and try to buy direct from them?" I asked. "No, because their business methods made an undercover operation very difficult," Meyers said.

I convinced my lieutenant, Bob Shaw, to allow me to work the case undercover.

I met with the marketing director at Mallick Tower, who in turn introduced me to the president. After chatting, they welcomed me to their executive offices.

They made me swear I wasn't a cop nor was I affiliated with any law enforcement agency. Then they trained me – how to spot undercover officers and what to say to avoid arrest. I let them know how thankful I was for their help.

I made numerous purchases from them. Then it was time to arrest them. I staged local television reporters outside, and with other vice officers, we all trooped into the porn office. I identified myself, arrested both men and read them their Miranda rights. Reporters then started asking questions.

Courts convicted both the president and national marketing director; their numerous companies were shut down.

Chapter 4

Patrol, Fights, Pursuits, Trains and Challenges

Every society gets the kind of criminal it deserves. What is equally true is that every community gets the kind of law enforcement it insists on.

-Robert Kennedy

The Giant and the Hostage

Told by J.C. Williams Jr.

In the turbulent landscape of Fort Worth's east side during the early 1980s, my tenure as a patrol officer unfolded amidst a tight-knit group led by Sergeant Dub Bransom.

One incident stands out vividly – the tale of "The Hostage and The Giant." In those days, we patrolled the streets without the modern luxuries officers now have at their disposal. The call that day was a hostage situation - a woman was being held captive by her ex-boyfriend, a menacing figure with a violent criminal history. The woman planned to escape when officers arrived and she needed help, dispatch told me.

As I neared the house, youthful confidence clouded my judgment though caution remained my ally, my first mistake was parking too closely to the front on the house, hoping another officer would show up before I approached. The woman, traumatized, saw me and burst out the front door in a panic, running circles in the street. At the same time, the ex-boyfriend barged out, his eyes fixed on me. He was a towering 6-foot-7 giant with a violent history.

"This is my woman," he bellowed, coming toward me. I knew he would try to hurt me if I intervened. I called for help and one of my academy classmates, Officer Dean Cunningham, rushed forward.

I wanted to delay the inevitable confrontation, but that didn't happen.

I improvised, telling the suspect he could take the woman inside, because it was a civil matter. I hoped to avoid a street brawl. The giant believed he was in control and agreed. The woman screamed louder, believing I was setting her up to be hurt.

As he turned toward her, I seized the moment and lunged at the giant, wrapping my arms around his neck in a chokehold.

A chaotic struggle ensued as he carried me across the street and through yards. Eventually, I brought him down, pinning him until he stopped fighting.

Cunningham arrived to witness the aftermath.

"My God, J.C., that man is a GIANT! How did you get him down?" he exclaimed.

The bulldog takedown was necessary, I told him. Handcuffing the giant proved challenging because of his massive wrists. The cuffs only clicked once, but that was enough.

In my patrol car, the suspect acknowledged my unconventional approach.

“You really like to do that, don't you? Bulldog people and choke them out," he said.

I told him that technique was a last resort, preferable to using lethal force.

This incident underscored the imperative for officers to resolve conflicts quickly without resorting to extreme measures.

Over the years, these experiences molded my understanding as a commander, particularly when justifying the use of deadly force to the police chief, the media, the community among others.

The Big Fight, Police Van and Jail Elevator

Told by J.C. Williams Jr
with help from Larry Alphin
& Ronnie Gouyton

There once was a time, not that long ago, when Fort Worth Police officers didn't tolerate disrespect, threats and confrontation from lowlifes at bars. Fortune didn't smile on those that crossed that line, bless their hearts.

I worked in the department's Special Investigations Unit with my friends that included Larry Alphin and Ronnie Gouyton during the 1980s.

One day, I heard from two Texas Alcoholic Beverage Commission (TABC) officers who, the night before, had been chased out of a bar on the city's southeast side during one of their investigations. The bar was the subject of numerous complaints including alcohol violations, drug abuse and gang activity.

While investigating the complaints at the bar, several patrons confronted them, forcing the officers to flee before they finished.

We jumped at the chance to go back to the bar with them the next night. We had the feeling, given the hostile environment, we'd make lots of arrests. We got one of the FWPD transport vans (paddy wagon) – we were going to need it.

A crowd of several men who were known crooks and hated cops, met us when we showed up. These men controlled the criminal activity at the bar and thought, foolishly, that they could intimidate us, forcing us to retreat. Wrong.

Their mistake led to a brawl stretching from the front of the bar to the street – fists flying, feet kicking and language that would make any mother blush.

Handcuffs adorned most of the bad guys. A few others we simply launched into the back of the van. Then off we went in our one-vehicle, loud, chaotic parade. When we arrived at the city jail, we parked next to an elevator where my sergeant, E.W. Usrey, and the on-duty jail lieutenant met us.

Other officers in need of some laughs, heard about our arrests and showed up to watch the circus. Of course, if needed, they'd jump in to help. Regular people stopped to stare at the pandemonium.

Our suspects in the van never stopped hollering, cussing and making vile threats at a volume that ensured they were heard up and down the street.

"This fight isn't over," I told the sergeant and lieutenant. "So, if you want to stay and watch, that's fine."

With that, I jerked open the van door, jumped into the back and started throwing suspects to other officers in the parking lot. The supervisors had disappeared.

Now, this elevator was small, designed for maybe four people in close quarters. It also served the city courts and other business areas on the first floor.

On this night, cops and suspects alike – eight or nine of us – crammed into that elevator, bodies on top of each other, suspects upside down, all of us twisted together as the slugfest continued.

Ding. The elevator door opened onto the public area outside the courtroom on the first floor. Those poor people. Each got quite an eyeful - I still remember their shocked and disbelieving faces before the door shut and continued down to the jail.

Our prisoners complained to the judge and people standing around about how they were treated by us. But then they ruined it by threatening the judge, everyone in eyesight and all their mothers as well. That skewered any sympathy they may have hoped for. High bonds were set.

Phil South & the Branch Davidians

Told by J.C. Williams Jr.
With help from Phil South

People love watching televised police pursuits. In reality, however, pursuits are dicey affairs, with each one carrying the potential for property damage and catastrophic injuries and deaths.

Police departments, the subject of many wrongful death lawsuits spawned by deadly pursuits, have been forced to change or update pursuit policies.

In the early 1990s, the Fort Worth Police Department issued a restrictive pursuit policy, calling for more intense scrutiny of pursuits, allowing only two police units to be involved and limited, for the most part, to its own city limits. Numerous other restrictions were included, and violations of the policy were severe, including indefinite suspension (tantamount to being fired.)

In 1993, I commanded the Weed and Seed community policing project. We were tracking a suspect we believed killed one of our elderly residents. The community was terrified another slaying would occur before he could be arrested.

Sgt. Phil South – a mentor of mine when I was a rookie – worked for me and headed the search for the killer. I told Phil to do anything he needed to do with our resources to make an arrest.

We set up surveillance at a place we knew the suspect frequented. That night, we found him inside an 18-wheeler semi-truck. When officers neared the truck, the suspect took off, and the pursuit began.

The truck driver led the chase east of Fort Worth, throughout Dallas County and then headed south toward Waco, where at the time, the Branch Davidian stand-off was ongoing. Federal, state and local lawmen by the dozens were there in response to the siege. It was about 70 miles south of Fort Worth.

Our suspected killer knew nothing of the stand-off in Waco as he headed straight for it. Our entire midnight shift was chasing the truck, most of whom were running out of gas. They'd pull off the highway, grab gas and shout at attendants they would be back to pay later. It resembled pit stops during NASCAR races.

Texas Department of Public Safety troopers helped bring the pursuit to an end, shooting the truck's tires to prevent our suspect from driving into the Branch Davidian compound. No one was injured and we arrested our suspect. It all happened near where scores of reporters and cameramen were camped to cover the siege. Most were ecstatic to have a wild pursuit to cover to break the tedium of the day-to-day siege coverage.[23]

South kept me apprised of the activity and it was my job to spread the news up the command chain. Deputy Chief David Reagan was on duty and when I called in the early morning hours.

"I hope this is not bad news because I just woke up Chief (Tom) Windham. He's not happy about problems in dispatch," he said. I told him the chief would "forget all about that shit" when he learned Weed and Seed officers were in Waco outside the Branch Davidian compound.

I couldn't help but laugh at Reagan's silence. I know he was terrified to call Windham about our pursuit that had been covered by the national press corps. And my officers had landed right in the middle of a national news story. Reagan didn't want to be the messenger.

I talked with South again for more details. We'd been friends for years and I could tell he was having too much fun, getting tours from local agencies on the security perimeter around the compound. He was enjoying this crazy moment. South asked if he and his officer could stay during the day for more tours.

Like you do with your children, I had to pull the plug.

"Phil, I know you are all having fun, but this is not 'Weed and Seed' on vacation,'" I told him. I added that play time was over and they needed to come back.

We both laughed. I gave them a few extra hours. In Fort Worth, I was waiting for the axe to drop.

I didn't get a call from any supervisor or commander in the department. Rumors ran crazy that my operation was in trouble and the chief might fire me.

When I finally saw Windham, he asked if I had planned any more out-of-town vacations for Weed and Seed officers.

"To be honest, I'm not sure," I said. "We are kind of spontaneous when we plan our trips."

He stared at me, shook his head and walked away, as if he had no idea what to do with me.

I had no idea what, if any, discipline would be handed out over the pursuit. I was thrilled we'd arrested the suspected killer. At the end of the day, the chief was happy. He just didn't want anyone to know.

Fight at the Jail

Told by Kevin Foster
with Kathy Sanders

Leaving a knife concealed on someone you're taking to jail is a big mistake, with big consequences. I committed that sin once early in my career and earned the right to work jail intake on a Saturday night in the early 1980s. Intake is where suspects are "processed" into the jail – searched, fingerprinted, photographed and put in jail cells.

And that's where I found myself one incredibly busy Saturday night - in the company of thieves, dopers, prostitutes, drunks and other misbegotten folk.

A particularly combative suspect came through and instead of cooperating, he decided he wanted to fight with the jail staff. That was a bad decision any time but especially bad on a busy weekend night when the jail was fully staffed.

After the suspect was booked in, a jailer helped me take him to the only available "single cell", in this case where the light bulb was burned out. The cell was long and narrow, and the only light came through a small window in the cell door. But the cell was empty and the only one available.
As soon as our guy walked into the cell, he renewed his fight and attacked me, smacking me right in the face. The fight escalated from there. I pushed him further inside and we battled to the back of the cell. When I tried to leave, the suspect regained his footing and attacked me before I could reach the cell door.

The jailer ran for help, and I again fought the man to the back of the cell, finally knocking him off his feet, as the jail lieutenant and another officer ran into the cell. But our bad guy just wouldn't give up. Still on the floor, he looked up at the lieutenant then latched on to his leg, entwining his arms around his knee and thigh.

It was dark, cramped and crowded in the cell and at this point, almost impossible to see. The last thing you would want to do was to get down on the floor to fight with the suspect to get him to loosen his grip. I thought the best way to help end the fight and help the lieutenant was to kick the bad guy in the midsection, hopefully causing him to release the leg. I gave him a solid kick and though he grunted loudly, the lieutenant didn't move and as far as I could see, the suspect still held onto the lieutenant. I kicked the suspect again, but nothing happened – just another grunt. The third time I delivered a kick, there was a loud grunt from the suspect and the lieutenant ordered everyone out of the cell – except the bad guy.

"I didn't think he was ever going to release you," I told the lieutenant as the cell door slammed shut and locked.

I was shocked when he smiled and said, "Hell, son, he let go the first you kicked him."

30 Seconds

Told by Kevin Foster

with Kathy Sanders

Police officers receive their share of injuries from violent criminals – seemingly calm people who turn into hell-fire demons in a split second, putting cops in life and death struggles. When it's a vicious one-on-one fight, they pray they'll be victorious.
Sometimes those prayers show up in the form of regular people. Like telephone linemen.

Police officer Randy Whisenhunt, a Vietnam vet with two purple hearts, was a training officer I worked with on the city's north side in 1990. He was a good and well-respected and popular officer that worked the midnight shift with me.

One night in February of 1990, Whisenhunt went to a traffic accident, where a car struck a utility pole and knocked out power in the area. He checked to see if the driver, Jesus Torres, was injured. Torres did not appear to be hurt, but he smelled like a booze barn and spectacularly failed the "field sobriety evaluation." The man was drunk.

Whisenhunt – riding solo – handcuffed Torres on suspicion of drunk driving and sat him in the patrol car. He then began paperwork for the incident and waited for a tow truck and an electric company worker to take care of the power outage. All this happened in a relatively isolated area, with no houses, businesses or help nearby.

A few minutes later, Torres said he needed to pee and asked Whisenhunt to remove the handcuffs so he could relieve himself beside the car. The officer knew they faced a long wait and agreed to let Torres do his business.

As soon as the handcuffs came off, all hell broke loose.

Torres attacked Whisenhunt, repeatedly striking him with his fists while trying to take the officer's gun. Whisenhunt, who had just enough time to radio for help, fought fiercely to keep his handgun. He was a tough, experienced officer, as well as a Vietnam vet, and he wasn't giving up his gun.
Torres instead got the officer's heavy-duty flashlight and savagely beat Whisenhunt in the head and face. Covered in his own blood, the officer was hurt, alone and losing the fight.

And that's when help arrived in the form of a Texas Electric lineman, we'll call Frank – he was a big man and a fellow Vietnam veteran. Frank arrived during the worst of the beating. He saw Torres sitting on Whisenhunt's chest and heard the thuds of the flashlight as it was striking Whisenhunt. Realizing the officer was defenseless and needed help, he bailed out of his truck and ran toward Whisenhunt, who he thought was dead. When Torres saw the lineman barreling toward him, he abandoned the fight for the gun and ran away.

Frank scooped up the officer's gun and ran after the suspect, who was struggling up an embankment. The lineman took aim and opened fire on Torres, the bullets ripping into the suspect's legs several times. Frank climbed the hill, saw Torres still trying to escape and said, "You move and I'll shoot you again."

Officer "Torch" Wilson heard the gunshots when he arrived and promptly threw himself on top of Whisenhunt to shield the downed officer from an unknown shooter. Within seconds, I arrived, ran to Randy, and thought he was dead. I looked up the hill and saw Frank standing over Torres, pistol in hand. I knew then what had happened.[24]

Other police officers swarmed into the area – I took Whisenhunt's pistol from the lineman while a fellow cop handcuffed Torres. I went back to Whisenhunt and began talking to him in case he could hear me.

"Randy – you're okay, you're going to be okay," I said repeatedly. At first, there was no response. Then, his head moved and, without opening his eyes, Whisenhunt said, "I don't feel okay." With that, we knew he was going to survive.

Medics worked on Whisenhunt as soon as the ambulance arrived. Several minutes later – and more an afterthought on our part – treatment began on Torres who had lost a lot of blood from his gunshot wounds. Ambulances rushed both men to the hospital – Whisenhunt went home later that day; Torres's injuries required a much longer stay.

Frank – who jumped into the fray with no thought of his own safety – earned hero-like status among the lawmen on the scene. But the story wasn't over.

A few months later, Torres received a life sentence and was fined $10,000 for assaulting Whisenhunt. The convict promptly decided to sue Frank and his employer, Texas Electric, for the injuries he suffered. That didn't sit well with Whisenhunt, who in turn filed a lawsuit against Torres for attacking him. Local Attorney Jim Lane represented Whisenhunt at no charge.

Texas Electric refused to settle, and the civil cases went to trial, ending in a $1.75 million dollar judgement against Torres.[25] As he expected, Whisenhunt never saw a penny from the case, but that wasn't his point. He was merely standing by the man who saved his life.
As it turned out, the utility pole didn't belong to the electric company. It belonged to the City of Fort Worth. Frank didn't have to be there. It was just luck.[26]

If Frank had arrived 30 seconds later, this would have been a much different story.

The Berryhill Drive and Canberra Court Gang

Told by J.C. Williams Jr.,
With help from Naymond James

As a rookie, I worked evenings for Sergeant Dub Bransom, an experienced lawman who'd been partners with my father for years. We worked Fort Worth's east side neighborhoods at a time when crime was rampant.

Bransom's keen insight into policing and the high crime in our district led him to mandate that two officers would ride in each patrol car. Two officers working together could accomplish more and be more effective in handling calls and making arrests than a single officer. It also provided enhanced safety for officers.

I often worked with Officer Naymond James, an eastside native and standout high school track star. Though both of us treated residents fairly and respectfully, we didn't tolerate aggressive, arrogant and threatening behavior, particularly when aimed at police.

One day, James and I answered a burglary call in the Berryhill Drive and Canberra Court area. We didn't know at the time that two other officers had been sent to address a minor theft in the same area while we were off work. The officers, not familiar with our area, were confronted by several aggressive young men who slung threats at them. They left the area, thinking it was best to diffuse the situation.

These thugs had started a small gang and claimed the area as theirs. They thrived on intimidating residents in the community, stealing from them and wreaking havoc in the neighborhood. They even set a horse on fire in a nearby pasture. We also didn't know initially that a detective, J.J. Lee, was working on all these cases.

We gathered the burglary details from the victims, who obviously didn't want to go outside because these hoodlums scared them. As we left the house, we heard shouting next door. "Get off our hill, now!"

Shocked, we saw five young men standing in front of an old, run-down vacant house. Naymond and I looked at each other, both thinking the same thing: "Did these five punks just say what we think they said?"

One of the thugs sauntered toward us with the others following. He looked at us and said, "This is our hill and get out of here now." We turned toward them and asked for their identification. But something in our voices, expressions or physical stances caused these men to realize they should be alarmed.

They didn't expect us to confront them. It certainly was not a repeat of what had happened the day before. Their situation was rapidly going downhill. Their excitement at having a gang and a territory dissipated – they spun on their heels and raced to their clubhouse. They didn't know Naymond had been a state champion track star in high school.

Into the house they scurried, but James was there to stop them from closing the door. He was trying to force his way – two of the gang were trying to push him back, while the other three were inside trying to push the door close.

I didn't think. I ran full speed at the door and hit it, sending the three inside flying through the air. James grabbed the leader by the throat, picked him up off the ground and engaged in a heart-to-heart chat with the young man. The others went from being neighborhood predators to bawling babies.

Arrests were made and they were held on "investigation fugitive." It meant they would be held for three days until the detective in charge of the cases filed formal charges or released them.

What Naymond and I both knew is you don't walk away from this type of confrontation. Doing so sets the next officers up for a difficult time. We often responded to high-risk situations because so many residents knew us and our reputations. We had fewer problems than most officers. The community also knew we didn't tolerate nonsense – everyone causing a problem was going to jail, particularly if we had to summon the "paddy wagon."

Young men like these, if not dealt with firmly, continue be a threat to their neighborhood and cause decay in the community. This set up our model later when establishing Weed & Seed.

The Glass Key

Told by Kevin Foster
with Kathy Sanders

Huddled in the shadows of downtown Fort Worth, a brick box building stood next to rundown housing projects, reveling in its disheveled state and infamous reputation. They called it The Glass Key.

Born in the 1950s, the café/gathering spot once sat amidst a small neighborhood with homes and streets. While known for serving good chicken at a lunch counter inside, The Glass Key soon became better known for all the wrong reasons and the neighborhood died, morphing into vacant lots that the Key used for parking.

Every sin and vice thrived in and around the Glass Key – violence, gambling, murder, prostitution, drugs, bootleg alcohol, theft. It also served as a market for stolen goods, supplied by thieves from around the city. It reeked of poverty and despair.

In 1989, cops were dispatched to the club 344 times and 67 arrests were made. That made the Glass Key the most active location for police activity that year.

Police made daily, if not hourly, calls here and God help any unwitting person who stumbled into the area by accident. It truly was hell on earth.[27]

So many memorable stories stem from The Glass Key – here are just a few.

Pocket Change

The 1980s was Fort Worth's most violent and deadly decade. One Saturday night, there was a shooting at the Key. FWPD Officer John Marcellus and I arrived and found a man lying in a large pool of blood just outside the front door. Someone had shot him in the chest. He wasn't breathing and had that vacant, wide-open stare we'd seen so many times before - he was dying or dead.

As this was a typical weekend night here, about 200 people stood around, including children.

Paramedics with MedStar Ambulance arrived just when we did and frantically tried to save the shooting victim. They sliced off his clothes and moved him around to better reach his injuries. As a result, a few dollars' worth of loose change fell from the man's pockets, littering the ground near him.

A group of kids – 12 to 15 years old – watched intensely from the sidelines, particularly when the change hit the ground. Their muscles tensed, ready to spring and scoop up what money they could. But they looked at me first. I held up my hand, pointed a finger at them and gave them my meanest, "don't-you-dare" look. They froze.

The medics loaded our shooting victim on the stretcher and ran to the ambulance while still trying to save this man. He died anyway.

At this point, the only thing stopping these kids from grabbing the pocket change on the ground was me – it lay between us. They all looked me in the eye for a few seconds. Then, I yelled, "Go!" sending all five of them diving to the ground, clawing to get every coin they could reach.

Marcellus laughed so hard; he had trouble speaking. He did mention, however, we both probably were going to hell.

Running away

The Glass Key fell into my district when I was a sergeant on the northside, as did the volatile Butler Housing Projects and the downtown area.

It was summer. It was 1989. It was a weekend night.

It was when an officer we'll call Bill was working off-duty as security for a food and beer distributor warehouse, just north of The Glass Key. Bill was very tall, physically fit and known for his legendary strength among fellow police officers. He also lacked patience with suspects who failed to obey him.

He'd been hired to provide security for the business that was reeling from a rash of thefts and vehicle burglaries at the warehouse. Owners were adamant the crime had to stop. So, Bill donned regular street clothes and patrolled the business.

About midnight, Bill radioed that he'd spotted a man breaking into a truck. Within seconds, the bad guy was fleeing toward the Key with the cop on his heels.

On this night, up to 300 people hung around The Glass Key, with liquor sales in the parking lot and drug sales conducted around the building. Another 50 people crowded inside, where a dice game was underway inside the front door.

The would-be thief headed straight to the Key, his bastion of safety. Or so he thought.

This was no place to be on your own - every police officer in the city knew that. And Bill was running right into the thick of it.

With lights flashing and sirens blaring, officers raced to the Key, desperate to prevent any calamity befalling Bill. His last transmission let us know the bad guy had run inside the building. Then there was radio silence. Another officer and I arrived within a minute.

We were stunned – throngs of people jammed the doorway trying to get out of The Glass Key. They were stuck two abreast in their stampede to get away from whatever was happening inside. Initially, we couldn't get inside. Suddenly, a gap formed, and we rushed in.

A group of patrons cowered near the bathroom and juke box while Bill stood on top of the food counter, like a winded avenging angel. He had pinned the bad guy backwards over the counter, grabbed his throat and slapped him with a huge hand. Then he slapped the man again, with the backswing.

Bill appeared to be lecturing the terrified suspect, something about never running from a cop who tells you to stop. He also questioned the would-be thief's poor life choices.

Hoping to end the ordeal, I yelled at Bill that we had arrived. He turned, greeted me by name with a smile on his face and handed us the bad guy he'd been chasing. Then he asked for a ride back to the warehouse.

Our runner didn't require medical attention and earned a trip to jail. When we emerged, the crowds had dwindled. I assume they preferred a quieter venue; grateful they weren't caught up in the mayhem. That included officers as well.

Surprise!

Trying to sneak up on The Glass Key was a fool's errand – lookouts were posted everywhere to alert those inside if enemies or police tried to encroach on their territory. It took clever plotting to best them.

Once, I assembled an ambulance, a yellow taxicab and a group of police officers to raid the illegal gambling den.

The officers loaded up in the taxi – like the clown cars at the circus – and waited. The ambulance crew waited for my signal and then took off, racing down the adjacent highway access road with its lights and siren causing a scene. The lookouts were distracted long enough for our taxi to pull up to the Key's front door. Out we jumped, barging into The Glass Key just as the owner, Albert Huey-You, was about to throw the dice. It was a win for us, as well as memorable experience.

An Accidental Discharge

One day, Rick McDaniel and J.R. "Smitty" Smith came up with a plan to get the drop on the drug dealers and gamblers at the Glass Key. Knowing that most of the patrons were illegally carrying guns, they decided to rush in through the back door and Smitty would be carrying a sawed-off double barrel .12-gauge shotgun. Jim Wade, Jimmy Little and J.C. Williams Sr. would be coming in through the front door to prevent any escapes.

As they made their grand entry, Smitty tripped and fell with his knee hitting the ground hard. He accidentally fired off a round from the shotgun that luckily, went right through the ceiling and roof. Not missing a beat, Smitty stayed in that position and pointed the shotgun in the direction of the inhabitants and yelled at them; "Put your hands up!" People were diving for cover and checking to see who had been shot.

Suddenly, there were a series of loud "thumps" as handguns and narcotics began hitting the floor.

J.C. Williams and Jimmy Little got two 5-gallon "pickle buckets" from Albert and they went around picking up the guns. They filled both buckets.

The Death of the Glass Key

The end of the Glass Key came explosively early on Monday, May 14, 1990. Huey-You had hosted an all-night gambling extravaganza featuring two high-stakes dice players. Thousands of dollars had changed hands and lots of people saw the money. The game had pitted two men against each other, Robert "Austin" Satterwhite, 30, and Billy Edd "Unc" Farmer, who lost nearly $150,000 that night – $60,00 in cash and another $90,000 he owed Satterwhite.

As dawn broke, Satterwhite was tired and wanted the game to end. People started leaving. About 7 a.m., a stolen brown 1983 Oldsmobile screeched to a halt in the gravel parking lot and four men jumped out.

One man wore a wolf mask, another sported a gorilla-head mask and the other two had donned ski masks, witnesses told police. They all had guns.

The wolf robber burst in the Glass Key first and ordered the remaining 20-25 people to put their money on the table, police said. Different witnesses reported hearing, "Task force! Task force!" "Get, Austin!" a reference to Satterwhite, and "Put all your money on the table!"

The only person inside not scrambling for cover was Satterwhite, who was wearing a bulletproof vest. The lead robber walked up to him and shot Satterwhite point blank in the head. He fell to the ground dead.

Witnesses said the robbers started gathering the goods and suddenly opened fire on everybody. Joe Wafers, 54, was shot in the head and died. James Lacey, 56, received two shots to the head. Timothy Carter, 45, was shot in the chest while he slept.

In the parking lot, Earl Edwards reportedly was sitting in a car when he was shot in the chest. He died five days later at a nearby hospital. All the deaths were caused by high-velocity gunshot wounds, autopsies concluded.

The robbers grabbed all the cash they saw. They missed Satterwhite's money belt with $60,000 in cash in it. Then they disappeared.[28]

Police arrested two brothers days after the rampage. No evidence linked them to the killings, and they were released.

On April 26, 1996, police announced a breakthrough in the six-year-old case. A group of four men – friends and acquaintances from Benbrook, Texas – were accused of being the masked killers.

Julian Burt, who was 21 when the killings took place, was the man behind the wolf mask, responsible for most of the gunplay inside the Glass Key, investigators said. Burt hatched the plot after seeing thousands of dollars at the dice game when he stopped by earlier.

"He and maybe others were at the Glass Key before the shooting...left the Glass Key and gathered up the group of people and put together the robbery plan," according to Homicide Sgt. Paul Kratz.

Aiding Burt was Malcom Griffin, who was 18 at the time; Anthony "Tony" Fennell, who was 17, and Robby Robinson, who was 31.

Burt pleaded guilty to two counts of capital murder and one count of murder in 2003. He is serving those life sentences in prison as well as another conviction for a drug-related killing that occurred eight months after the Glass Key.

Griffin pleaded guilty and received a life prison term. He was the gunman who killed Edwards in the parking lot. He died in 2002.

Fennell pleaded guilty and received a 35-year prison sentence. He was the group's look-out in the parking lot.

Robinson pleaded guilty and was sentenced to 42 years in prison. His role, he said, was to gather the stolen money and jewelry.

The Glass Key Café never re-opened.[29]

A few years later, I saw Huey-You at a downtown hospital. He was accompanied by his son, who'd been the cook for years at the one-time café. Huey-You motioned me over with a smile. When I shook his hand, it was like reconnecting with a long-lost friend.

We swapped war stories for about an hour – police sneaking up on them, the crooks hiding things we never knew about, laughing the whole time. I never saw him again. I did, however, hear when he died.

Despite the headaches, crimes and dangers, Huey-You respected police officers – for him it was all part of a game between the gamblers and cops.

A Pursuit and the Trinity River

Told by Kevin Foster
with Kathy Sanders

Car chases have existed nearly as long as cars. Police want cars to stop, drivers don't want to stop and think a better idea is to run away. It usually doesn't end too well for the drivers, whether they've stolen a car, are dodging arrest warrants or just don't like being told what to do. Some end tragically. Others are near misses.

One bitterly cold night, two of my officers spotted a stolen Chevrolet Suburban on the city's south side. When they tried to pull it over, the driver decided to take off.

As supervisor, I joined in the pursuit to monitor it. The cars headed north to downtown Fort Worth and then the cars made their way east on Belknap and then north on Oakhurst Scenic Drive.

None of us knew how the chase would end, particularly when the Suburban made a sudden detour into a park. The suspect then drove straight into the freezing water of the Trinity River.

His passenger jumped out just as the Suburban plunged into the river. He yelled at his partner that he could not swim. "Good luck," the driver told him, and then he started swimming.

He surprised us with his resolve to evade capture – the driver kept going with the current. While he was swimming, a large rat or maybe a nutria traveled beside him, eventually outpacing the driver. I telephoned my lieutenant to let him know the situation and that the man might not survive. We called the Fort Worth Fire Department for a rescue boat and crew. When it arrived, the exhausted swimmer was under a bridge, clinging to a pillar, apparently too cold to continue.

Fire officials launched the boat, jetted to the man and offered to help him. The driver refused to give up, so the firefighters gave him a life jacket and patiently waited. It wasn't long before he climbed into the boat and returned to shore, where we promptly arrested him. Paramedics on the scene treated him before we took him to jail.

Firefighters noted the location of the submerged Suburban so it could be retrieved the next day. When recovery crews arrived, they discovered the Suburban had traveled several hundred yards further downstream.

Against the odds, the driver survived to steal another day.

The Old Motel

Told by Kevin Foster
with Kathy Sanders

Every big city and town has those sleazy, downtrodden places that attract the misfits of society – the dopers, the drunks and the sex workers, to name a few. Fort Worth has had more than its fair share of them.

But the Victorian Inn on Hemphill was one of the worst and well-known to cops. No one remembers when a fire destroyed the south half the building back in the day, but its boarded-up windows and doors bore testament to years of neglect.

The owner was a Chinese immigrant with a heavy accent and very bad English skills who became known as "Hop Sing" (a character from the Bonanza television series). He didn't care for police officers and their frequent interruptions of his business. He rented rooms by the hour, day and week and didn't care who rented the rooms as long as they paid.

He married a young woman - referred to in the area as "the prettiest whore on Hemphill" – but he had trouble keeping her home. She stayed out late and disappeared for days on end, which drove her husband crazy. I don't think she cared.

Traffic at the Victorian Inn was constant, with a steady flow of prostitutes, drug dealers, thieves, hoodlums and killers loitering and conducting business in the rooms, the sidewalk, and the parking lot. Police and code enforcement officers stopped by daily, but business kept booming. It was annoying and frustrating.

One night, a group of very young and enterprising south side officers conceived an idea to impact business there.

The electrical wiring of the motel was in shambles with the breaker box in the hallway. The plan was to have a plainclothes cop start throwing random breakers in the box - it would cause chaos, disrupt illegal activity, and be entertaining. And that's what happened.

Lights began going on and off, people emerged from their rooms and Hop Sing carried a three-ring binder full of notes to the breaker box to stabilize the lights. Our plainclothes officer insisted on helping, purposely throwing further wrenches into the system. Cops surrounding the outside kept a lookout for wanted criminals and when they spotted one coming out of their room, the foot chase was on. People ran all over the neighborhood that night.

Drug dealers, realizing they'd been had, started throwing away their dope and frantically trying to re-enter their rooms. Some made it – others didn't.

Hop Sing remained confused over what had happened, he was mad that his wife once again was missing (she showed up later) and a number of crooks went to jail. Better yet, the officers had a good time doing their job. A few years later, what was left of the Victorian Inn burned to the ground, leaving nothing but memories in its wake.

Joe Wallace and the Rookie

Told by J.C. Williams Jr.
with Joe Wallace

Undercover work has extreme highs and lows. When you're in it, your sense of humor follows those extremes – it's hilarious to "bump" a car full of your cop buddies going 70 mph an hour on the highway or jacking with a friend's rookie until you almost get a flashlight upside the head.

When I was assigned to Special Investigations, my partner was Larry Alphin. One night, in 1982, we had decided to focus on some current gambling and prostitution complaints. While driving down Interstate 30, we spotted another undercover car with four of our friends in it. They were assigned to narcotics and had been targeting drug dealers aligned with local gangs. We figured they were going to meet their informant to make more drug buys.

Both of our cars were traveling between 60 and 70 mph, and they hadn't seen us. Alphin laughed quietly and I knew then he was going to do a high-speed "bump." Alphin sped up, moved behind them and bumped into their car, with a hearty thud.

We could tell they'd gone for their guns, wondering what the hell had happened and who had done it. We laughed and sped around them.

Once we were on the east side, we headed to the Valley View Motel to check on the prostitution complaints. We spotted my friend, Officer Joe Wallace, patrolling with his rookie officer.

Wallace was one of the smartest, calmest, most caring, fun and dedicated cops I ever worked with – everyone liked him.
So of course, we had to mess with them.

Larry drove up next to their patrol car, waved at Wallace and yelled, "Officer, we need to talk to you. Will you pull over?'' We were undercover, looking a little rough and the rookie didn't know us. Wallace did and braced himself for whatever prank was coming.

The rookie pulled into a parking lot, and I sauntered up to the passenger door where Wallace was sitting.

"Officer, I guess you know why we wanted to talk to you," I said.

"No, not really," Wallace replied. I raised my voice, pointed my finger at the rookie and accused her of speeding. "I demand you write her a ticket right now."

Wallace turned to the stunned young officer, waved his hand and told her to just leave. "I am not going to write her a ticket," he told me. As she put the patrol car in gear and started to pull away, I reached in the open car window and wrapped my arms around the door frame.

"You can try to leave, but I am not going to let go until that officer is issued a ticket," I yelled.
The officer saw a crazy person hanging on to the door and refusing to budge. Wallace could barely keep his laughter contained, hanging his head down to hide his grin.

Suddenly, the rookie slammed the car into park, jumped out with her big flashlight and ran toward me. "Go ahead and tell her who I am," I told Wallace.

"I don't know who this crazy guy is," Wallace told his trainee instead. With those words, my friend turned everything around on me. Just as she raised her arm to hit me with that flashlight, I managed to get my badge out and identify myself. It was hilarious. And Wallace gave his rookie a rave review for initiative.

Trains vs. People

Told by Kevin Foster
With help from John Marshall

When I worked on the south side of town, I learned about the power of trains and the carnage they can inflict on a person or a vehicle. One of our most frequent police calls involved people dead from train accidents.

An area of ours had many railroad tracks and only a few crossings – except for the train noise, it was a quiet area.

One night many years ago, while John Marshall and I were patrolling this area and on an unlit side street, we saw a body half on the road and half on some grass. We thought this man was dead – he wasn't moving, and one leg was mangled with the foot missing.

After calling in our discovery, we moved closer. Suddenly, the "body" moved. He bent his knee on the destroyed leg and raised what was left of the leg with exposed bones and flesh flapping. He said not a word and never looked at us. We both jumped, making sounds like we'd just been tackled on the football field.

While awaiting the ambulance, this man who we'll call Steve, told us he was trying the cross the railroad siding and was on a train when it started to move. Steve said he tried to jump but his leg got caught in the wheels and he was tangled.

A couple of turns of the wheels and his foot was torn off and Steve fell free from the train.

When no help showed up, he rose and walked several hundred yards down the road, his leg bones digging into the ground with each step. He collapsed where we found him.

When medics arrived, they searched for the foot in case it could be reattached by surgeons. The medic who found the foot, still encased in the tightly laced shoe, held it up in the air like a trophy. The damage was so severe, Steve's leg was partially amputated, and his foot was disposed of.

Several months later, we ran into Steve, who had sued the railroad and received a token settlement to dismiss the lawsuit. He was wearing a good prosthetic leg and told us he was doing well.

A few days later, we saw Steve again. He was drunk, holding a 40-ounce bottle of malt liquor and was carrying a .45-caliber handgun he'd just used to shoot someone. Steve went to jail that night and we never saw him again.

Sleeping Between the Rails

Told by Kevin Foster
with Kathy Sanders

Urban myths or legends kill people – particularly when involving trains.

I learned some migrants - just passing through on their way north – truly believed that sleeping between railroad rails kept them safe from snakes when sleeping outdoors.

The myth declared that snakes can't cross the rails, but I never saw evidence confirming this. The theory continued that the person asleep on the tracks would hear any train approaching and give them ample time to escape. All bets were off, however, if they were passed out drunk or incredibly heavy sleepers.

I was summoned to a set of train tracks in the early 2000s, where a train had run over and killed a man who had been sleeping between the rails. The train was stopped and a private railroad police officer was present.

We learned the train crew spotted the man as they drove over him. They stopped the train as fast as possible and went to check on him. Crew members thought he was dead because of a massive head injury and notified their railroad police department. The nearest officer was in Denton, Texas, and it took him more than an hour to appear.

I believe they should have called local officials first – the police or fire department – who could have helped immediately, but that's not what happened.

When the railroad officer arrived in Fort Worth, he did a cursory examination of the victim and pronounced him dead. That's when we were called.

I immediately had issues with this officer, from his smirk to his cockiness, and how he tried to order us around. I looked at the victim – they are referred statistically as trespassers – and saw the large, gaping head wound with his brain partially exposed. Then I saw him take a breath, exhale and take another breath. He wasn't dead and about two hours had elapsed since the train struck him.

I asked if an ambulance had been called and the railroad officer sneered at me, asking why he would do that for a dead man. I informed him the man was still alive. He glanced at the victim and was visibly shocked to see him breathe again.

One of my officers called for an ambulance with specific directions to the accident site. The man was taken to the hospital but died a few hours later. I don't believe this was a survivable injury, but his chances would have been greater had he gotten immediate help.

Another Elevator Ride

Told by Told by Kevin Foster with Kathy Sanders

I'm not sure what it was about the jail's elevator. It just seemed to bring out the worst in suspects. Dingy and dark inside, the elevator was cramped and too small for large groups. And it boasted a steel mesh door that required a jailer to unlock it before anyone could exit into the jail.

Once, I escorted a seemingly calm and cooperative handcuffed prisoner to the jail. But once we entered that elevator and I pushed the down button, this guy started fighting. It didn't last long and when the door opened, he was sprawled on the elevator floor with me forcing him to the floor while trying to grip the walls for balance.

The prisoner was screaming obscenities and thrashed like he was possessed by a demon. Not the best way to enter that jail.

One of the jailers heard the commotion inside the elevator and rushed over to unlock the gate. As the gate opened, I jumped out of the elevator and dragged the prisoner inside and got him into the "chute" the holding area next to the booking desk.

Through the years, the elevator had seen hundreds of incidents like this.

The Best Police Cars Fort Worth Was Willing To Buy

Told by L.E. Webb

A constant struggle exists between the costs of running a police department and limited public funds. Some administrators cut corners, even foolishly, whenever possible to maintain the budget.

Such was the case in 1978, when a fleet of police cars were bought at a bargain price. Lemons, every one of them
.

Assistant Fort Worth City Manager David Ivory opted to buy Ford Fairmont sedans to be used as patrol cars – even though the manufacturer warned these were not designed for police use. And the cars would not have warranties. The bargain deal apparently superseded the need for the officers to drive safe patrol cars.

The cars produced more carbon monoxide than nearly any vehicle on the road. The back seat was made of foam rubber and the catalytic converter was underneath the driver's seat. If the car didn't gas you, fumes from a burning back seat would. Those of us who had to drive these death traps have the memory of them burned in our minds.

Since Ford Motors had warned the city about the cars before they were purchased, they refused to fix them. "Not our fault: and "good luck with that" punctuated discussions about the cars.

The city told police officers to roll the windows down and bail out of the car if their eyes began burning. We could accept that unless it was raining, hailing, snowing, extremely hot or extremely cold.

Finally, they announced a solution. It happened on my days off, so I was excited to see what had happened with the cars.

Their solution was a triangle-shaped gauge hanging on the dash. If a red dot on the gauge turned black, we were to roll all windows down and immediately head to the city's garage. Fifteen minutes into my shift, this gauge turned black, so off I went to the garage. The mechanic happily announced they had a fix and handed me a large plastic bag with about 20 more similar gauges. He removed the blackened gauge and replaced it with a new one.

I was to keep the bag sealed and away from the back seat, so the gauges wouldn't be contaminated. I put the sealed bag in my briefcase on the passenger seat and resumed my shift. That lasted 20 minutes before the new gauge turned black. Much to my surprise, the sealed bag of replacements had also turned black – the bag must have had a hole.

And back to the garage I went. This time, I was scolded for driving too slow to keep a flow of fresh air in the car. I left with another new gauge and parked in a grocery store lot. I rolled the windows down, turned off the engine and answered calls from there. I don't know what the day shift officers did to avoid heat stroke.

Chapter 5

The Unexpected & Unusual

"There are a lot of law enforcement officers out there who work according to their own set of what is right and what is wrong. And that doesn't always include respect for administration cops, you know, people that are higher up the food chain".

-Bruce Willis

“Exorcism at the City Jail”

Told by J.C. Williams Jr.

I was all of 20 years old when the Fort Worth Police Department hired me as a police recruit. Since classes did not begin for another month, the department assigned me to work at the city jail, built and in operation since the 1930s, processing suspects during nights and weekends.

It was not a glamorous job by any means, but it was “police” work with hands-on experience. And it was only for a month.

The inside of the jail – this was the late 1970s – resembled a mini version of an old crumbling prison you see in movies. Cramped, dank and dirty, the jail reeked of vomit, body odor, urine and other foulness I could barely comprehend. Officers escorted the handcuffed suspects to the basement, then used the elevator or stairs to put them in a holding room (the chute). There they stayed until they were booked into jail.

It was a large jail but could barely house everyone brought in during a wild weekend.

One night, several Fort Worth cops brought in a stocky 30-year-old man who started fighting with other suspects, jailers and officers. This guy, who we’ll call Damien from now on, was wanted on several felony warrants out of neighboring Dallas County. It seemed Damien had a penchant for violence and assault. And he was a problem for us as soon as he arrived.

Damien’s eyes were wild and crazed and he repeatedly growled in a deep, low guttural voice.

It fell to me to force Damien into a solitary cell reserved for the meanest, most combative bad guys. During the next few hours, this suspect crawled around the floor of his cell, hissing like a snake and claimed that he was Satan. Though he had no visible cuts to his face or mouth, he spit blood out of his cell onto the opposite wall. As the blood dribbled down the wall, Damien laughed in a low voice, got back up and jumped around his cell.

His behavior scared other "problem" inmates, despite them being in different, separate cells.

When Damien's infamy reached its peak, in walked two older Dallas County warrant officers to retrieve their wanted man. These lawmen had a good 20 to 30 years of experience under their belts and were nearing the end of their careers.

As we walked back to the cell, I offered to drag Damien to the front of the jail, fully expecting a fight. I described what he'd been doing and that he was calling himself the devil.

"Son, just open the door and step back. There is just a misunderstanding here," one of them said. "You see, he thinks he is the devil. But what he doesn't realize is that the devil has just arrived."

With that, he stepped in the cell, struck Damien in the neck and lifted him about a foot off the ground. His partner stepped in and both warrant officers carried Damien out without his feet touching the ground.

Whatever possessed Damien, left him immediately – he was completely silent on the way out. I couldn't help but laugh and admire the warrant officers' skill.

The Blind Policeman

Told by Kevin Foster
with Curtis Chesser
and Doug Phillips

Fort Worth police patrolled and worked the downtown area to have high visibility. One of these officers was Horace Phillips. For me to say that Horace was a unique person would be an understatement.

Phillips and his rookie were looking for tickets to write on a Tuesday about 10 a.m. They spotted a car going the wrong way and stopped it. Exiting the police unit Horace stopped and leaned back against the car then turned toward the other car. With one hand on his police car and his left arm outstretched, he began to walk towards the car he had stopped. When he reached the end of the police car, he extended both arms and walked toward the violator's car.

Arriving at the violator's car he put his right hand on it, extended his left arm and walked down the side. As he passed the driver's window he bumped into the outside rearview mirror and had to back up. He bent over and started to talk in the direction of the steering wheel then heard this voice say, "I am over here." Horace redirected his voice to the sound of the woman's voice and identified himself. He told the woman she had been stopped because she was going the wrong way on a one-way street, and he needed her driver's license. He extended his hand, and she placed her DL in it and asked him "Can you see?"

Horace told her he was legally blind, and would she mind helping him fill out her ticket? The lady responded by howling with laughter along with the other three females in the car. The woman kept saying, "You've got to be kidding me!" as she began to fill out the ticket. When she got to the weight blank, she told Horace that she did not know her weight. His reply, "Sure you do. Just put it down." The woman asked Horace, "Well suppose you tell me how much I weigh?" Not missing a beat, he said, "Sure. By the sound of your voice, you're about 5 foot tall with long brown hair, blue eyes, and weigh about 120 lbs." At the completion of this sentence, the car erupts into howls of laughter by all the women in the car.

The woman passenger seated behind the driver leaned forward, stuck her head out the window and stated, "Officer, Tammy Lou is 6 feet,1 inch tall and weighs 222 pounds, has green eyes and bright red hair worn in skull curls." Tammy Lou yelled at the lady in the back seat "I do not weigh 222 pounds! This morning, I weighed 220 pounds and that is what I am putting on this ticket. Now, Officer, what goes in this box that says, 'Violation Code'?" Horace told her that box was for the ticket code for the law she broke and if she would just turn the book over, she could find the code by looking for one that says, 'one-way street.'

Horace asked her if beside the violation code box if she would write, 'going the wrong way on a one-way street.' Tammy Lou asked him how he knew she was going the wrong way, and how did he drove his police car? He said that when she came through the intersection, he heard her car engine and knew she was going the wrong way. "As to how do I drive I use the Bump Braille method. If you look at the street, you will see reflective buttons glued to the street marking the traffic lanes. By hanging my head out the window I can hear the tires making the bump noise and I count the bumps and can tell what street I am on."

With that he tore the pink copy out of the ticket book, handed it to her, and told her she had eleven days to either pay it or set the ticket for trial. He then told her she could turn left at the next street, and she would be going the correct way on the next street.

As he walked back to his police unit, he heard the lady saying to her companions, "I was just given a ticket by a blind police officer, but the worst part is I wrote my own ticket!" Horace listened to the howls of laughter coming from the car, as it turned left on Jones Street. As

Horace entered his police car he turned to his rookie and stated, "Another satisfied customer."

Murder, Mayfest & Mayhem

Told by J.C. Williams Jr.,
With help from Kathy Sanders,
David Thronton
& Curt Brannon

May 5, 1995, dawned relatively quiet in Fort Worth, an unremarkable, cloudy spring day with a promise of storms later.

The major news of the day continued to be the homegrown terrorist bombing of the Alfred P. Murrah federal building in Oklahoma City, that occurred just two weeks earlier. Search efforts continued to recover all 168 victims' bodies.

"This Is How We Do It," was the number one song in the nation. And the Boston Celtics were scheduled to play their last basketball game at Boston Garden.

Before the sun set, however, events conspired to shove all that to the back burner in the minds of cops.

It started with a car blaze behind a derelict and condemned house in the Polytechnic Heights neighborhood – an area besieged by criminals and violence.

Inside the remnants of car, firefighters discovered two men who'd been shot to death. The killer doused them and the car in gasoline and lit it up. The blaze was so intense, the bodies melted to the upholstery. Most of the skin stayed on the seats as coroners removed the remains.

Homicide Det. David Thornton and his partner, Det. Tom Boetcher, showed up at the scene and worked into the evening. Thornton uncovered information that led him to the identity of the man in the trunk – he was owner of a nightclub on East Lancaster where he funneled drugs.

He'd been targeted by narcotics officers who had secured wiretaps on his phone. Thornton and Boetcher went to listen to the recordings on the east side. They heard their victim planning a deal to sell $20,000 worth of crack cocaine to a Waco man known as Popeye. The time and place he set coincided with where the burning car was found.

During their investigation, the detectives started hearing frantic calls on the police radio – all hell was breaking loose on the west side. Particularly at a favorite outside festival underway on the banks of the Trinity River – Mayfest.

At 7:10 p.m., a supercell thunderstorm unleashed its fury on Fort Worth, slinging huge hailstones that measured up to 4.5 inches across. It came down so furiously, some streets had up to two feet of hail covering the pavement. Winds gusted to 70 mph, the National Weather Service reported, and more than five inches of rain fell in 35 minutes in the city. Tornadoes also threatened.

Mayfest – which draws thousands of people each year for live music, food, vendors and kids' activities – offered no shelter.

Organizers, volunteers, festival attendees and off-duty police officers working security, had nowhere to go to escape the unrelenting storm. Some sought safety inside their vehicles, which were demolished.

Several cops made Herculean efforts to save people - Billy Holbert, an auto theft detective, hunched over several children to protect them and his back literally was beaten black and blue.

Homicide Det. Curt Brannan, also working off-duty at Mayfest, was enjoying the dinner his wife brought him before the hail hit. Both their cars were destroyed, but Brannan raced to a locked National Guard Armory nearby and broke in.

It was imperative that casualties had a safe place until the hail stopped and ambulances arrived. His wife joined in, caring for bleeding babies, wrapping them in army blankets until help arrived. The storm surged to the east side, where Thornton and Boetcher raced outside, valiantly trying to save their brand-new police cars while dodging softball-sized hailstones and rotating clouds.

"It was crazy," he said 29 years later. Their sergeant "was more pissed off about the cars getting damaged than us getting killed," he joked.

Eastward the storm churned, causing deadly flash floods and building collapses in Dallas. Rain fell at a rate of 2.25 inches in 15 minutes, the NWS reported in their analysis of the storm.

One man died in the Fort Worth area and 15 people died in Dallas - most swept away in flood waters.

At Mayfest, 400 people reported injuries, including 60 that required hospitalization. No one was killed.

The storm remains one of the costliest hail events in history with damages totaling $2 billion in both counties.

Thornton, though enmeshed in Friday's double homicide, had to spend time the next morning patching a hole in his house. More rain was expected, but a storm of a different sort was about to make his life worse.

Thornton drew four more homicide cases before the weekend ended, including another double homicide. Boetcher took the lead in another three slayings.

The homicide unit also was hosting agents from the Federal Bureau of Investigation that weekend, working with Fort Worth's detectives to gain practical experience.

One of the agents – tasked with a second homicide – asked Williams, "When do you add more detectives to help?"

I laughed. "Welcome to real police work."

The Detachable Leg

Told by Kevin Foster
with Kathy Sanders

I've said it before, and I'll say it again – a cop never knows what weirdness he's going to encounter on any given call.

I was a relatively new officer in 1982 when I was sent to roust a transient who'd passed out in a Safeway parking lot.

He was exactly as described – this older man was pretty drunk and smelled horrible. I decided to wake him and send him on his way without taking him to jail.

When I finally roused him, he responded with a barrage of insults and threats, and defiantly declared he had no intention of leaving. Okay, jail it is, I thought.

I got him to his feet and spread him against my car to search him. He continued his verbal assault and adamantly resisted having his legs spread apart for the search. Undeterred, I held onto his waistband and, using my foot, attempted to move his right leg. Unexpectedly, the leg seemed very hard and stiff, and as I applied more force, it took an awkward angle about mid-thigh and appeared to detach.

Realizing he had a prosthetic leg, I had him sit down and I pulled the detached leg from his pants and placed it in the back seat of the patrol car.

His animosity towards me did not waiver as I drove him to jail. Unbeknownst to me at the time, he was a familiar face at the jail, and everybody knew his name.

In the years that followed, I learned that the man had been murdered and his body dumped along the Jacksboro Highway. Suspicions arose that he might be another victim of serial killer Ricky Lee Green. His murder remains unsolved.

A Closet, a Mattress and a Bucket of Chicken

Told by Kevin Foster
with Kathy Sanders

Mark Twain once said, “It’s no wonder that truth is stranger than fiction. Fiction has to make sense.”

And the bizarre case of Anthony Fleming makes no sense. No one could make this up. I have, however, changed some names.

In 1985, one Fort Worth man shot another, truly not unusual nor newsworthy. Though seriously injured, the victim survived. He told detectives he knew his assailant, a man we’ll call Anthony Fleming.

The attempted murder case landed in the lap of Fort Worth Police Det. Danny LaRue who gathered details from the victim. After researching police records, LaRue was confident he’d identified his suspect – he had the name and matched the height, weight and age the victim had described.

He obtained an arrest warrant and Anthony Fleming was arrested. Everything seemed to be going smoothly. Until the victim said, uh-uh, that's not him upon viewing Fleming.

Apparently, two Anthony Flemings lived in Fort Worth and they'd arrested the wrong one.

Unfortunate, but not unheard of. Most folks would be unhappy, if not downright mad, about the arrest, but this Anthony Fleming wasn't. He had been a professional boxer, albeit not a very good one, and he had been previously shot in the head.

Fleming just didn't act right, whether because of repeated blows to the head in the boxing ring, the gunshot to the head or a combination of both. He battled other mental disorders. Some described him as "punchy" while others spent scant minutes with him to know something wasn't right.

Fleming didn't like being arrested and it wasn't his first time in jail. But he didn't mind it because he ended up with a roof over his head, a mattress to sleep in and three meals a day.

LaRue released Fleming from jail then started working on the case again.

Satisfied he'd gained enough information about the "real" suspect, LaRue had the warrant reissued.

Guess what? They arrested the same man the second time. Again he was released, they worked the case some more and officers went out to finally arrest the suspect.

I kid you not, they got the wrong one again.

Well.

Police had entered the embarrassment phase and they still had a gunman running the streets. They said farewell to Fleming and released him a third time.

Not long after that ordeal, Fleming moved to Honolulu, Hawaii, and made his home in a small rent house.

I'd love to tell you that was the end of the story. It wasn't.

Fleming and his neighbor had an argument. The former Fort Worth man thought he'd solve the dispute through their dogs. Fleming put his largish pit bull terrier in his neighbor's backyard to kill the neighbor's much smaller dog. His plan worked, but Honolulu police weren't amused when they arrived.

They hauled him to jail, then discovered he was named in an outstanding attempted murder warrant out of Fort Worth. Fort Worth police were called.

LaRue had long since retired and another detective had been given his old cases. While reviewing those, he ran across the shooting done by one Anthony Fleming. He didn't know about the earlier debacle. He talked with prosecutors and another arrest warrant was issued.

Round four began. Two Tarrant County Sheriff's deputies of the extradition unit flew to Hawaii to fetch Fleming. The Tarrant County jail again was Fleming's address. No detective came to see him

No one visited him, no one interviewed him.

Six weeks later, Fleming went to court and an attorney was appointed to represent him. He told his lawyer the saga of mistaken identity and the wrongful arrests.

The attorney listened, checked his story and discovered Fleming's tale was true.

A court hearing convened, the shooting victim and detective testified, and Fleming was released. Again. Now he was stranded in Fort Worth.

The lawyer knew Fleming's mental issues were a severe handicap in getting him home. He needed help and headed to the police department.

Police Chief Thomas Windham listened to the account and agreed immediately to get Fleming a plane ticket back to Hawaii.

Windham summoned Lt. Greg Bradley who oversaw the Major Case Unit. The chief often called on Bradley when he needed something done quickly and quietly. This was one of those times.

The first thing the lieutenant did was summon patrol officers to take Fleming to the Presbyterian Night Shelter – at the time it served as the drunk tank for the Fort Worth jail. A sheriff's deputy stationed there could watch out for Fleming. Then he came looking for me.

Bradley was my lieutenant when I headed the fugitive detail. He gave me an outline of the situation – Windham coughed up cash to get a plane ticket to Hawaii and I was then anointed as the one to get the ticket and make sure Fleming was on the flight the next day.

It turned out more difficult than it sounded.

About 10 minutes after I learned about Fleming, I got a call from the shelter deputy. Fleming had been kicked out in record time for starting a fight and other behaviors deemed somewhat disagreeable to others in the shelter.

He was on foot somewhere near downtown Fort Worth. I had Fleming's information broadcast on the police radio. Luckily, an officer spotted Fleming and brought him back to police headquarters.

I realized Fleming was not all there, mentally. Not by a longshot. I took custody of him.

For Fleming, he was happy with all the attention turned his way and that he was going home the next day. I knew I couldn't trust him to stay where we could find him.

Bradley suggested getting Fleming a motel room, but I knew it wouldn't work. I came up with a different plan I felt certain would work.

I knew of a storeroom that held only some empty lockers. It had lots of floor space. I sent two of my officers to the jail and they returned with an almost new jail mattress,

We began to create a room for Fleming for the night. Bradley saw what we were doing and nearly bolted for the door – he wanted plausible deniability.

This sounds bad, but it wasn't. The bathroom was nearby, the storeroom was clean and air-conditioned and Fleming was accustomed to sleeping on a jail mattress.

We lacked food. Fleming wanted fried chicken. Off we went.

One of my officers accompanied me and Fleming to a nearby restaurant where we got him a bucket of chicken, a bag of rolls, French fries and a big soda.

We took him back to his "room." He was delighted. Not long after that, Fleming went to bed, sleeping soundly through the night. I stayed overnight in the office with another officer, just to make sure Fleming didn't leave.

With dawn, came two Major Case Unit officers who were taking Fleming to the airport. They were to go to the airline counter, pay for ticket and absolutely not identify themselves as police officers.

They'd treat Fleming to breakfast, then sit at the gate with him until he boarded the flight to Hawaii. They were to stay put until the plane left the taxiway. Just in case.

It went perfectly. We never saw nor heard of Fleming again.

With Windham aware of this case, the gunman Fleming finally was identified and jailed two days later, charged with attempted murder.

I've always wondered who was lucky enough to sit next to Fleming on the plane. I'm certain it was a memorable trip.

The Severed Hand

Told by J.C. Williams Jr
with help from J.C. Williams Sr.
& Hondo Porter

My father, J.C. Williams Sr., worked as a patrol officer on the east side of Fort Worth in the 1950s. A colorful character, he had a legendary, storied career at the police department until his retirement.

One night, he was summoned to a barbecue restaurant where an armed robbery had just occurred. The owner, Benny Bateman, knew my father well and was shaken. Bateman said two robbers barged into his business, demanding money. The restaurant owner said one man held a gun on him as he stood behind the counter, while his partner stood watch by the front door.

The gunman held his weapon in his right hand and rested it on the counter; his left hand was free to grab the cash and two barbecue sandwiches he'd ordered.

A terrified Bateman believed he was a dead man even if he handed over the cash. So, when the gunman glanced at the door, Bateman grabbed his meat cleaver and, with all his might, chopped down on the robber's wrist, severing the hand.

The now-handless robber, with blood pouring from his stump, fled with his partner. Behind, on the counter, lay his severed hand, still gripping the gun.

Williams told Bateman he doubted the robbers were local, and probably came from Dallas. The officer would check local hospitals but couldn't promise they'd be found. Williams asked for a gallon pickle jar, took the pickles out and inserted the hand and gun combo into the brine.

Williams shot Bateman a smile and left, carrying the pickle jar under his arm.

In the ensuing months and years, Williams hauled out the pickle jar when working with other lawmen on task forces, showed it off and claimed that was how he dealt with robbery suspects and other criminals with whom he had issues. It made an impact. When asked if the robber was dead or alive, Williams just smiled and kept the secret.

Two decades later, Williams had a new partner in undercover narcotics. The partner spent vacation hunting with Bateman who related the hand story. When he next saw Williams, the new partner asked if he still had the pickle jar. Again, Williams just smiled, then said, "Sometimes, you don't need to know all the details."

The Batman Burglar

Told by J.C. Williams Jr.

It's no secret in the news business that the sensational stories grab headlines and airtime. There's absolute truth in the saying, "If it bleeds, it leads."

Media-savvy and sometimes bored cops used that knowledge to make the mundane come alive. At the same time, they brought elusive attention to their operations.

When I was a sergeant, I worked with a team of great detectives on Fort Worth's east side. I looked for any chance to promote those officers and their work.

One day in 1991, as I sauntered through the office, I caught a glimpse of a burglary video where a guy was breaking into a building. He was wearing a Batman shirt.

Officer Kelly "Cowboy" Caruthers had arrested him and his partner in crime the night before. I turned to the detectives with a big ol' grin. "We just caught the Batman Burglar," I announced.

Smiles all around, I turned around and picked up the phone. The media needed to know this dastardly fiend was in custody. Zoinks!

I let local television stations know and they scrambled to get news crews to me. My friend, Kathy Sanders with the Fort Worth Star-Telegram, headed over to see me. It was, she said, a slow news day.

"What do you have?" she said when she arrived.

"I was bored," I told her. I laid out the Batman Burglar case – we arrested two men responsible for breaking into at least seven businesses and stealing cigarettes. One suspect wore a Batman shirt.

Sanders looked at me, incredulous. She covered the likes of killings, explosions, massacres and national disasters. Then, we burst out laughing. I started to truly understand how the media worked.

"Clang! Click! Duo put behind bars," the headline on her story read the next day. "Police believe they caught Batman Burglar, sidekick."

In truth, part of my motivation was my fascination as a 7-year-old kid with Batman, the movie that debuted in 1966. I was dropped off at the movie theater where I watched it five times in a row before my mom picked me up.

Holy Smokes, Batman!

The Prostitute and the Wheelchair

Told by Kevin Foster

Society's criminal element always boasts some truly unique people who, although unwanted, embed themselves in police officers' memories.

Enter a gal that we will refer to as Camille.

No one knew where this drug-addicted prostitute came from, when she showed up in the 1990s peddling her wares in the hospital district, just south of downtown. And she didn't stay long, preferring a transient lifestyle.

Hobbled by a disfigured foot, Camille hustled at dilapidated hotels and flop houses. Her favorite was The Victorian Inn that we discussed earlier. Unable to walk normally because of her foot, Camille coasted through the area on sidewalks and streets with a motorized "Hover Round"- type of wheelchair that had seen much better days.

She disliked police officers with unwavering resolve and wouldn't know the truth, even if it up and bit her. Camille was also usually drunk or high.

While she was embracing her new home on the city's south side, a naïve, young officer entered our FWPD ranks – he brimmed with compassion and a genuine desire to help the downtrodden. He was an exceptional young man with a big heart.

One afternoon as I was patrolling that area, I noticed movement in a vacant lot, near the tree line. There, I saw Camille sitting on a fallen utility pole and performing a sex act with a man. Her wheelchair lay abandoned in the nearby street.

After I radioed for assistance, our big-hearted young officer appeared. I assigned him the task of interviewing Camille for her side of the story. I began talking with the man, who didn't know much about the prostitute, other than he had paid her for sex. I left him momentarily to see what Camille had told the other officer.

Smiling, he told me that Camille knew the man as an old friend and hoped to borrow money from him. I stepped by him, went to Camille and asked for the man's name since they were such old friends.

A defiant silence and murderous glare met my question – the young officer's jaw dropped when I described what I'd seen them doing. The plan was to issue tickets to both. We told Camille to head back to her chair.

She couldn't walk, she said, and now she was stranded in the vacant lot without a way to get back to her chair.

Then how did she get to the utility pole where she was when I arrived, I asked.

She had crawled, Camille said. I told her – in what was not my finest policing moment – to crawl back.

With ticket in hand, Camille awkwardly walked back to her chair. She didn't crawl.

I saw her a few more times after that, always using crutches. Another transient stole her chair, Camille said, and pawned it.

Head in a Jar

Told by Kevin Foster

Weird things happened in the early days of the Fort Worth Police Department, as well.

One morning in 1919, two officers were on foot patrol downtown when they made a gruesome discovery just a few blocks from the police station. It was a human head, severed from the body at the neck. The head was found in a trash pile.

The officers collected the head, placed it in a box and rushed it to headquarters. Detectives scrutinized the head, looking for any clues to the man's identity. It had wavy locks of hair; a chin beard and it appeared rats had gnawed on the face. The detectives were quickly joined by other officers and news reporters.

Police summoned medical professionals, who determined that the head had been preserved in alcohol and exhibited in a doctor's office. When it was found in a storeroom, workers put it on the trash pile. Mystery solved.[30]

A desk sergeant, who didn't want the head to go to waste, found another glass jar, poured in alcohol and put the head in. He proudly displayed the head on his desk inside the front doors of the police station. That lasted all of a day, until the chief encouraged the sergeant to get rid of it, properly.

It disappeared. There is no record of where it went.

The Clumsy Burglar

Told by Kevin Foster

Patrolling the downtown district comes with a certainty – a slow night can turn "interesting" in a heartbeat. The area encompassed some notorious high-crime sites such as Butler and Ripley Arnold public housing, as well as The Glass Key and the night shelters for the homeless.

So, when two cops showed up at 3 a.m. one Saturday to deal with a burglary alarm, it turned exciting pretty quickly.

The alarm was called in at the I.M. Terrell High School, sitting on a hill beside Butler Public Housing. The officers watched a man run downhill after he spotted the patrol cars arriving at the school. An experienced officer knows foot chases are easier if you can chase them with your police car – so these officers drove behind this guy until he began to tire. Realizing he couldn't outrun the cars, he changed course, sprinting toward the Butler Housing apartments.

Each two-story building had steel doors set into steel frames. Concrete steps led to a covered porch at each doorway and thick, sturdy concrete trellises bookmarked the porches. Our burglary suspect couldn't kick his way in to hide, so he climbed a trellis, hoping to get inside through a window above the porch. When he saw the officers watching him and knowing he was out of options, the burglar laid down atop the covered porch and pretended to be incapacitated.

Of course, the officers weren't going to allow their suspect to rest. One of the officers climbed the trellis and handcuffed the man with his hands in front – this would help the bad guy climb down.

Perhaps they could have called the fire department for a ladder to use in the descent, but they didn't. Instead, the officer dragged the suspect to the edge to get him ready to climb down. But the suspect slipped, falling 10 feet to the ground and landing with a hollow thump that sounded like a melon bursting.

After checking on him, the officers called for an ambulance and the man was rushed to John Peter Smith Hospital for his injuries. In the past, one officer guarded the patient while the other officer filed the police report, and the case was passed on to the next shift.

But Fort Worth police had instituted a new policy – any time someone suffered serious injuries while in custody, the department began a "Critical Incident" investigation to figure out how that person was hurt.

Investigations were conducted by Major Case Unit detectives. On this morning, it fell to Det. Danny LaRue and his partner, and it went something like this:

LaRue: Hey, partner, how'd you get hurt?

Suspect: I fell off a roof when I got arrested.

LaRue: Did anyone throw you off the roof?

The suspect didn't answer, just glared at Larue.

LaRue determined the case was not a critical incident.

The Elephant Man

Told by Kevin Foster

Fighting with a cop rarely ends well. It really doesn't if you decide to fight three cops at the same time.

I went on a disturbance call on Hemphill with two of my officers one hot summer night in the late 1990s. I don't recall what led to the call and it really doesn't matter. A man had been placed under arrest and handcuffed. He was drunk, uncooperative and when we tried to put him in the police car, he started kicking and fighting.

My officers were struggling, trying to get the man into the car from the passenger side. I went to the opposite side of the car and leaned across the back seat, grabbing the man by the collar, and pulling him in. It worked great until the man hauled off and kicked one of the officers in the chest, knocking him down to ground. Now it was serious.

I used an "open hand distractionary strike" on the still fighting man. Translated, I slapped him hard on the side of his face. Maybe twice.

I inadvertently hit this guy's "sweet spot," knocking him unconscious. I yelled, "He's unconscious!" just as the kicked officer was ready to dive into the car.

He missed the fight, yelled an expletive and shut the door. Normally, this would have been the end of the story. While we discussed the jail paperwork, we noted the man's head began to swell up like a pumpkin (remember I said I found the sweet spot). Knowing we couldn't take him to jail in that condition, we took the man to the hospital. He was treated in short order and released back to us. The man, now completely compliant with a very swollen face, looked like the "elephant man." Once at the jail, the jailers were wary and asked the man how he had been injured. He replied, "I don't know – I must've got my ass whipped in the last bar I went to." We declined to give the man any clarity and back then, there was no such thing as a "Use of Force" report.

I don't know if we ever dealt with the man again, but he certainly didn't make himself known to us in the future.

Good Morning Officer

Told by Kevin Foster

When you are a patrol sergeant, you move around different parts of the city. After working the city's southside, I was sent north, closer to where I was raised. I worked the midnight shift in an area that included two cemeteries, Mount Olivet and Greenwood.

I was raised visiting the graves of family members. My father also liked to take our family to old cemeteries to walk about and look at the headstones. As a result, I always felt comfortable in graveyards.

On some slow shifts, I liked to take my breaks at my favorite spot near the back of Greenwood Cemetery, close to the Trinity River. Wildlife wandered up from the river – mostly raccoons and foxes. It was peaceful and relaxing.

I was there about 4:30 a.m. one day. I finished my coffee and the newspaper. With my windows rolled down, I turned off the dome light and listened to the car radio. It was a quiet night and after 10 minutes, I was pretty relaxed. "Good morning, officer," came a loud voice at the same time a man ran past my window. I nearly jumped through the roof. It was a jogger.

Apparently, many people enjoyed early morning jogs through the cemetery with its paved roads and lack of traffic. It certainly was safer than any city street. Once my heart settled back into normal rhythm, I started my car and left. I never went back there at night for my coffee and newspaper. I began sharing a spot with Officer Marcellus in the parking lot behind Mount Olivet funeral home. It wasn't as tranquil, but the joggers left us alone.

An Errant Gunshot

Told by Kevin Foster

When a police officer buys a new gun, everyone wants to see it, hold it, and admire it, much like a newborn baby. One Fort Worth officer brought his "new baby" to work and it didn't take long for him to regret it.

This officer answered a call with fellow officers Rick Williams and Fred Pruitt. Afterwards, they all relocated to a west side parking lot to examine the new gun.

Pruitt asked to see the .357 Smith & Wesson Magnum and when he had it in hand, he opened it and dumped the cylinder into his hand. Pruitt, did not, however, count the bullets. Pruitt took aim out the window of the patrol car and pulled the trigger a couple of times. Impressed, he commented that the gun had nice action.

He then pointed the gun at the radio and pulled the trigger. This time, the gun fired – there was still a bullet in the chamber. Oops!

The bullet struck the radio support cover and ricocheted through the floorboard of the car. The .357 left a big hole in the floorboard. They quickly discussed what to do and decided to go to one of their homes not far away where they hoped they could fix the damage.

The officers removed the radio support cover. They hammered out the large dent, spray-painted it black and remounted it. To repair the hole in the floorboard, they cut the shag carpet under the car seat and squirted lots of Elmer's school glue in the hole. They stuffed the carpet in the hole and that was that.

Meeting New People

Told by L.E. "Spider" Webb

Training officers test their rookies in some curious ways. Perhaps there's a lesson there and perhaps, it's just for grins.

Take young officers from the city's north side midnight shift during the 1980s.Their training officers loved to introduce them to an eccentric local informant known as "Cochise." Cochise viewed all rookie officers as fun prey and relished her chance to welcome them to the north side.

If anyone ever knew her real name, they'd long forgotten.

Training officers took these newbie cops on a bar check where they knew Cochise would be holding court. After finishing the check, they would stand next to the bar and, eventually, they'd summon Cochise to introduce her to the rookie.

Typical encounters saw Cochise talking with the rookie while slowly moving closer. She then touched the front part of the gun belt, running her fingers along it. When the rookie was used to her touch, she pounced, grabbing the belt, jerking the officer close to her and grabbing his crotch. It was always a one-time occurrence that left an indelible impression. She then gave officers tips about criminal activity in the area, some of which led to arrests.

Normally, Cochise was good-humored and ready for a prank. Once, a woman officer walked into her bar and Cochise reached into her pocket, pulled out a cigarette lighter shaped like a derringer. She pointed the lighter at the officer and pulled the trigger, causing a flame to pop out of the top. Before she could finish lighting the cigarette dangling from her mouth, that officer punched her in the face. Cochise didn't go to jail and didn't complain – she knew she'd deserved that punch.

The Midnight Caller

Told by Kevin Foster
with Kathy Sanders

Many of the buildings that housed our neighborhood police offices were simply crap. I worked out of one on the city's south side that boasted huge wall cracks, leaky roofs, horrible air conditioning that didn't work half the time and furniture that was all donated and used. We'd leave the doors open on nice evenings to let the air in and circulate.

Such was the case one evening in the late 1990s, when a pleasant couple came in to ask a question. Neatly dressed in jeans and a white, button-up shirt, the man stood about 6-feet talk, weighed about 190 pounds and was muscular. We'll call him Mike. I don't recall much about his companion except she was seated in a wheelchair. They got their answer and left.

Six hours later, I was standing outside the sergeant's office by the lobby, when I saw Mike walk back in. He'd lost his shirt; he had several cuts and blood on him. And Mike was ready to fight.

When he walked in, he growled, yelled, and struck a pose like the Incredible Hulk. Mike stared at me with such rage, it quickly became an "Oh, shit!" moment. Officers John Thompson and Barry Swain – who were also in the office - heard the screams and ran to the front lobby.

Mike charged and the fight was on. We needed to drive him out of the building and we succeeded, fighting and scrapping the entire way. Our battle raged from the sidewalk, down the street and to the corner coffee shop. Finally, we overpowered Mike, flipped him on his stomach and handcuffed him. Mike made a lot of noise during the fight, but he never said a word to us.

We believed the fight was over. But when a car drove close by us, Mike flexed his entire body like a huge, flopping carp, flipped two feet in the air, spun and landed on his back. Using both his legs, he kicked Swain in the chest, knocking the officer off the sidewalk into the path of an approaching car. It didn't hit him.

We were back in the thick of it, the three of us trying to control Mike's movements. Finally, we flipped him back on his stomach and I stood on his shoulders, while clinging to a street sign for balance. Mike remained pinned until an ambulance arrived and took him to a nearby hospital. Officers followed.

After catching my breath, I started the paperwork. We discovered Mike lived in a little house behind our building. Originally from Houston, Mike received a head injury in the past that left him with what doctors called "intermittent explosive disorder." No one knew when it would surface.

Mike's parents had sent him, alone, to Fort Worth to learn how to live independently. Officers at the hospital reported Mike had changed back to the engaging individual we'd met earlier in the evening. He was pleasant and very apologetic to the officers guarding him, though he cried each time medical staffers touched his injuries. He moved back to Houston.

Always be Ready with your Lucky Strike Cigarettes

Told by J.C. Williams Jr.

Some of the best plans for police raids go screwy in the rush of excitement.

In the 1960s, Fort Worth Police Sgt. H.L. Smith knew that firsthand. He never lived it down.

As supervisor of the narcotics unit, Smith was a tough, respected man, though not physically large. It didn't matter for he would fight anyone at any time. Smith also chain-smoked Lucky Strike cigarettes, a pack of which was always found in one of his pockets wherever he went.

A known drug house in full swing needed a take down. Smith and his men – among them were my dad, J.C. Williams Sr., and Curtis Henderson - made plans to raid the place.

At the house, plainclothes narcotics officers stealthily moved around to the back of the property. The sergeant went to the front door, showing uniformed officers where he wanted them.

All the cops expected the bad guys to be in the back of the house. They also "knew" their suspects would try to run out the back door.

That just didn't happen.

Instead, Smith found the front door open and walked inside. Alone.

All 10 suspects stood in front of Smith and stared at the gun-wielding plainclothes man.

In the excitement of identifying himself, Smith mistakenly pulled out his pack of Lucky Strikes instead of his badge and identification.

Yelling, he continued holding up those cigarettes and identified himself as a cop to the men assembled before him.

In his street clothes, he looked like an old-time gangster. The people inside that dope house thought they were being robbed.

Officers who had started entering the house, wondered whether Smith even knew he was holding the suspects at cigarette-point.

"Sergeant, those are your Lucky Strikes you're holding up, not your badge," my father told him as he stepped in from the back corner of the room. Williams held his badge high for the suspects. They were thrilled it was "only" the police.

Of course, everyone on all future raids made sure Smith always had his Lucky Strikes.

Oswald's Grave

Told by Kevin Foster
with Kathy Sanders

Being a cop entails abhorrent and repugnant tasks. Guarding the grave of a presidential assassin and cop killer for several years was one of the worst for Fort Worth cops.

President John F. Kennedy died in Dallas at the hands of a man with deep Fort Worth roots. It was November 22, 1963, when Lee Harvey Oswald took up his rifle and shot Kennedy in the head.

In the 81 minutes before police arrested him, Oswald also killed Dallas Police Officer J.D. Tippit. Two days later, while being transferred to the Dallas County Jail, Oswald himself was shot to death in the basement parking garage of Dallas City Hall.

Incredibly, all three men were buried on the same day – a surreal happenstance that saw two sophisticated and elaborate ceremonies, while the third was a small, bizarre, rushed affair in Fort Worth, coordinated by the U.S. Secret Service.

In less than 24 hours after Oswald died, Secret Service agents took his small family into protective custody, reporters became pall bearers and Fort Worth cops were drawn into the unwanted detail of guarding the killer's grave.

While a nation grieved, few cared about what happened to Oswald. Rose Hill Cemetery hosted his funeral where his mother already owned a plot. [31] Preachers didn't want to conduct the service. And law enforcement agencies were on high alert, expecting violent and hateful repercussions.

New President Lyndon B. Johnson instructed Secret Service agents to protect Oswald's family at all costs – "Protect them as you would the president of the United States."[32] So they did, housing Oswald's widow and their two small girls, Oswald's brother, Robert, and his mother, Marguerite, in an Arlington motel.

That had its own "drama."

A distraught, some say grief-crazed, Marguerite tried to escape the hotel, with agents racing after her. One tackled her, just as a submachine-toting police detective stepped out, ready to fire.

Agents waved him off as Marguerite screamed, cussed out the agents and demanded to know why Oswald wasn't being buried in Arlington National Cemetery alongside Kennedy.

Robert Oswald had already bought a $300 wood casket and paid $710 for the service. The funeral would be at Rose Hill.

Someone needed to guard Oswald's body – the powers that be chose Fort Worth Police Officer Rocky Stone. From the time the body was at Miller Funeral Home, "I never lost sight of him, from the time they dressed him until we dropped him in the hole at Rose Hill," he said. [33]

Stone accompanied the body – prepared and dressed in a suit – to the cemetery's chapel and remained with the casket throughout the day.

Which inadvertently led to the inception of the empty casket rumor.

An "obnoxious" reporter pestered Stone about whether the casket contained a body. He repeatedly said Oswald was inside it, but that

didn't satisfy the reporter. Frustrated and fed up with the reporter, Stone popped off and said the body had been taken out and buried somewhere else in the cemetery. He told the reporter it was a big secret. In fact, it was a big lie.

That reporter raced out of the chapel and across the cemetery to find a phone.

Not long after, Police Chief Cato Hightower showed up and he was pissed. Hightower complained that "someone" had started a rumor that there was no body in the casket.

"We're not going to have any of that," the chief said. He ordered the casket opened, then, when convinced it was Oswald's body, he ordered photos to be taken and the casket resealed.

"(The rumor) took on significance it shouldn't have," said Mike Cochran who at the time worked for the Associated Press. But reporters were standing around waiting on the Oswald family – the only mourners – and boredom leads to speculation and rumors.

"Cato Hightower entered the chapel, opened the casket and assured us it was Oswald," Cochran said in a Fort Worth Star-Telegram video recorded for the 50th anniversary of the Kennedy assassination.

"We got past that crisis and the family still hadn't arrived," he recalled.

The preacher who'd agreed to conduct the service was a no-show, so organizers had to find someone else. And there were no pallbearers to carry Oswald's casket to the gravesite.

Scores of agents, local cops, reporters, photographers and cemetery employees milled about. Fort Worth cops stood every 10 feet along the cemetery fence line to keep gawkers and potential troublemakers at bay.

Fort Worth Star-Telegram reporter Jerry Flemmons turned to Cochran after surveying the scene.

" 'You know, Cochran, if we're going to write a story about the funeral of Lee Harvey Oswald, we're going to have to bury that SOB ourselves,' " Cochran recalled. "And it turned out, we did."

A handful of reporters agreed to be pallbearers at the graveside service. "At the time, not a single one of us gave it that much thought about becoming a historical footnote," Cochran said.

The family and their protectors finally arrived. The service was quick and simple.

At the end of the funeral, Hightower again ordered the casket opened to display the body. Marguerite, Robert and Marina identified the body as Oswald. After the family left, the casket was lowered into the grave and sealed in a concrete vault.

Everyone left, except a detail of Fort Worth police officers who embarked on a yearslong tour of guarding Oswald's grave.

The unique duty became tedious quickly, but it had to be done, Hightower said. Officers guarded the grave from their patrol cars, the front gates and they patrolled just outside the cemetery's fence closest to the gravesitc. Occasionally, people showed up wanting to see Oswald's grave, but they were turned away.

Some officers literally fell asleep on the job, but no one faced discipline if they were discovered by supervisors.

Retired officer Roger "Honky" McDonald told me that nearly every officer that guarded the site made a point to "piss on Oswald." Not only had Oswald killed the president, they believed, but he brutally killed a fellow officer. They took that personally.

So, at shift change, many officers lined up to relieve themselves on the grave, McDonald said.

The guard detail was scaled back more than three years later until cops only guarded the grave after sunset.

Oswald's mother was the only known, regular visitor to the grave, placing flowers on her son's grave at least twice a week. An elaborate $100 headstone she had bought was planted at the grave.

Eventually, Fort Worth stopped the guard duty.

Until Oswald's headstone was stolen on Nov. 22,1967, exactly four years after the assassination.

Thieves simply dug up the 135-pound marker, hauled it to their car and took off for parts unknown.

A man delivering flowers to the grave noticed the missing marker and called police. Oswald's grave was making national headlines. Again.

Parts unknown turned out to be Bartlesville, Oklahoma.

Mike Dempsey, a 20-year-old Army soldier preparing to leave for Vietnam, and his friend, Raymond Greenwood, 19, drove to Dallas to visit the assassination site. They also decided to visit Oswald's grave at Rose Hill Cemetery.

When they saw the headstone, Greenwood later said, they felt having it as a souvenir was imperative. The two men took it to their motel room, scrubbed it clean in the bathtub, took showers with it and loaded it back in the car when their visit ended.

Back in Bartlesville, they immediately started showing the headstone to their friends and soon the story was everywhere. A "neighbor lady" called the Bartlesville police department, saying she'd seen the marker in Greenwood's car. A full investigation began.

After some back and forth between police departments – with a Fort Worth police lieutenant saying, "Just find it!" – Bartlesville Police Capt. Joe Glenn met with Greenwood's father, Lenard Greenwood. Daddy Greenwood got the headstone from his son and gave it to Glenn.

Five days later, Fort Worth Det. J.D. Roberts and Det. Sam McGee met an Oklahoma highway patrolman and retrieved the marker. Marguerita Oswald was given the headstone the next day. [34]

No charges were forthcoming, though Tarrant County District Attorney Frank Coffey wanted them prosecuted and raised hell about it.

Dempsey went to Vietnam and in 1968, he was awarded the Distinguished Service Cross for his actions in combat.

Marguerite never learned the young men's names. That was probably for the best.

She believed the two unpunished young men would be gloating. As a result, she bought a new headstone that simply read "OSWALD" and used it to mark the grave on Dec. 5, 1967. It was set in 10 inches of concrete to prevent theft.

Fort Worth police, Hightower said, would not guard the grave again.

Oswald's mother died in 1981. Neighbors Ida Coffman Card and her family bought her house. In the crawl space under the house, the Cards found the stolen/recovered headstone. It remains with the family today. One would think the saga ended there. Nope. Contrary to what Hightower avowed, Fort Worth police were back to guarding Oswald's grave.

Although the chief went to great lengths to dispel rumors that Oswald was not in the grave, they persisted through the remainder of the decade and into the 1970s.

British author Michael Eddowes, in a book published in 1976, claimed a Soviet agent was buried in Oswald's grave instead of the assassin. He filed suit three years later, demanding the body be exhumed for identification. The lawsuit was thrown out.

He went to Dallas County Medical Examiner Dr. Charles Petty and convinced him to ask his Tarrant County counterparts to exhume the body, citing "certain information" that caused him to doubt the identity of the body. The author also convinced Oswald's widow, Marina, the grave was empty.

Legal wrangling took two years until October 1981. Oswald's body was exhumed and taken to Dallas County. The examination determined the remains belonged to Oswald.

His casket, cemetery officials discovered, was damaged beyond repair because it had been sitting in water throughout the years. Oswald's brother, Robert, arranged for a new casket with Baumgardner Funeral Home to hold the remains, and it was lowered into a new waterproof vault.

The only people present for the burial were cemetery workers, cops and security guards.

Grave guard duty began when the first of several lawsuits were filed, ensuring the body wasn't moved.

Marguerite Oswald died of cancer in 1981 while the legal battles continued to rage. She was buried next to her son. [35]

Robert Oswald assumed the funeral had destroyed the rotting casket. Nope. Turned out, the funeral home owner kept the casket in storage for close to three decades. Then someone decided to sell it.

The casket – peddled with a death certificate and embalming tools used on Oswald – sold at an internationally advertised auction in California.

The casket sold for $87,469 The death certificate brought another $49,374.[36]

Robert learned of the sale and promptly sued the funeral home, the owner and the auction house, claiming breach of contract and fiduciary duty, invasion of privacy, gross negligence and mental anguish.

An attorney for the funeral home claimed that Robert never owned the casket. Instead, the attorney said he had gifted the casket to his dead brother.

The Oswald family won. Part of the deal included shipping the casket back to Robert Oswald.

I heard he destroyed it.

The “Japanese Flag” Incident

Told by Kevin Foster

Every once in a while, encounters between cops and bad guys leave, um, special “marks.” This was one of those times.

When I worked on the city’s south side, we often had special details that targeted various law-breaking individuals.

One night, I was partnered with a young officer, and we had our eyes out for criminal transients, violent parolees and general troublemakers. On West Magnolia Avenue, we spotted such a man.

We stopped and, after speaking with him, we decided to arrest him. I walked him to the back of the "paddy" wagon. I told this man to put his hands on the back door.

He didn't budge. I told him again. He didn't respond.

"Knife!" the other officer suddenly yelled.

I hadn't seen a blade, but I wasn't going to wait until the last minute. I hit our suspect in the back and knocked him into the van to get him off-balance. I heard something hit the ground. It was a folding knife with the blade open.

Also hitting the ground was the suspect. He wasn't conscious.

I looked at him and realized he hit the wagon face-first. I turned to look at the wagon and there, right in front of me, was a "rising sun" mark displayed on the white door.

Luck was with me that night, but not so much with the transient. He came to within a couple of minutes.

He still went to jail.

Chapter 6

How to Handle Animal Calls

"Anyone who hates children

and animals can't be all bad."

-W. C. Fields

The Runaway Hog

Told by J.C. Williams Jr
with help from Mike Miller

A police rookie is subject to all kinds of taunts, tasks and terms depending on your police destiny.

In my first year, I became the hog whisperer.

Driving back to our patrol beat from downtown, my partner Mike Miller turned to me.

"There is a giant pig running on the other side of the freeway with the traffic," he said.

Constantly leery of potential pranks, I replied, "Really, how much have you been drinking!"

Miller said it was the biggest pig he'd ever seen.

All of a sudden, the dispatcher told us to be on the lookout for a huge "bear" running amok on the freeway, alerted by people who'd seen the monster running down the highway.

I turned our car around and Miller yelled, "There it is! A giant pig!"

Living in the country with livestock, I recognized that it was neither bear nor pig. It was a giant white Poland China boar hog – a large, heavy-jowled, lop-eared porcine with short legs. The average weight is 600 to 700 pounds.

Miller wasn't about to miss the chance to be in the first-recorded police pursuit of a hog, he told the dispatcher to close the radio channel because we were in pursuit of the boar at the whopping speed of 5 to 10 m.p.h. The dang thing refused to stop, pull over and appeared infuriated with a seriously bad attitude.

An animal control officer joined the chase as the hog moved closer to the road's edge. Using a rope provided by that officer, I lassoed the boar around the neck. Even more incensed, the animal charged toward me – I tied the end of rope around a street sign pole and kept it tight.

A large livestock trailer was dispatched to us, but until it arrived, I was in a standoff with the hog – I couldn't let it get loose and cause a wreck.

Miller, who couldn't wait to be in the pursuit, spent his time on the hood of our patrol car and summoned other cops to come by and watch the circus act. He wanted nothing to do with big "pig."

It kept charging at me and I ensured my safety by making sure the post remained between us. When the animal tired and began to slow down, my helpful fellow officers threw small rocks at it to keep him mad and chasing the rookie. The trailer arrived, officers loaded the hog and that ended the ordeal.

For more than a month, each time I received patrol calls I would hear random squeals on the radio, just to remind me I was the official "hog catcher" of the department.

Jerry Milo Brown

Told by Kevin Foster
with help from L.E. "Spider" Webb
& Kathy Sanders

Jerry Milo Brown was a huge guy with a freaky obsession for snakes.

So much so, in fact, that the 6-foot-5, 300-pound man, often carried rattlesnakes inside his shirt. And if this Scorpio was mad at you, he'd toss those rattlers right at you.

Brown was a legend at the police department.

One morning at roll call, our captain warned us: "A white male driving a black Ford pickup by the name of Jerry Milo Brown is back in town and will have rattlesnakes on his person or in his truck, so all officers beware of him." We all paid close attention.

A few days later, I showed up to help at a traffic stop on the south side. Other officers were already there – they had pulled over Brown. His hands were in the air, but one hand gripped a snake by the head and the tail nearly reached the pavement.

I stood 20 to 30 feet away and I could have sworn I heard that snake rattling. One of the officers told Brown to secure the snake and he

moved to the truck bed, raised the snake, and put it in a wire container. I moved closer and saw this container holding four to five snakes.

The officer who had stopped Brown directed him to secure the snake. Brown moved to the bed of the truck, raised the snake and put it in some type of wire container. The officer directed him away from the truck where he began writing tickets.

I looked in the bed of the truck and that wire container held four to five snakes. None appeared to be terribly happy. Brown accepted his tickets and drove away.

"He pulled that snake out of his shirt! It had been inside his shirt," said the officer who stopped Brown.

Through the 1970s and early 1980s, officers encountered Brown and his rattlesnakes numerous times. But police officers who thought they knew him had no idea he was a convicted cop-killer.

Brown grew up in Fort Worth and police knew him and his brother, Gaye, as problem children. As a teenager, Brown palled around with a convict named Arnold Jernigan, who was four years older. They were thieves and hoodlums who thrived in burglaries, robberies and counterfeit schemes.

On Dec. 22, 1960, about 1 a.m., Brown, 24, Jernigan, 28, and two other Fort Worth men, Burt Mullins, 23 and Melvin Renfro, 22, were in Ardmore, Okla, intent on stealing a grocery store safe.

To gain entrance to the inside, at least three of them started chiseling through an outer wall. They'd cut the phone lines to stop a night watchman from summoning police if he noticed them. But when he saw the thieves, the watchman asked a passing motorist to notify police.

The motorist quickly found two Ardmore police officers – Bobby Rudisill, 29, and his partner, Robert Neasbitt - who immediately headed to the burglary. When the officers confronted the burglars, gunfire erupted, with Rudisill fatally wounded. He was able to fire his gun twice before losing consciousness. Neasbitt emptied his revolver before leaving to summon help. A swarm of lawmen, on and off-duty, descended upon the grocery store and fired about 200 rounds of ammunition and tear gas, thinking the burglars were still inside.

They found Jernigan, still clad in a stocking mask, dying in a pool of his own blood. He was alone. He was pronounced dead at a local hospital about five hours later. Officer Rudisill had been pronounced dead shortly after the shooting.

Police theorized the other burglars had escaped and started searching. They knew through ballistics that Jernigan hadn't killed the officer and believed one of the other burglars had shot the officer, possibly from a rooftop.

The search discovered Brown sitting in a car within a couple of miles. Brown claimed he knew nothing of the burglary nor the officer's death. Yet, in the car, police found burglary tools, a rifle and the handle of a drill found with Jernigan.[37]

Three Texas Rangers had been tracking the four suspects involved in an interstate burglary ring. They shooed local officers out of the interrogation room and began beating and torturing information out of Brown. Though he denied being at the grocery store, he gave up the other three men's names and where they were headed. He didn't know Jernigan was dead.

Mullins and Renfro made it back to Fort Worth and turned themselves in to Fort Worth police in the company of attorneys. Brown, Mullins and Renfro all received life sentences in connection with the burglary and slaying of Rudisill.[38]

However, in 1963, the Court of Criminal Appeals in Oklahoma reversed Brown's conviction and dismissed the case partially because of the actions of "three Texas tormentors, who beat and abused the defendant, so they say, into making admissions connecting him with the crime." The tormentors, the court said, were the Texas Rangers.

Dr. Frank Clark, a physician who examined Brown on Christmas Day 1960, said the inmate had black eyes, multiple bruises on the nose, elbow, leg, right ear, his genitals and his back where kidneys were. The court also ruled Brown's right to a speedy trial was violated.[39]

When Brown was set free, he came home to Fort Worth. Police who encountered him had no idea about his past. Or what sparked his snake obsession. Which is usually when they ran into him.

In 1974, a fire broke out in Brown's house and firefighters found hundreds of rattlesnakes loose in the house. They opted to fight the fire from the sidewalk across the street. Little water made it to the house.

A couple of years later, trouble erupted at a bar when an off-duty officer came under attack from four cowboys. Brown, a customer, didn't like the odds against the officer, so he fought three of the attackers and the officer fought the fourth. The cops talked with Brown a long time after the fight and learned he liked and respected police officers but said had no respect for the legal process. He didn't explain.

Brown and the off-duty officer developed an unusual friendship. Oddly, Brown often said that he knew he would die a violent death.

Other officers benefitted from Brown's warped sense of right and wrong. When an officer saw Brown walking alone down the middle of a south side street, he parked his patrol car and walked with Brown to his home about two blocks away. Brown never forgot and at times would pass on tips about local criminal activity.

But the snake man crossed the line a few times – he threw a snake on an officer once thinking it was hilarious. The cops didn't agree, a fight ensued and Brown "got a good whipping which he never forgot." Brown complained to the city council. One of the councilmen responded that he would have shot Brown if he'd thrown a snake at him.

Brown worked as a bouncer at a biker bar in Fort Worth and frequented many others. A few bar disagreements resulted in Brown deploying snakes at men who annoyed him, whether sitting at his favorite table or just being obnoxious. He was arrested once when he took his snake into a donut shop.

"Get the crazy mother------ out of here," the donut shop customers shouted at police. Brown took his snake outside, kissed it on the head, then dropped it in a wooden box with air holes.

Another time, two panicked men ran up to officers, complaining that someone had thrown a huge snake at them.

It happened outside the Crazy Horse Saloon when they saw what they thought was a tall "cowboy" handing out fish. They walked up and asked to have some of the giveaways.

The cowboy grinned and threw a large rattlesnake at them. They ran, fell, skinned their knees and broke the key to the car. One told the cops he had never hotwired a car so fast in his life.

Of course, it was Brown, the officers said. The snakes he had in the trunk had their mouths sewn shut and Brown liked to throw them at and on people. Officers searching his car also found snakes loose inside, something Brown had neglected to mention.

About 1979, Brown was speeding and was stopped by an officer. Jerry stepped out of the truck and all the officer saw was a moving bulge under Brown's long sleeved western shirt. Having already been warned about Brown, the officer just yelled, "Brown, slow that truck down!" and left. If it was a rattlesnake inside the shirt, the officer reported, he would have shot Brown.

Never to be confused with a saint, officers noticed that Brown's disposition seemed to worsen as time went on. He began having more run-ins with police and apparently was reverting to his burglary and robbery ways.

About this time, an officer's wife was brutally attacked by a man who subsequently was arrested. The officer, who knew Brown only by reputation, reported that the snake man approached him.

"I know the pain and hurt you and your family are going through. I am going to ask you a question, you don't have to say anything. Just shake your head yes or no," Brown told him. "Would you like for me to make this man go away for good so no one would ever have to worry about him doing an assault again?"

Dumbfounded at the proposition, the officer stared at Brown. After a moment, the snake man handed the officer a piece of paper bearing Brown's phone number. The officer was to call him if he wanted Brown to handle the problem. Brown turned and walked away.

In 1981, a barroom brawl on the city's north side resulted in the arrest of 45-year-old Brown and his wife, Mary Kitchens Brown, 26. The bartender told police a fight started after several men flirted with Brown's wife. Brown took exception to it. Brown's wife had instigated the flirting, witnesses said.

A year later in another bar, Brown was shot to death.

He and his wife were enjoying the 4020 Club on Nov. 16, 1982. Just before last call at the bar, Mary was perched on her husband's lap, passionately kissing and hugging him, witnesses said. While making out with him, Mary took Brown's pistol, put it against his chest and pulled the trigger. Mary told officers she'd just put an end to several years of spousal abuse.

It was her second attempt to kill him, she said. Mary said the previous year, she started flirting with men at another bar, hoping he'd die in the subsequent fight. Instead, she and Brown were arrested.[40]

Mary was convicted of killing Brown.

Brown was taken to a local hospital, where he was declared dead. He was 46 and survived by three daughters, his brother, Gaye, a sister and four grandchildren.

After the shooting, one officer who knew Brown went to check on him, unaware he'd died.

Seeing him dead on the hospital gurney, the officer was struck again at how large Brown had been, when he saw his legs hanging off the edge by about a foot.

Wild Animals

Told by L.E. "Spider" Webb

Side hustles and off-duty jobs keep the money flowing for police officers, who have never earned enough as lawmen.

Take for example a Fort Worth detective named Tommy Wright. He owned a 24-hour convenience store called The Hitchin' Post. When I first started at the police department, I worked midnight shift in the Stop Six neighborhood, where there was always crime and officers were always busy.

The Hitchin' Post was one of two all-night stores police watched closely because they were prime for robberies. The other was a Mr. M food store that was robbed on a regular basis, despite our best efforts.

To my knowledge, The Hitchin' Post never got robbed. There may have been a good reason for that.

Anyone who knew Wright knew he had a side hustle other than the store.

He hunted rattlesnakes, keeping them in a storage room at the back of the store. Wright saved them until he had enough. Then he killed and skinned them.

We tried to watch the two stores closely and curiosity caused me to check on the snakes at The Hitchin' Post. As soon as I walked into the back room, those snakes started rattling.

One woman had worked there for years. Every once in while she would have help, but usually it was just her. I asked if she was ever afraid of being robbed.

She wasn't because she had a plan, she told me. If a robbery ever occurred, she would run to the back room, open the snake boxes, and throw them out the door before closing herself back in. She also told me it was common knowledge among most of the customers and potential bad guys that there were a lot of rattlesnakes there.

One night, Wright announced he was having a snake kill that morning if anyone wanted to watch. Several officers, including myself, showed up. Wright had so many snakes, he had filled five or six trashcans with them. Those snakes were angry and making a hell of a racket.

The detective had a pump sprayer filled with gasoline that he used to squirt into the trash cans. He put the lids on and waited. He told us the gasoline would kill the snakes or at least knock them out long enough for him to kill them. Some of his snakes were at least seven feet long and as big around as a roll of bologna. After a while, the cans grew quiet, and Wright began to dump the snakes on the ground to skin them. They appeared lifeless.

A fellow officer, who'd brought his camera with him, asked me to take a photo of him with one of those snakes draped around his neck. The snake he chose had a head about the size of a woman's hand. As I got ready to take the picture, I noticed the snake appeared to twitch and I told my friend the snake had moved.

It was then we discovered that this snake was neither dead nor unconscious. It was wide awake. The term "chaos" doesn't come close to describing the next several minutes. Wright eventually killed snake. After about 20 minutes, our heart rates dropped from about 400 to 120.

After that, I figured The Hitchin' Post employee had a fairly good robbery prevention plan. My fascination with rattlesnakes pretty much died that morning.

Lion on the Loose

Told by J.C. Williams Jr.

When it came to wild, troubled men, my father counted many among his friends.

Jim Landers was one of them. An agent with the U.S. Drug Enforcement Administration, Landers worked with my dad, J.C. Williams Sr., on federal narcotics task forces around the area. Landers came from a wealthy family and owned an exotic game ranch near Waco, Texas.

He had a wild javelina as a pet and brought it with him when he visited us. Landers and my father would hit the bars on Fort Worth's east side, javelina in tow. The animal sat quietly in the corner of whatever bar they were in until someone began playing the pinball machine. The javelina didn't like pinball. With teeth snapping, he charged the person and chased them out of the bar.

Landers gifted me with all kinds of animals while I was growing up, to add to the Williams' family menagerie. I wasn't surprised, then, when he gave me a lion while I was in high school. I already had plenty to feed Searcy – goats, pigs, rabbits and deer meat.

Searcy went with me everywhere – she sat in the back seat of my car, put her paws on the front seat and put her head next to mine.

One day, I took my lion to Eastern Hills High School, waiting to see my girlfriend. Eldon Ray, the football coach, saw me and asked if I could control Searcy. Of course I could, I had a thin chain I used as a leash when we got out of the car.

Ray wanted to scare the other coaches so he asked me to follow him into the athletic field house where we would scream, "Lion on the loose!"

One young coach got a face-to-face meeting from Searcy when she jumped up on his desk and looked him straight in the eye. He sprinted out the front door. He didn't look back until he ran the length of a football field.

Ray laughed so hard, he dropped to his knees. That young coach later became the head basketball coach and swore he'd never forget that day.

The man who started it all, Landers, ended up shooting and killing his girlfriend, an airline attendant. For three days after he killed her, he hid at our house while police were looking for him. My father believed Landers would be safe there until he could explain what happened.

A jury gave him a 10-year probated prison sentence in the death. The DEA fired him. Landers eventually became the security manager for ZZ Top.

When the Circus Came to Town

Told by Kevin Foster

About a hundred years ago, Fort Worth experienced its first and only African lion hunt.

The lion escaped from a circus train and ran into a heavily populated neighborhood near the train station, causing residents to run amok in fear.

The Al G. Barnes Wild Animal Circus train was headed to Dallas on Feb. 11, 1923, when one of the lions escaped its cage in an express car, forcing the man in charge to run for his life. As the train neared Fort Worth - it was scheduled to stop at the Fort Worth Rock Island railroad yards on the edge of downtown - it rounded a curve, the express car door flew open and the lion leapt to freedom.

It happened to land beside two switchmen who ran for their lives, screaming at the top of their lungs. The lion raced into the neighborhood, prompting at least 50 telephone calls in five minutes to the Fort Worth Police Department. Callers begged for help and told police where to find the wild beast.

The switchmen's yells alerted residents of the danger and they began to panic. One man carried his small dog outside, announcing he would use the canine as bait and capture the lion. His plan lasted until he saw the lion. The dog was not too keen on the idea, either.

Three police officers – Ed Lee, W.B. Hinkle and B.F. Griffith – received the lion call. They first raided the department's armory of rifles, shotguns and ammo. They found the neighborhood in a full-blown panic with residents running, screaming and pointing to where they'd seen the lion.

The lawmen quickly found the lion curled up in the backyard of a house at 408 Wall Street. Lee, who normally drove the Patrol Wagon, took careful aim and fired, killing the lion with a single shot.

The trio of big cat hunters loaded the carcass and hauled it to the police department, where someone skinned the lion and put the hide on display. The hide was next displayed at the Fort Worth Star-Telegram offices. That's when the circus called, wanting the lion back. They also demanded the hide.

The remains of the lion were packaged and sent to the circus still in Dallas.[41]

Fourteen years later, The Three Stooges released a film short, "Hold That Lion!" that includes slapstick scenes of a circus lion escaping its cage on a passenger train. Art imitating life, perhaps?

The Stolen Suitcase

Told by Kevin Foster
with Kathy Sanders

When you want to cause chaos, all you need is a big old suitcase and a really large raccoon.

In 1966, a new Fort Worth police officer arrived at shift change with a huge boar (male) raccoon in a tow sack. This officer, who we'll call Jake, had an affinity for catching wildlife, including raccoons, opossums and snakes.

Jake and three other officers devised a scheme that involved putting this raccoon in a suitcase. One of these officers just happened to have an old hard-sided suitcase in his car and they put it to use, punching holes in it to give Mr. Raccoon plenty of air. Then he was packed away.

The loaded suitcase was at roll call the next day. It was placed by the door and kicked each time an officer left the room. Each kick enraged the raccoon which apparently was the intent.

Jake and his buddies took the suitcase to the southeast side of the city. They put it on a curb at a street intersection, then hid nearby to watch the fun. They were convinced someone would steal it.

Within minutes, a brand new four-door Buick drove by and two people hung their heads out of the window, assessing the suitcase. Four times, the car passed by before the front seat passenger opened his door and grabbed the suitcase.

The Buick sped away but came to an abrupt halt when it hit a telephone pole. Officers watched as all four car doors flew open, four men bailed out and our misunderstood raccoon sprinted away.

The car occupants called police after they'd calmed down and our quartet of officers, of course, responded to the wreck.

Apparently when they opened the suitcase, the crazed animal burst out, running across the men and the car. Mr. Raccoon ended up spread across the steering wheel as if he was trying to drive.

The cops reported that the interior looked as if someone had shredded the upholstery with a sharp knife. The driver required 120 stitches for his cuts and scratches. The others also bore deep scratches and bruises. Jake and his buddies said the men looked terrified.

They maintained, however, that their injuries came from the wreck. Someone had pulled in front of the driver, who had to swerve to avoid hitting the car and struck the pole instead.

They made no mention of the suitcase or the raccoon.

Bathroom Monster

Told by Kevin Foster

Sometimes, we need a reminder that there is a considerable overlap of intelligence between an average human and a smarter-than average raccoon.

I took a call from an elderly woman who was one of our frequent customers. Those of us who dealt with her regularly thought she was a bit loopy. At 3 a.m. on this day, she reported that a raccoon was in her bathroom. I had my doubts but headed to her house in the Arlington Heights neighborhood.

I went inside her tidy, well-furnished home and she led me to the master bedroom at the rear of the house. Two French doors led to a back garden and on the other side of the room was the bathroom. And inside that bathroom on a stack of clean towels in a cupboard sat a large raccoon. He looked comfortable.

All I had to do, I told myself, was open the doors to the garden and encourage the raccoon to run out through those doors. I retrieved a broom, intent on giving this critter an unobstructed path to the garden and a little push in that direction.

After a couple prods with the broom, I realized this was a bad idea. That raccoon stood on his hind legs, stretched out his paws and claws, then growled as loud as any dog I've ever been around. I'm fairly sure the next thing I thought was, "Oh, crap!"

Trying to save an incident that was careening toward disaster, I used the broom to shut the cupboard door, then wedged it shut. I walked out and shut the bathroom door, too.

I told the woman I was incapable of solving her raccoon situation and warned her not to open the bathroom or cupboard door. Animal control officers would be happy and qualified to help her if she called the office when they opened, I told her and handed over their phone number. I guessed she didn't go back to bed that night.

I left feeling incredibly grateful that my poorly thought-out plan didn't result in a more painful lesson that I would have had to explain at the hospital later.

The Body Bag

Told by Kevin Foster
with Kathy Sanders

Circumstances often dictate unique and, sometimes, awkward solutions to problems. Resourcefulness is imperative.

When I was a midnight sergeant, we had two rottweiler dogs running amok in the hospital district – the dogs were attacking and killing other dogs and cats in a frenzy.

After we received several calls from residents, two officers searched for the dogs. They saw the mutilated remains of the other animals and tracked the dogs with help from the neighbors. These cops ended up outside a vacant house with a fenced backyard. The gate was open. My officers found the dogs at the same time the dogs noticed them. The dogs charged and the Officers knew they couldn't outrun the dangerous dogs and knew they'd be badly injured if the out-of-control dogs got to them. They opened fire, killing both. That's when I was summoned to the scene.

Whenever a cop fires her or his service weapon on the job, an investigation is conducted.

Ensuring the dogs were dead and the officers were uninjured, I started the investigation. We also needed to dispose of the huge dogs and that presented a problem.

The city's animal control unit only dealt with live animals, so they wouldn't be assisting.

I suddenly thought of an idea and sent one of the officers to John Peter Smith Hospital to get a body bag. This grinning officer took off and soon returned with the bag that was large enough to hold a person.

We ensured that bag was large enough for both dogs and loaded them on the curb for the trash trucks in a few hours.

A few chuckles came at the sight of the stuffed body bag lying on the curb. Officers left and I didn't think about the next day.

When daylight came, some residents of the neighborhood unaware of the night's events, were aghast when they saw the bag. They summoned police – the day shift officers.

Apparently, no one was aware of our dog call - more officers arrived, the crime scene unit showed up and detectives stood by in case a human was in the body bag.

They were a bit flummoxed when the bodies of two dogs were revealed inside. They didn't have answers, but no one called me.

A few days later, I turned in my supervisory incident review and never heard another word about it.

Chapter 7

Police Pranks and Entertainment

Even the gods love jokes.

-Plato

Camping on the Brazos

Told by J.C. Williams Jr
with help from Larry Alphin

Involvement in long-term investigations takes its toll on everyone involved. It's imperative to take time to relax and blow off a little steam.

So it was in the fall of 1983 when four of us from the vice unit decided to embark on an overnight camping trip along the Brazos River, west of Fort Worth.

Captain Ray Armand, Sergeant Bob Bishop, Officer Larry Alphin and I hiked quite a way before finding a sandy island in the middle of the river – it was the perfect camping spot with an area for a campfire far enough away from the sleeping bags.

The fire slowly burned down to smoldering ashes after we cooked dinner. We moved toward the sleeping area, about 30 feet from the fire.

Armand had set up his new, expensive sleeping bag atop a small, raised cot. Bishop and I stood talking to Armand while he got in his sleeping bag because he was cold. He zipped it up to his neck to keep the heat in. Alphin was busy gathering a few more things to bring to the sleeping area.

But with Alphin, anything could happen at any time, anywhere.

Out of the corner of my eye, I spotted Alphin pouring Coleman fuel to make a line in the sand, from the fire embers to our sleeping area. He motioned me to stay quiet and not rat him out. If it had gone as he planned, Alphin would have a fire line run along the ground toward us and stop right behind us.

He wanted a movie effect – fire racing across the sand and scaring everyone. I should have known it would be an epic disaster.

Alphin walked closer to Armand and Biship, pouring his line of fuel, when the campfire embers suddenly ignited the fuel. The flames rushed toward a shocked Alphin while he was still holding the can of fuel. The fire line was impressive, burning about four feet off the ground. The small isle glowed like a war zone.

Of course, Alphin slung that fuel can so it wouldn't explode in his hand. That in turn caused the fuel to soak Bishop from his waist down to his toes. When the flames reached him, Bishop was engulfed in fire from the waist down – he never had time to run.

Alphin's thrown fuel can landed next to Armand's cot, about three inches from his head, shooting a flame about six feet in the air. Armand flailed around, trying to escape from his sleeping bag, but he struggled with the zipper.

I yelled at Bishop to run into the river to extinguish the fire and I followed him. Armand finally ripped out of his sleeping bag and joined us. In shock, the three of us checked each other for injuries. Bishop lost the hair on his legs, which bore a smoky black look. It was miraculous we were fine.

Almost on cue, the three of us pivoted to look at Alphin, standing in the water holding a beer in one hand.

He raised his beer to us and said, "You know guys, it doesn't get any better than this."

We laughed with relief, but we probably should have killed him.

Memorable Church Presentation

Told by J.C. Williams Jr.
with help from Dub Bransom
& J.C. Williams Sr.

The best laid plans of mice and men would definitely go awry if my father was around. A notorious prankster who viewed nothing as "off-limits," J.C. Williams Sr. would do anything to amuse himself. He loved targeting his partners and supervisors at the police department and did so with relish.

In the late 1960s, my father and his partner at the time, Dub Bransom, were assigned to narcotics. Officer Bill Hardin also was in the unit and spent much of his time giving public presentations about drugs and the people who abused them.

With the rise in heroin use, demand for these presentations was high. Occasionally, Bransom was tagged to help. Hardin and Bransom used a slide projector with photographs of drugs, weapons, paraphernalia and mugshots of those arrested.

One day, Chief Cato Hightower sent a note requesting that Bransom conduct one at the largest Catholic church in the city. At first Bransom (coached by Williams) declined, saying he was too busy. The chief sought Bransom out to personally extend the invitation again and Bransom said he wasn't about to get on Hightower's bad side.

"Yes, sir, Chief. I'll do it," he said.

The next evening, Bransom finished preparing for the presentation and made sure Hardin had left the slide projector and slides for him.

"J.C. was around the office going over case files and said he would stay and finish some officer work while I finished with the presentation," Bransom recalled.

About 1,000 people showed up at the church to learn about the rise of narcotics and everything was going as planned – Bransom's notes matched up with the slides. As he looked down at his notes, and clicked for the next slide to appear, a huge gasp of shock came from the audience. Bransom looked at the screen which had a nude woman in a pose that typically was seen only in pornographic magazines or movies. Dumbfounded, Bransom tried to change the slide, but the projector and the image were stuck.

Out of panic and desperation, Bransom yanked the electric plug from the wall to stop the obscene projection. The priest walked up to Bransom and put his arm around the younger man's shoulder.

"It's obvious you are the victim of a prank, but it could have been worse,'' the priest said into the microphone. "You could have been doing this presentation at a Baptist Church."

The audience chuckled, but Bransom wondered if his chief would be as understanding. Bransom said he was furious because he knew he'd been set up.

When he entered the narcotics office, he saw my father and knew right then that Williams had put the woman's photo in the slide show.

"You did it, now get up and fight," Bransom told him. "I didn't know if I could win the fight, but I was ready to take the chance," he said. Williams was laughing so hard, he couldn't get out of his chair. He was ecstatic the prank had worked.

By happenstance, the next day Bransom ran into the chief.

"I understand you had a very interesting and memorable presentation last night," Hightower said. Bransom could only reply, "Yes, Chief." And that was the end of that conversation.

The Bogeyman and The Sergeant

Told by J.C. Williams Jr.

Halloween always manages to bring out fabulous prank gizmos.

My partner Larry Alphin and I stopped in a novelty store to grab some stuff for our kids one Halloween season.

While there, our eyes fell on the scariest, full-faced robbery mask we'd ever seen. It came with a black cloth toboggan, and we absolutely had to have it. The possibilities seemed endless. We are going to have fun with this, if we were careful.

Several others helped us plan our pranks – Ronnie Gouyton, Larry "Duck" Taylor, Wane Fitch, Clyde Martin, Craig Gouyton and Benny Thompson.

Early victims included friends and fellow officers who came to our lair on the third floor without their guns or who used the bathroom off a narrow hallway.

To disguise myself, I took off my shirt and donned the mask. I carried a 16-inch knife we used to carve the office's Thanksgiving turkey. Then I scared the bejesus of them, particularly when they came out of the bathroom.

The reactions were predictable and unforgettable.

After scaring several friends, we decided to take on our night supervisor. Sergeant Curtis Henderson was a respected and tough supervisor, who had worked undercover before his promotion. I was willing as long as I had help and they made sure Henderson didn't have his gun.

Henderson's routine rarely varied – he'd be back in the office at 1 a.m., turn on all lights and wait for the detectives to get back in the office before their shift ended at 2 a.m. He always parked next to our building and took the elevator up to our office and he left his gun in the car for that hour.

My co-conspirators and I showed up before Henderson one night and I waited in the hallway outside the elevator on the third floor to surprise the sergeant. We kept the lights off so when the doors opened, the light would shine on me. The other officers crouched down and hid – they had a good view of the elevator and Henderson's reaction but couldn't be seen.

The sergeant showed up on time and rode the elevator alone to the third floor.

But when the doors opened, I immediately saw the gun on his belt. Henderson wasn't the only one terrified. I saw him reach for his gun with his fastest quick draw.

Still in costume, my only option was to jump in the elevator with Henderson to stop him from pulling his gun. I don't know why I still had the knife in my hand. I tried to force him against the elevator wall while trying to tell the sergeant it was me.

We danced around the elevator until I got him pinned against the wall so I could convince him it was me. About that time, the other officers started popping up out of the shadows to help, but they were too late. They said they were laughing too hard to realize the prank had gone bad at first.

Henderson, finally realizing it was a prank, relaxed and slumped to the floor. I was just happy to be alive.

The sergeant didn't talk to the other officers for a month. It took longer for him to speak to me until I agreed that I'd retire the robbery mask.

A Little Respect Please

Told by J.C. Williams Jr.

Another prank pulled frequently, actually was more of a re-training activity of new detectives.

Veteran detectives and officers took offense if these newbies failed to show proper respect to them. Whoever needed "corrective action" was held out the third-floor window of the police department by their feet. This usually improved this disrespectful behavior.

Unfortunately, agents from the Federal Bureau of Investigation witnessed one of the re-training sessions and believed police officers were hanging suspects or inmates out the window during the evening.

Concerned, the agency sent two agents to the department to investigate the practice and see if anyone needed to be charged with cruel and unusual punishment in treatment of prisoners.

Oops! The practice was stopped.

Pranks and Payback

Told by J.C. Williams Jr.

Cops love a good prank. Always have. Always will. Even those pranked eventually smile about it.

Like the detective who spent too much time in the bathroom every day.

His fellow detectives all had one car to share and every day, they had to wait for him to finish his extended restroom constitutional before they could leave the office. They were annoyed.

One July morning, they opened his stall and found him with dropped drawers, reading the newspaper and in no apparent hurry. Each day, he read most of the paper before ending his ritual.

The other detectives photographed him on his throne – he didn't care. It didn't stop him. No one discussed it after that. Until Christmas.

Our detective didn't understand why people passing him in the hallway broke out laughing and wished him a Merry Christmas – he was puzzled because it had never occurred in past years.

He found out soon enough.

A Christmas card sent to all the Special Investigations Unit employees, featured the photo of this detective reading the newspaper while on the toilet, wishing them all a Merry Christmas.

Well played.

The Nash Metropolitan Car

J.C. Williams Jr.

My dad enjoyed helping his friends.

One of them was H.L. Smith, a vice and narcotics sergeant who lived in the country while working in the city.

Smith complained to Williams about the amount of gas his old pickup truck was burning through during his long commutes to work.

Williams offered to talk with Darius Willis, who supplied police with undercover vehicles and usually had many used cars for sell.

"If he gets in a cheap, used, economy vehicle, you could buy it," Williams told Smith. "The gas you would save compared to what your old pickup is using would almost pay for it."

In short order, Smith had bought a used Nash Metropolitan, one of the first economy cars made in the 1950s. For the first few days, he reported getting 30 mpg (miles per gallon), a vast improvement over the 12 mpg for his truck.

Smith was thrilled, so Williams decided it was time to mess with him.

"I heard from Darius Willis that your car's mpg will keep getting better as you drive," that sly old dog told Smith. "Try to drive it each day and consistently keep your foot steady on the gas pedal."

Smith did what his friend said.

Williams took to carrying a gas can to work and, without telling Smith, added gas to the Metropolitan every day.

Astonished, Smith reported gas mileage of 40, 60, 80 and then 100 during the next few weeks.

All the cops in on the joke, including my father, praised Smith for his ability to drive so perfectly smooth – that was the only explanation for the outstanding mileage, they told him.

Of course, Williams wasn't done. He started decreasing the amount of gas he added to the Metropolitan. Then he started taking gas out of the tank.

Soon, Smith was down to 20 mph. He decided new spark plugs and a complete overhaul would improve the gas mileage. Others agreed with him.

Williams kept siphoning gas from the car and the mileage dropped to 10 mph.

A man with a short fuse, Smith stalked into the office mad as hell. Not to let things alone, the pranksters poured fuel on the flame: the mechanic probably saw the sergeant as an everyday sucker, an easy target and took advantage of him.

What no one saw coming: an enraged Smith stormed over to the garage, got into a physical fight with the mechanic and ended up in the department's Internal Affairs.

Williams convinced everyone they better wait an eon before telling Smith about the prank. He'd probably shoot every one of them.

Chapter 8

Faith and Police Work

Faith

In the midst of darkness, light persists.

Mahatma Gandhi - 1869-1948

Chapter Introduction by
Kevin Foster & J.C. Williams Jr.

Police officers face death daily.

Just as "there are no atheists in foxholes" during wartime, many cops discover a higher power when faced with flying bullets, brandished machetes and truly evil people.

The most intensely spiritual motivators that inspire law enforcement officers include a desire to make a positive difference in the world; champion noble ideals, like freedom, justice, and the sanctity of human life; protect the weak and innocent; and battle evil.

Many officers enter the profession motivated by spiritual ambitions just like these. They might not recognize their motivation as intensely spiritual, but if they become aware and train accordingly, that spirituality can grow throughout a career in policing.[42]

Many times, I found myself uttering a quick prayer while driving to a risky and unstable call. My prayer became more urgent if I had a bad feeling or the crime was still in progress – those calls that can often result in serious injury or death. The prayer may have lasted mere seconds, but my prayers were heartfelt. It wasn't out of habit - it was a simple request to survive and live another day. Some officers believed divine intervention saved their lives, others could come up with no rational explanation for escaping a certain death. Some felt compelled to change their lives, others heard "the call" to serve their God.

Faith and police have been intertwined since the beginning. In the early days, the Fort Worth police department held mandatory Sunday morning worship services for on-duty officers. In later years, police chaplains became more of the norm – either they were drawn from within the police ranks or were church leaders with ties to individual officers. The background of the chaplains was inconsequential.

What mattered the officers was having faith in each other and faith in God.

The Beginning of Weed and Seed

"Policing from the past can save policing for the future."

-J.C. Williams Jr.

Told by J.C. Williams Jr
with help from Kathy Sanders

In 1992, Fort Worth earned the infamous honor of being among the highest crime cities in the United States. As such, our city was awarded grant money to help reduce crime, along with 16 other cities nationwide.

Known as Weed and Seed, the goal was to "weed" out crime and "seed" the community with social programs to help residents.

Officers chosen for the program would be paid for two hours of extra patrol at the end of their regular shifts.

Our target areas centered in the near southeast neighborhoods of Stop Six and Polytechnic Heights, normally referred to as Poly. Parts of these areas were run-down, filthy and infested with drugs and crime.[43]

Police Chief Thomas Windham chose me to lead the project that started July 2, 1992. With City Administrators present, I advised that we would decrease crime 50% and cross train officers to do things they had never done.

Chief Windham, who was not at the meeting, came to my office the next morning. He said downtown instructed him to tell me to never make promises to the community again. Their reason was that previous initiatives had failed and they didn't want to raise expectations.

I told the chief, I would not change and he could transfer me if he wanted. In my onion, the reason other efforts failed was because no one had faith or believed in what they were doing. For us to succeed, I had to have faith; then supervisors, officers and the community would have faith we could decrease crime to that level.

Chief Windham became silent and was very mad at first, then after several minutes, got up and said, "J.C. – do what you have to do and you work for me." He later told me because he knew me well, that he did not know if we would both get fired before it was over. Additionally, he said that was the most stressful time in his 30-year career.

In the first few weeks, I met with community members and leaders to talk about problems in the neighborhood.

Longtime resident, Callie Pollard – who became one of my best friends – pointed to increasing drug traffic in the 300-unit Cavile Place Housing Projects in Stop Six. It was out of control and Callie had tried in vain to get help. She voiced her concerns to Windham and filed complaints with the narcotics unit – narcotics officers said they were unable to make undercover buys in the complex, with few, if any, criminal cases.

A Fort Worth Housing Authority representative told me there was a persistent concern that a police supervisor "protected" the drug dealers at Cavile and that person might cause problems.

I told them nothing mattered. We would eliminate the drug problem and anyone who had problems with that could take it up with me.

I formally requested narcotics to make buys in the neighborhood, but I received the same response – they couldn't get anyone to make buys from the dealers.

Having worked undercover for seven years, I knew there was always a way. I summoned J.D. Franklin, one of my patrol officers.

"J.D., can you make drug buys at Cavile?" I asked.

“Sure, I can,” he said without hesitation.

Our plan was taking shape. Franklin would work that night and I arranged to have a narcotics officer help with the undercover buys. Det. Roger Dixon was on tap to coordinate the criminal cases and write search warrants for each of the places where Franklin would buy drugs.

We worked with Housing Authority officials on how to keep drug dealers out of Cavile. The answer was to evict everyone involved in drug trafficking. Eviction notices would be served whenever we made an arrest. Residents were given three days to leave and if they didn’t, a civil suit would be filed against them.

Franklin proceeded to buy drugs several times from different peddlers and the purge was on. Weed and Seed officers, S.W.A.T, other police officers and members of the housing authority took part, witnessed by television and newspaper reporters. We even provided some journalists with bulletproof vests.

Nine people were arrested, several raids took place simultaneously and 11 eviction notices were issued. In one night.

Callie walked proudly with me during the operation. She was thrilled they were reclaiming their home. Other residents and neighbors came outside to support us.

It was the first of many celebrations through the years involving Weed and Seed officers and our successes.

Next, we targeted a house in the Weed and Seed territory. Fenced, this house had steel doors, guard dogs, camera surveillance and armed guards hanging out on the porch. The fortified fortress posed a challenge to S.W.A.T officers, but we resolved that with a wrecker and heavy tow chains.

They just pulled off the front porch and the front part of the house. The S.W.A.T Commander agreed to help hit as many fortified drug houses as possible.

Weed and Seed couldn't rely on other units to help serve search warrants – they were understaffed and overworked – so our officers were cross-trained to cover any eventuality. We also found a huge uninspected and unregistered commercial van to use during raids – I told Sergeant Phil South to send Weed and Seed officers to fetch it from California. I knew we needed it and knew it would never be approved. We got it and used it for the first seven years for our program before being asked about it.

Our results? In the first year, we seized more than $1 million in cash and made more than 5,000 arrests for felony crimes and other drug and firearm violations.

We reduced crime nearly 50 percent and earned praise from then-U.S. Attorney General Janet Reno as the "best in the nation."

More importantly, however, was the positive impact on the residents and Cavile itself.

As significant as enforcement was the positive efforts of the seeding initiative. I knew local media wanted to go on all dynamic warrants, however, would not prioritize news of seeding efforts. We had local teenagers at the start of Weed and Seed doing surveys of residents on their needs. The organizers told me they contacted the media but all said they were too busy to cover this story. I called and warned all media that if seeding efforts were not covered , I would not call them on any dynamic warrant operations. They quickly came out and covered this story along with other future efforts.

The "seeding" part of the program included establishing innovative programs such as a job bank, transportation for residents to access jobs, a neighborhood newsletter and after-school programs for children.

Leaders organized clean-ups that included painting homes and cleaning vacant lots.

Combined with the crime-fighting efforts, it all helped to turn a one-time cesspool into a safer, livable neighborhood.

Heroes in the community included Callie Pollard, Quincy Taylor, Deborah Hernandez, Rev. W.G. Daniels, the pastor of Pilgrim Valley Missionary Baptist Church and Rev. LeRoy Haynes, the pastor of the Carter Metropolitan CME Church. Others involved were Patsy Thomas with the Crime Commission and Barbara Holston and Dianne Cook with the Fort Worth Housing Authority.

Weed and Seed officers, up and down the roster, still say their time working in the program was the most rewarding, successful tour they experienced in their careers.

They point to the fact that they were allowed to do "real" policing they'd always wanted to do; support a community and be supported in return, particularly when under fire from drug dealers and city officials; and to actually help.

Weed and Seed eventually ended in Fort Worth, but its lasting effects are seen throughout the police department. Our community policing gave birth to the city's Neighborhood Police Districts to solve problems and reduce crime.

You're on Your Own

Told by J.C. Williams Jr.

Criminals often complain about the success of police programs that target them and their illegal trade. Sometimes, outstanding officers are unjustly transferred or disciplined to make the commotion go away. Enter the reality of local politics.

When I commanded the federal Weed and Seed project in Fort Worth in the early 1990s, a cluster of complaints nearly derailed the innovative, successful program.

Weed and Seed was the 1991 community-policing brainchild of the U.S. Department of Justice.

Its goals were simple: reduce violent crime, drug abuse and gang activity in high-crime neighborhoods, then improve the residents' quality of life with support, new growth, jobs and assistance programs.

Fort Worth was tagged as one of the first 16 cities to take on the federally funded challenge.

My officers and I hit crime hard from the beginning as we took on the bad guys who terrified the residents in our target area, the neighborhoods of Polytechnic and Stop Six in the southeast part of the city. Weed and Seed officers and supervisors made drug buys, raided drug houses and arrested dozens of dealers and gang members we knew were responsible for the high crime rate.

We also worked tirelessly with community leaders to gain their support. Two of the faith leaders, Rev. W.G. Daniels, pastor of the Pilgrim Valley Missionary Baptist Church, and the Rev. LeRoy Haynes were among our staunchest allies. I met monthly with Rev. Daniels – sometimes more frequently – and each time, he prayed for me, my officers and the operation's success.

With our accomplishments, the complaints started coming in. In 1993, a group of "residents" attended a city council meeting, demanding that Weed and Seed be shut down for police brutality and an investigation be conducted into all law enforcement actions taken in the community. They also mentioned an officer-involved shooting. The officer already had been exonerated of any wrongdoing.

We were shocked, however, when the council immediately created a task force to investigate us without determining the validity of the complaints or the people complaining.

Many of the people who spoke against us at that meeting weren't residents. They had strong ties with the drug trade, gangs, and other criminals. They'd even used fake names.[44]

The next day, I sought a meeting with then-Police Chief Thomas Windham to inform him about these people. I also wanted him to call a press conference to defend the Weed and Seed operation.

Word came back, through the chief's public information officer: "You're on your own."

At the same time, Windham told a lieutenant he was disappointed with the city administration's lack of support, but he couldn't do anything to support me or the operation.

Realizing this could end Weed and Seed, I decided to go all in and fight. This was a battle officers had always lost over the years and it was time to change it.

I released undercover surveillance videos to the media that depicted several of those people who'd been at the city council meeting engaging in crimes. I showed the footage to neighborhood leaders to discuss the complaints. The department would never have released the videotapes, but as the chief had said, I was on my own.

The television stations aired stories every day based on the footage until the next council meeting.

The mayor, council and city manager heard a different message that night – police brutality was a bogus issue in the neighborhood. Residents primarily worried about drugs, crime, and gang violence. Daniels and Haynes voiced support for Weed and Seed and spoke on behalf of their congregations. Deborah Hernandez, of the Polytechnic Heights Hispanic Home and Business Owners Association, called for the city manager's resignation and the mayor's ouster if they didn't support the program and its officers.[45]

"As all of this unfolded in City Hall, it was like sitting at a heavy weight boxing match," said Ralph Mendoza, who became police chief following Windham's death in 2000. "The bad guys come in to council and lay out all kinds of (alleged) illegal actions by the Weed and Seed officers. Next the true residents of the Weed and Seed area come in for the knock-out blow." "They took the bad guys and the Council and (Police) Department to task," Mendoza said. "I can recall the citizens standing up and saying that the previous people filing their complaints don't speak for us. They are the problem. They are the drug dealers and criminals."

"I have never seen anything like that before. I'm sitting at ring side thinking to myself, 'Yahoo!'" Mendoza said.

Within two weeks, the political winds had changed again in our favor. Windham, who had failed us, publicly voiced his support and adapted to our innovative approach. It resulted in a seismic shift in police operations and spurred the creation of Neighborhood Policing Districts.

Billie Daniels

"In man's light, it was his time to die. In God's light, it wasn't."

Told by J.C. Williams Jr.
With help from Billie Daniels

Weed and Seed Officer Billie Daniels should be dead.

One of my 74 original Weed and Seed officers, Daniels died on the operating table once while a team of talented surgeons tried to repair the devastation caused by a bullet that hit both femoral arteries.

But his doctors said it wasn't them.

"In man's light, it was his time to die," Daniels recalled Dr. Jim Sloan saying. "In God's light, it wasn't."

Even during his life and death struggle, Daniels implored his police chief to keep the Weed and Seed program going. "We are making a difference in the community," he told Fort Worth Police Chief Thomas Windham.

I had led the program since it began in 1992, but I had just left to command the department's Violent Personal Crimes Division, when the shooting occurred.

Daniels, a strong leader in the program, was part of an eight-person team raiding a house where undercover officers had bought drugs. It was also home to thugs who'd been terrorizing the neighborhood, down to pathetically robbing school kids of their lunch money.

Armed with a search warrant, officers set the raid for Nov. 9, 1994, at the house that was across the street from an elementary school.

Daniels and his friend, Officer Rudy Johnson, were tasked with tackling a back bedroom during the raid. They had known each other five years since Johnson's earliest days on the police force. Both officers were big and determined. Daniels was a Second Team All-American football player in high school and Johnson enjoyed bodybuilding.

Within seconds, the two officers stood outside the back bedroom, they noticed their view into the bedroom was partially blocked. Suddenly, an elderly man rushed out of the room and plowed right into Daniels. At the same time, he saw a younger man sitting on the bed and reaching for something, he told me.

He shoved the older man to the floor, looked up in time to see the younger man turning a gun on them. "Gun!" Daniels yelled, and pushed Johnson out of the doorway just as a barrage of bullets came flying at them.

Both officers collapsed, shot.

Daniels told me that his vision started growing dark, but the gunman wasn't finished. He forced himself to sit up and return fire with his revolver while he watched the suspect moving about the bed. Dizziness started enveloping the officer, but he managed to fire three times before collapsing again.

Police officer David Ukle took over, coming upon the bedroom as Daniels fell. Another officer with military medic training, Chip Gillette, dragged Daniels to the porch outside. Johnson rose and made his way away from the shooting.

Two other officers, Brent Ladd and Corporal Robin Krouse, joined Ukle to fire a barrage of bullets at the suspect through the bedroom wall. Daniels said when the officers paused to reload, the gunman tried to flee out a window. Ukle shot the suspect in the back of his leg, leaving him dangling half in and half out of the window.

Officers stationed outside arrested the man, identified as Harold Curtis Edmonds.

On the porch, Gillette found Daniels' wound in his upper thigh and raced to place makeshift tourniquets around the affected areas.

"I'm not going to die, man," Daniels told Gillette. "You got to get me to the hospital. I'm not dying!"

Johnson had been shot in the thigh as well, but the wound didn't appear to be as severe.

An ambulance showed up almost immediately and a paramedic sought specific help, Daniels told me. Officer Fred Myers volunteered. His sole job, according to the paramedic, was to smack

Daniels hard in the forehead anytime the injured officer closed his eyes. The attendant told Myers that if Daniels lost consciousness, his body would start shutting down.

After being smacked by Myers several times, Daniels told me he was so mad, he wanted to hurt Myers. He, however, was strapped down to the gurney.

"I would feel my eyes closing or feel myself closing down, and then Fred would start hitting me again," Daniels said.

When they got to the hospital, time was nearly up for Daniels. Surgery took more than six hours. His body stopped at the four-hour mark, but surgeons revived him.

The bullet that struck him entered his left upper thigh, he said, severing the femoral artery. It continued to tumble in Daniels' body, ultimately nicking the femoral artery in his right thigh.[46]

"The first thing Billie said to me after the shooting was, 'Please do not stop what we are doing because we are making a difference in the community," Windham told me later.

Hospitalized for 24 days, Daniels had surprising visitors in the hospital, including a group of Blood gang members, he'd been working with. They offered to kill Daniels' attacker and his entire family because they didn't like Edmonds or what he did to the officer.

Stunned, Daniels declined the offer, saying he didn't want repercussions against the gangsters on his conscious.

Daniels and several other officers sat in the courtroom when Edmonds was convicted of trying to kill him. They were also there when the jury handed Edmonds a 10-year probated sentence.

Daniels said it was so quiet after the sentence was announced he heard another officer unholster his gun. He grabbed the officer's elbow, trying to stop him from shooting the defendant. A sergeant approached, telling the enraged officer shooting Edmonds wasn't worth his life and career.

At one point, Daniels said he looked around at the courtroom scene: Edmunds was under the defense table under his attorney; crying jurors hid behind their seats, the judge remained behind his bench and the older bailiff was shaking but had his hand on his gun.

Others convinced the officer to release his gun. The officer then ripped his badge off his shirt and flung it to the floor, Daniels said. He pointed to the jurors and vowed he'd be back in the courtroom when the defendant sold crack cocaine to their children. The officer then left.

A Glimpse of Heaven

Told by Kevin Foster

The Fort Worth Stock Show & Rodeo is a huge deal.

It draws more than one million visitors, runs over three weeks, and brings in millions of dollars to Fort Worth's economy.

It also provides great off-duty jobs for police officers.

That's where I was camped in January 2009. I was the midnight officer with relatively simple duties – watch for trespassers and thieves and keep track of the night workers.

The stock show is a busy place at night. Everything is cleaned, trash is gathered and arenas are prepped for the next day's events. Some teens stay with their animals, getting ready for their show. And livestock must be rounded when they escape their barns or pens.

People who do those tasks, men and women, are otherwise unemployed, disabled or in need of extra money. Sometimes, they have health issues.

That night, I went back to the police office after completing my patrol rounds, walking the barns and visiting people working at the gates. It was about 5 a.m.

Within a few minutes, security was calling to inform me about a worker " that was down" at the John Justin Arena. There was no urgency in the call, they just needed me there.

I assumed someone had gotten drunk and passed out – I was the one to get them on their way.

When I reached the arena, I saw a circle of 10-12 men facing inward, looking down on the dirt floor. As I got closer, I saw they were watching an unconscious man lying on his back.

I thought he was dead, based on my more than 30 years of police experience.

He was older, possibly 60 years old, his face was dark purple, his mouth hung open and his eyes were fixed in a cloudy gaze. He exhaled and his breath and saliva formed a bubble the size of his face.

It was his last breath.

I believed he had been dead 10-15 minutes by the time I arrived. If it had been in a hospital setting, the odds of his survival would be less than 10 percent. In that dirt arena, his odds were far worse and probably close to zero. He was dead, I told myself.

Before I could say anything, the men's supervisor asked me if I was going to administer cardiopulmonary resuscitation (CPR).

Well, hell.

I had no desire to get down in the dirt and livestock waste and do CPR on someone I knew was dead. But I knew I had to try even though I thought it was a waste of time.

I called for the fire department personnel stationed at the show and an ambulance. I told them the man wasn't breathing. Then I started CPR. After several minutes, I needed a break. He was still without a pulse and help hadn't shown up. I called dispatch again and resumed compressions.

Again, after a few more minutes, I needed a break and I was getting frustrated. This seemed pointless and I had no idea when help was coming. I began again and after a minute, the man's head rocked back and he gasped for air. It scared the hell out of me. The supervisor who had suggested CPR said: "I saw it, too!"

I gathered my wits and went back to CPR to keep him going. Eventually, firefighters arrived as did the ambulance. They took over.

Our man, an unemployed Vietnam veteran, made it to the hospital and regained consciousness. He became alert, spoke with doctors and began to improve. He had been estranged from his family for some time, but they came to his bedside where amends were made.

Two years later, he was again at the Stock Show, this time as a guest. I don't know what became of him. I never saw him after he left the arena that cold January morning.

What I do know, with certainty, is that every one of those workers prayed hard that night. They all had faith that the man would live, unlike me, who was certain he was dead.

Still, I have no doubts he was pulled back from Heaven's gate.

Good Luck and a Good Dog

Told by L.E. "Spider" Webb

Police dogs are invaluable assets for police. Depending on their training, they can sniff out contraband such as drugs, guns and explosives, or hunt down people who don't want to be found.

Instead of searching buildings alone, many time officers summon the K9 teams to sniff out hidden bad guys, avoiding potentially deadly encounters.

Officer Lonnie Gilmore did just that one night in early 1976, after being called to a burglary alarm at a business on the north side. He wanted a police dog to search the nooks and crannies of the building.

Gilmer accompanied Officer Fryer and his leashed dog during the search. The trio encountered a long corridor with offices on each side. They carefully checked each door before moving on the next. Eventually, they came to a closet door at the end of the hallway – the dog indicated someone was inside. Fryer ordered the hidden person to reveal himself or he'd release the police dog. No one answered.

Cautiously Fryer opened the door and the burglary suspect hiding inside opened fire on the officers with a handgun. Multiple shots were fired in that close, confined area – the officers and dog were caught in a kill zone they couldn't exit.

Before Gilmore and Fryer could return fire, the dog did a U-turn through the men's legs, dragging them both to the floor. The officers managed to fire their guns while falling to the ground, aiming at the storage closet. They didn't know immediately that the gunman had been killed by their return fire.

The dog was still trying to move away, dragging the officers with him, so first they had to untangle themselves from the leash and gain control of the police dog. Then they found their suspect dead.

Gilmore spoke about the experience several times, always incredulous how both officers escaped the gunshots. "The guy was in spitting distance," he would say of the gunman. The miraculous escape was either part of God's plan for them or just dumb luck at being with a dog that inadvertently saved their lives.

Or both.

The Calling

Told by J.C. Williams Jr.
With help from Rod Corder

I tell my grandsons that wisdom comes from life experiences, understanding history, learning from others – especially our elders – and knowing that we are all part of God's plan. I stress that they are special and have a purpose even if they don't know what it is now.

And I think of my friend, Officer Rod Corder. And that night.

Early in my career, I worked with Corder during the midnight shift on the city's northside. We were nearing the end of our shift when we got one last call concerning a drunk passed out in a pickup truck. Because of all the bars in the area, this was a frequent call – people who drank too much just parked their cars on the side of the road and tried to sleep it off. This low-priority call had been waiting because of a busy night – which meant that, more than likely, the person was sobering up and might have already departed.

The truck was still there and so was the driver, who we'll call Carl. The truck leaned to the right where the road dropped off and we both were standing by the driver's door.

Corder opened the door to wake the snoozing man and get him out of the truck.

Carl wasn't drunk, and he was polite and courteous to both of us. Neither one of us were concerned at first. We saw nothing alarming when we looked in the truck through the windows – just some clothes. The truck, however, was filthy and stunk. Plus, Corder added later, suspects with felony warrants aren't known to park on the shoulder of main road. Corder asked Carl for his identification and Carl responded it must have dropped on the passenger floorboard. Corder didn't want us crawling around that nasty truck, so he told Carl to find it so we could check to see if he had any outstanding warrants.

Carl stretched out on the front passenger seat, supposedly looking for his ID. Immediately, I felt a rush of adrenaline and instinct led me to the passenger side of the truck. Because of the steep culvert, I grabbed hold of the truck bed and quietly and quickly moved to the passenger window.

Corder gave me an odd look, not sure why I was so concerned. The hair on the back of my neck was up – I felt something was wrong. Carl was talking over his shoulder to Corder, but I saw him slowly pulling out a .45-caliber automatic handgun from under the passenger seat. Corder couldn't see the gun. Carl was looking at Corder and started to turn toward him with the gun.

"Gun!" I yelled as I pulled out my gun. Carl appeared shocked, unaware I had moved to the passenger side. This gave Corder time to quickly draw his gun. With two cops holding him at gunpoint, Carl didn't know what to do. After a long pause, Carl put the gun down. He was wanted for capital murder and numerous robberies.

When I talked to Carl at the jail, he had decided he wasn't going back to prison and had planned to kill Corder, then try to surprise me with bullets as well.

Fast forward several years and I ran into Corder at Texas Christian University. He said I was the reason he was taking classes at the university on his way to becoming a pastor. Though we never spoke about God or faith while officers, I was still surprised the retired officer had chosen to become a minister.

Corder said that within a few years of our near miss, he knew that incident was a wake-up call for him to pursue a future in the ministry. He said God had used me to get the point across.

I would see Rod 35 years later in a town I would raise my family and now grandchildren. He became a pastor in this same town and each time I drive by this old rock church where he was a pastor, I realize I was only a small part of God's bigger plan.

Chapter 9

Leadership

"The ultimate measure of a man is not where he stands in moments of comfort and convenience, but where he stands in times of challenge and controversy"

- Martin Luther King Jr.

The Investigation of City Manager David Ivory

Told by J.C. Williams Jr.
With help from Danny Larue & Others

Fort Worth Police Chief Thomas Windham, was alerted by an anonymous tip from a new 24-hour hotline created to identify any corruption involving city employees that possible criminal activity was taking place.[47]

The tipster accused Windham's boss, Senior Assistant City Manager David Ivory, of accepting free trips to Las Vegas from Perry McCord, a contractor who had been awarded contracts to build multi-purpose centers and other buildings for the city.

Upon hearing this, City Manager Doug Harmon ordered a police investigation.

Windham instructed us to treat the Ivory's case just like it was any other employee probe.

My partner and I gathered details, names, business contacts, reviewed contracts and conducted interviews.

Ivory's attorney, William "Pat" Weir, met with us to explain all payments – gifts and cash – bestowed on Ivory. He said it was merely

loans from a successful business client – a masonry subcontractor who gave it to help Ivory's brother.

Weir showed us paperwork and the attorney was convinced this would clear up any misunderstanding. He controlled Ivory's trust account and knew we couldn't subpoena certain information.

We smiled and thanked him as we left. We had no intention of stopping the investigation and we didn't believe half of what Weir told us.

We immediately went to the client Weir had mentioned. We chatted about masonry which we had in common. I got the sense he wouldn't lie for anyone. So, we showed him the loan documents we'd just received and asked if he had made loans to Ivory.

Not only did he emphatically state he had never loaned Ivory any money, he said he didn't even know him well.

What was significant was that anytime certain annexations, zoning changes and multi-purpose center contracts were approved, Ivory received money from the trust account. That was bad news for Ivory's attorney – he now needed his own attorney.

Detective Danny LaRue, who I worked with in major case, approached me one day in the office. He'd talked with a good friend of his, a local defense attorney, who thought the Ivory investigation was merely a misunderstanding. Ivory was helping his brother Michael, who had medical issues and any loans and cash he'd received were for his brother.

It was a fishing expedition. LaRue's lawyer friend was a prominent and a good friend of Tarrant County District Attorney Tim Curry. I knew LaRue would never compromise the investigation and was relaying information so I went about my business.

I called a Kansas City, Mo., businessman who was involved in a 519-acre annexation project near Alliance Airport in far north Fort Worth. He was one of many I interviewed and I had the foresight to record the conversations, which cemented the case later.

LaRue said he'd give the defense attorney a couple of names from the case. I asked him to tell his friend that I thought he was right, and it was just a misunderstanding.

I still needed to meet with the Kansas City businessman and another person with the Waste Management Company in Oklahoma. After that, I passed on, we could clear up in the Ivory case.

LaRue came back the next day laughing and shaking his head.

When he mentioned the names to that attorney, the reply was this, "Well, that son of a bitch (me) is going to get us." The defense attorney said he had lied to LaRue to help Ivory and hopefully stop the investigation.

The games continued.

It was exceedingly difficult to work around a protected trust account. The investigation became so large, my partner and I moved into a separate office. We had the only access – we kept all documents and our notes there, as well as flow charts connecting the different players, locations, and types of transactions.

We interviewed numerous City of Fort Worth department heads who had any part in the contracts. Most were visibly angry and less than cooperative.

Newspaper reporters from the Fort Worth Star-Telegram reported on the investigation, quoting Ivory representatives who decried the probe, saying Ivory did nothing wrong.

My dad called me about this time, saying retired Capt. Garland Geeslin had called him about my work. Geeslin told my father he knew Ivory when Geeslin oversaw internal affairs during the 1970s. Ivory had contacted him.

Ivory wanted to know if Geeslin thought I had recorded conversations I had with the people involved. Ivory was unaware that dad and Geeslin went way back. Geeslin killed a suspect in an undercover operation my dad was involved in. He also didn't know I had done rock work on a cabin for Geeslin. The ties that bind.

In any case, Geeslin knew I recorded the conversations because of my background but kept that to himself while talking with Ivory.

Instead, he told the beleaguered assistant city manager that it would be unusual for a detective to record any conversation early in the investigation. I found out later that while he was still at the police department, Geeslin had a reputation for killing any investigation involving Ivory.

After that, Ivory's attorneys said I had lied about conversations I had with people involved in the investigation. The attorneys also proclaimed that Windham should be removed from office. They didn't know the tapes existed.

On the tapes, men involved in the payment scheme described how Ivory was paid for approving contracts and taking care of annexations.

Windham stopped by my office one day and informed me that if Ivory avoided indictment, the city council would vote 5-4 to fire the chief. I never discussed the case with Windham. I was comfortable with our work.

On July 29, 1988, a grand jury began hearing testimony in the case. City council members expressed frustration with the length of the investigation. I knew they were nervous because they had met many times with the same businessmen involved in the case.

Four days later, it was reported that Ivory received the equivalent of $1,000 per month in consulting fees from a Kansas City, Mo., firm involved in the Alliance Airport annexation. Ivory said he'd done nothing wrong and called the investigation "incredibly unfair."

Nearly two months later, the grand jury returned five misdemeanor indictments against Ivory for accepting a total of $33.000 in payments for preferred favors. Three indictments were levied against Weir, Ivory's attorney, accusing him of giving Ivory the funds.

After that, it was time to look at other people within the city government that were mentioned during the investigation. I told Windham we were ready to proceed.

"J.C., don't you think we have done enough?" he asked me. He abruptly said he had a meeting to attend and left to avoid talking about it.

The indictments drew the interest of the U.S. Attorney's office, who had started their own criminal investigation into Ivory's actions. A federal grand jury subpoenaed our files on the Ivory case and our local Federal Bureau of Investigation agents came to call.

They told me it was unfathomable what had occurred in the case. Elected officials in Washington, D.C., however, met with top officials in the U.S. Attorney's Office to discuss a deal involving city council members and Ivory. I was told all agreed to step down and not return to city government.

Ivory accepted a plea agreement in which he pleaded no contest to two misdemeanor charges. Weir, Ivory's attorney when the investigation began, also agreed to plea to offering a gift to a public servant.

In 1992, Ivory resigned and went to work for R.D. Hubbard Enterprises, which operated several horse and greyhound racetracks. Ivory went on to become the executive vice president of the Fort Worth Star-Telegram, the daily newspaper.

In March of 2007, I was contacted by a trusted friend who knew I worked on the David Ivory investigation. Fort Worth police officers and their association were not being supported by the Star-Telegram regarding benefit issues. An election on "meet and confer" - which would allow favorable changes for police officers in police civil service statutes - was coming soon, and the Star-Telegram continued to publish articles and editorials objecting to the change. My friend wanted to know if I had the original newspaper articles about Ivory's investigation that ran in the Star-Telegram.

I had saved every article because it was one of the biggest corruption cases in the history of Fort Worth. My friend made copies.

I was shocked that articles about the Ivory corruption case were missing from the Star-Telegram archives, including the front-page stories. Questions and requests for an explanation were made but never received an answer.

But several days later, Ivory suffered a heart attack while playing golf and died. His unexpected death shocked the community.

I can't help but think of how many other significant stories of Fort Worth police department history have been lost after the officers have died. Even worse are stories where an attempt was made to destroy history due to personal agendas that directly benefited a person in power.

Lieutenant B.J. Erby

A True Leader

Told by J.C. Williams Jr
with help from Paul Strittmatter

When I promoted to sergeant, the police department was trying a passive, hands-off approach to crowd control. It began during an annual July 3 parade in the Como neighborhood. In theory, they believed this was a better way to handle crowds in general.

In reality, it wasn't.

At least for the east side where I was working second shift.

My officers described bedlam on the streets in our district with crowds turning aggressive toward cops making routine traffic stops and arrests.

The crowds morphed into mobs, throwing bottles, interfering with arrests and threatening my men and women.

This crap needed to stop.

I expected immediate arrests of anyone causing a disturbance on the scene, no matter what they'd been told previously, I told my officers.

We were going to be tested and prepared for it.

Within a couple of weeks, hundreds of people descended on a car wash. Pretty soon, police were called to a convenience store next door – a suspect had warrants for his arrest and was carrying a handgun.

The crowd rebelled, confronted the officers and attempted to stop the arrest. I was summoned to the store and other officers raced there to help.

When I topped the hill, I saw a sea of people – the sea parted as I drove to my officers making the arrest.

I ordered every officer to arrest anyone fighting, hurling bottles or other disrupting the scene. The other sergeant on second shift, jumped in to coordinate the arrests and transportation to jail.

I called the midnight supervisor, Lt. B.J. Erby, and told him we needed help from everyone on the midnight shift.

Without waiting for officers to show up for roll call, Erby started sending officers as soon as they walked into the station.

Erby and Sgt. Paul Strittmatter showed up to help, as well. Every second and third shift officers on the east side were involved before it was all over. We arrested people until we had control of the area.

"J.C., we will stay just a little bit longer," Erby said, lighting one of his hand-rolled cigarettes. "Everyone must know that we can take the street or area anytime we need to for safety and keep it as long as we need."

And then our deputy chief called on the radio, ordering whoever was in charge to meet him immediately.

Erby offered to take the meeting, but I declined.

"No, I'm the acting lieutenant on second shift and it started with me and is my responsibility," I said.

It was not going to be pleasant.

"Okay. Stop and talk to me after you meet with the deputy chief," Erby said.

I met Culpepper nearby. He was red-faced and said in a loud, emphatic voice, "What did we do to start this incident?"

Equally red-faced, I spit back, "We were doing what cops do. We were making arrests, taking enforcement actions and will continue to do so."

Clearly, that was not what he wanted to hear. Culpepper wasn't finished.

"I want a full report and I will have this investigated," he said before stomping off.

Back at the station, I prepared my response to Culpepper and went to meet Erby.

He had put pen to paper, writing a long commendation letter for myself and the other evening shift sergeant. When I read it, you would have thought that a top general in the military was supporting his men.

"I will send this in now, because you'll need it," Erby said, smiling. He showed me in words and actions that he supported me one hundred percent, as well as any officers that did the right thing, regardless of politics.

After the reviews and screaming, there was no disciplinary action taken. Just commendations.

Sergeant Dub Bransom
The Very Best

Told by J.C. Williams

"I have fought the good fight. I have finished the race. I have kept the faith." 2 Timothy 4, cited in Bransom's obituary.

That was, indeed, D.W. "Dub" Bransom Jr., a salt of the earth Texas lawman who passionately fought for cops and against criminals most of his life.

Dub inspired generations of police with his effective common-sense approach to policing – on the streets and in the ivory towers of administrations. He was one of the most respected and influential supervisors in Fort Worth Police history.

As early as I can remember, Dub was present in my life – a benevolent father figure, a keen mentor as I cut my teeth as a Fort Worth police officer and a stalwart friend to both me and my dad.

He was brilliant, tough, relentless and a trailblazer in everything he did. Dub and my father were solely responsible for critical undercover narcotics innovations.

Dub had a strong "right and wrong" code and heaven help you if you crossed it, it didn't matter whether you were criminal or cop.

There wasn't a task Dub wouldn't do, even if it was assigned out of anger or revenge. Hell, he even decorated the results with sprinkles and a cherry on top.

A Fort Worth native, Dub joined the Fort Worth Police Department in 1966, quickly distinguishing himself among his peers. He and three other officers were ushered into the Special Investigations unit.

"We were the clean guys that didn't have any record," Dub said. "They told us we were going down there and instructed us not to talk to anybody. Everything we did was on our own. We were supposed to stay clean."

Within a year or two, Dub made sergeant and Williams planned a surprise for him – he and a handful of his biggest cohorts were making sure Dub commemorated his promotion properly.

Dub, he said, was getting three stripes tattooed on his butt. Dub vehemently disagreed and threatened the tattoo artist with bodily harm. "You ought to appreciate your stripes there," Williams laughed. Dub didn't get the tattoo.

Dub flourished in patrol with his commonsense approach to policing. The times were violent, with anti-establishment groups and mobs targeting anyone wearing a uniform.

A sniper killed Fort Worth Police Officer Edward Belcher in October 1971 because, he later said, he just wanted to kill a cop. Belcher was one of 25 officers working outside of the Electric Circus nightclub on south Riverside Drive that night following another shooting.

An angry crowd threw bottles and rocks at the officers. Then a rifle shot, thought to have been fired from the roof of a restaurant across the street, felled Belcher, Dub said. The gunman was 18 years old.

After Belcher was killed, Dub was placed in charge of that district, over his protestations.

He sat one night at Berry and Riverside and watched 800-1,000 people evolve into a mob in that parking lot at any given time. If police appeared, "blocks and bottles would start flying." Dub decided "that was enough of that shit."

He brought four other district sergeants together, elicited help from vice and narcotics and all available detectives to surround the area. "We're going to work until the damn parking lot is empty," Dub vowed. Four transport vehicles stood at the ready.

"You don't back off from anything," he said. "It was zero tolerance."

"We were fighting like urban warfare here with all the dopeheads and (anti-government groups)," Dub said. The groups turned their hate against undercover narcotics and vice officers at one point.

"They had an underground newspaper that had all our pictures in it, our home addresses, our phone numbers," he said. "My house got broke into twice."

His success didn't come without hiccups along the way.

Sometimes as a midnight supervisor, he would go to "choir practice" with men involved with the police officers' association in his district. Few liked or respected the current police chief, A.J. Brown, and they wanted him gone. Somehow, in 1977, Dub ended up being the man to deliver the association's no-confidence petition to the chief.

Within a few hours, Dub's phone was blowing up. His deputy chief ordered him to headquarters – Dub made sure they paid him for his off-time – and refused to tell him why. All he was told was the police chief wanted him in the office. Like now.

When Dub finally sauntered into headquarters, he eventually was ushered into Brown's office.

"He comes around and sits on the corner of his desk and he said, 'I'm tired of you bad-mouthing me and my administration. You're going to the goat farm,' " the chief said.

"I said, 'What?' " Dub said.

"GET OUT OF MY OFFICE!" Brown yelled at him.

"Well, what do you want me to do?" Dub asked.

" 'I want you to go to the goat farm. Now, get out of here,' he said to me," Dub said. "I come out and I'm thinking, "What in the hell is going on? Why am I going to the goat farm?"

Police called it the Goat Farm – it was a neglected, run-down rehabilitation facility operated by the city and staffed by the police department. If you were sent to the Goat Farm, you were in big trouble with the brass

Still clueless about what he'd done to deserve the assignment, Dub went to the jail. He was told simply that they needed a supervisor for the handful of tenants at the facility. A friend, jail Capt. B.J. Kirkpatrick, told him to go to the farm and he'd find out what prompted the drastic move.

Within an hour, Kirkpatrick called him. "Well, you got a budget of about $565 to run the goat farm. Do what you need to with that and go from there.

"They're mad at you over a petition," he said.

"I sat there so utterly depressed. For 12 years, I'd been on the department and never even had a reprimand.

"I was sitting there so mad, I didn't know what to do," Dub said. "That's when I started building. … Of course, them poor old guys out there. Pitiful. All of them were disabled."

The sergeant ordered a crew in to demolish much of the facility, clean the lumber for future use, burn 12-year-old piles of clothes, replace counters and lay tile. Residents showered and slept on new mattresses.

"They ain't laying in bed all day now. They're going to get up and go to work, doing something," Dub said.

"Next thing I know, we had a real deal going on out there," he chortled. "And I built me an office out of the stuff out there. I had the weed man come out there and build me a rose garden outside the window."

Two city council members visited the Goat Farm and laughed themselves silly.

"Brown thinks he's messing with you?!? You've got a better office than he does," one of them told Dub.

"We made the Goat Farm t-shirts and bought a whole new recreation area off the proceeds of those t-shirts," he said.

Then one day, boredom hit Dub. He was with a couple of residents that he laughingly referred to as his aides-de-camp.

"We're going to have a Goat Farm Olympics out here," he told them, as surprised as they were.

He envisioned contests like fire building and chili cook-offs, competitions like wine bottle throwing and goat roping. They would invite people from similar facilities in Houston and Dallas.

"They were all for it. 'We'll come over there and have the first annual Wino Olympics,' " he recalled.

Somebody told Brown about it.

He called Dub.

"What is this shit?" said the chief, already torqued about the Goat Farm's success with Dub behind it.

"You know what it is. We're going to do something out here," Dub said. "We're going to put the farm on the map."

"You're not doing anything else," Brown said. "You're coming back to patrol here and come back to the office."

Dub said he was happy where he was.

One of Brown's deputies piped in: "No, you're coming off that goat farm. You've caused enough problems out there. It's embarrassing. Everywhere we go, everybody's talking about the damn goat farm."

"Well, you put me out there." Dub calmly reminded him.

Negotiations began and Dub got everything he wanted – the same patrol sector with the same crew, with weekends and Mondays off. And he got it in writing.

Police Chief Brown left the department in April 1978.

Over the next few years, Dub once again distinguished himself as an outstanding leader, mentoring another generation of police officers, me included.

Because of his outstanding results, Dub was chosen to lead his patrol crew to work high crime areas. In the early 1980s, robberies and homicides surged.

"This is out of control. We've got to do something," Dub told us.

We moved over to the east side of downtown to do it. It went from at least 30 robberies a month to none within a month's time. It was zero tolerance.

We were lucky we weren't killed during that time. Federal agents learned someone was planning on putting hits out on us.

The most effective crime-fighting starts at the officer-sergeant-lieutenant level – that is where most crime is stopped and where cases are fought. It's where you make the stand.

Dub's knowledge and manner passed down to his officers. Many rose through the ranks, carrying that information with them.

Though Dub was president of the police officers association and chairman of the police retirement board, he outgrew the Fort Worth Police Department and retired in 1983. He didn't stop being a lawman, however.

There was an unsuccessful election bid to become Tarrant County Sheriff and then, in August 1990, Dub was hired as police chief for the small suburban city of River Oaks. While there, he was able to get incentive pay for officers and upgraded computers.

Six years later, Dub was appointed as U.S. Marshal for North Texas.

The interview for the job, Dub said, brought up things from his past with J.C. Williams.

"There was a rumor J.C. had buried someone at a construction site," he said. "They wanted to know about that. I told them there were always rumors about J.C. and I didn't know anything about that."

Dub served seven years as marshal. Even then, he wasn't done.

He won an election in 2004 to become Tarrant County Precinct 4 Constable, a feat he repeated twice more. Citing his declining health, the 79-year-old lawman retired on Dec. 31, 2016.

In August 2019, this innovative trailblazer and mentor to scores of police officers died.

He was buried in Oakwood Cemetery, the final resting place for many law enforcement officers from Fort Worth's history.

Getting Promoted

Told by L.E. "Spider" Webb

I always laugh when I think of my "promotion ceremonies," as I rose through the ranks.

In those days, at least for me, there was no fanfare or ceremony attached to promotions. My first promotion to detective was showing up in the chief's office and listening to an inspirational speech. Then we swore to do our best.

I didn't take the promotion tests for noble reasons such as leading officers. For me, it was the only way to get a pay raise, at the time. The police association tried to get collective bargaining passed in an election, but it failed. Officers went several years without a pay raise as a result. It was the city's way of letting us know they were in charge.

When I made sergeant, I received a memo to be in the chief's office to get my new badge. Another officer, David Eurto, was to be promoted at the time. We showed up outside the chief's office at the appointed time.

But we saw no one around – no office staff, no officers, no brass. All the office doors were closed, so we waited. I decided to head into internal affairs to ask what was going on.

Eurto wouldn't walk across the threshold of internal affairs, so I walked in and talked with one of the investigators. Some nut had been threatening to shoot up the police building and that explained the absence of people. He suggested I knock on the chief's door.

I returned to the chief's office and knocked. Someone hollered to come in. Now, the chief's office on the second floor had an entire wall of windows on the south side. A voice from behind the desk told us to "get down."

Eurto and I dropped to the floor and then Police Chief Herbert Hopkins appeared from behind his desk on his hands and knees. He told us of the threats to shoot up the office, gave us a truly inspiring speech and gave us our new gold sergeant's badges with the accompanying paperwork. It ended with a prayer from Hopkins and we crawled our way out of the desk.

"What was that," Eurto asked me when we were outside.

We both had our badges in hand and I told him it was our promotion and we needed to leave.

I kept my promise to Hopkins and did the best I could. A few years later, I was fortunate enough to be promoted to lieutenant and received the coveted increase in pay that accompanied the rank.

That time, I accepted my badge from Police Chief Thomas Windham in a pseudo-ceremony in the Memorial Room at police headquarters. It wasn't as interesting as the earlier one, but I still welcomed it.

The Compassionate Sergeant

Told by J.C. Williams Jr.

Before police departments espoused a more humane approach to their employees, some supervisors were hard-core officers from the 1950s who embraced more of "suck it up and deal with it" attitude. To say they were characters is being kind.

Personal problems and family needs had no place in the workplace, nor would they be tolerated, according to these good ol' boys.

For example, my pregnant wife called me at work to tell me the baby was coming.

I left work. She was in labor all night and well into the next day before doctors said they needed to do a Cesarean section to bring my son into the world.

Then it was time for me to go back to work. I hadn't slept and called my supervisor to see if I could take one vacation day.

"I didn't know you were pregnant and had a baby. I thought it was your wife that had the baby," came the curt retort. I got one day off.

A few years later, when I worked as a Major Case Unit detective, one of the other guys was going through a messy divorce. He also had a child with special needs and one day he was sick, with his head down on his desk at 8 a.m.

The unit was ready to start the day. Our sergeant, H.L. "Curly" Wyatt, walked over to the officer's desk and yelled at him.

"Let me tell you something! I don't care about your personal problems, your crazy wife, nutty ass kid or whatever is making you sick so get your ass up and get to work," Wyatt said. "If you can't do the job, I will replace you with someone who can do the job."

A kick in the ass was how he operated. The rest of us laughed because it was typical of our sergeant.

When my former partner, Larry Alphin, worked on the fugitive squad, he served a felony warrant on the east side. After a foot chase and a fight, Alphin shot and killed the violent suspect. I assisted on the officer-involved shooting.

At the same time, the department was operating the "Chicken Coop" jail because of prison overcrowding. Officers each had to work a mandatory shift at the Coop to guard inmates. Alphin's scheduled Coop day was the day after his shooting.

Alphin mentioned he had some family activities he wanted to do but Wyatt was still supervisor and he refused to let Alphin change his schedule.

At the time, there was no mandatory days off for the officer after shooting someone while on duty.

I told Alphin I'd try to talk to Wyatt, the last person willing to accommodate any officer's personal needs.

"You need to let Larry off jail duty," I told Wyatt.

"I'm not changing the jail schedule for Alphin and he doesn't need to be off over this shooting, so forget it,'' he said.

I knew I had to be creative.

"Sergeant, I know Larry isn't concerned about his recent shooting and that's the problem," I said. "If the prisoners try some kind of violent breakout or conflict and have weapons, Larry won't hesitate. He'll do what he's supposed to do and won't be scared to kill a dozen if needed to protect others.

"Sergeant, even if it's completely justified, you'll be asked who assigned Larry to jail duty a day after his recent shooting," I continued.

"The perception of this is going to look horrible on you, but I understand this is your decision."
Mind games.

A short time later, Alphin got the day off from jail duty.

Leading by Example

If The Shoe Fits

Told by J.C. Williams Jr.
With help from J.J. Lee

Before the East Division moved to its new building, a few officers and sergeants got into fights to resolve their conflicts.

These fights took place in the basement, in the parking lots and inside the office areas. I know – I broke up a few fights and supervised a few others.

I was sergeant for the Eastside Criminal Investigation section. supervisor. A new captain, B. Ray Armand, had moved to East Division as well.

Armand, who had worked undercover narcotics with my father, was a strong commander who supported his officers. He also wanted everyone to know he was in charge. Armand had a "big" personality, forcing other administrators to avoid conflicts and fights with him. I had worked for him in the past.

I was a popular leader in the division – everyone was my friend and trusted me to help them. Instead of going to the captain, they came to me regularly.

One day, Armand apparently believed it was time to let everyone know who was in charge and it wasn't me.

I was on the phone to someone involved in one of our criminal cases. I'd worn leather slip-on shoes that day and one of my legs was propped on a chair next to my desk.

Armand walked by desk, pulled my shoe off and walked into his office.

He should have known better.

When I finished the call, I walked into Armand's office, that had a door opening directly to the detectives' office. Detectives Rick Ramos and J.J. Lee sat just outside the door working on the computers.

"Captain, where's my shoe?" I asked.

Armand laughed and loudly replied to others could hear, "I don't know, I guess you'll just have to look around."

"Captain, I want my shoe and I want it now!" I stated.

He laughed some more. "Start looking."

"I won't be doing that because I'll just take your shoe," I shot back.
"I don't know about that big boy," he replied sarcastically.

The next thing happened fast.

I grabbed him, turned him upside down and held his legs up in the air with one arm. I pulled his shoe off with my other hand.
Lieutenant Bentley heard the struggle and ran in, saw the captain's legs in the air, then turned and ran out.

As I tossed Armand back behind his desk, I said, "When you find my shoe, I'll be glad to give you yours."

I walked past Lee and Ramos, both staring at their computer screens.
"Sergeant, you're going to get fired, but we didn't see a thing," they whispered to me.

A few minutes later, Armand brought me my shoe. I returned his.
"If you want to trade shoes again, just let me know," I said.

Nothing more was said that day.

The next day, I was downtown at police headquarters dropping off paperwork. Police Chief Thomas Windham walked into the hallway and saw me.

"J.C., I need to talk to you," he said, serious. "I'm going to have to get (Internal Affairs) to do an investigation on you. What can you tell me about taking a captain's shoe?"

"What captain's shoe are you talking about?" I said back.

The chief's face turned red.

"J.C., just how many damn captain's shoes do you take around the Fort Worth Police Department?" Windham demanded to know.

"Chief, you can investigate it, but under the same circumstances I would take your shoes," I told him.

He paused.

"You know, J.C., I think you would. I'm not going to mess with your shoes," he said and walked away.

I was not contacted by IAD and I continued to work well with Armand.

15 Minutes?

Told by Kevin Foster

In an earlier, simpler time, sergeants always helped keep their officers out of trouble. This was years before body cameras and technologically advanced equipment. Young officers thought chasing criminals was the greatest sport ever. Few officers would ever disagree.

One night in the late part of the 20th century, several officers chased a car burglar on foot and a very senior sergeant headed to their location to assist them. Before he arrived, the officers broadcast that the suspected burglar was in custody. A few minutes later, they asked for the sergeant to come to the scene.

When he arrived and surveyed the scene, he noticed the suspect, lying in the street, had a broken jaw and his clothes were torn and scuffed up. Needless to say, he couldn't speak. Paramedics were already on the scene treating the injury.

The cops involved in the foot chase huddled together until one approached the sergeant. He asked him if he could leave for about 15 minutes, grab some coffee at the 7-Eleven and then return to the scene with his questions.

A long look took place between the officer and the sergeant.

With a sigh, he said; "Okay, I'll be back in a few minutes."

Upon his return – with coffee, – he asked how the suspect was injured.

The apparent spokesperson for the group of officers looked the sergeant right in the eye and said, "He fell and hit the curb with his face while we were chasing him."

Ten seconds passed without a word.

"It took 15 minutes to come up with that answer?" the sergeant asked? The officer hung his head a little lower and the others had the "Oh, shit!" look on their faces. Silence.

The sergeant broke the silence saying, "That answer works for me, but that took 15 minutes?" There was a look of relief all around.

The suspect later refused to talk to the sergeant and no reason was ever found to believe any differently than what the officer said.

The man fell, hitting his face on the curb. No one ever said anything different.

"Big" Joe Bellar
Tough and Committed

Told by J.C. Williams Jr.
With help from Dub Bransom

When I finished training in 1980, Sgt. Dub Bransom made sure I was assigned to him on the city's east side.

I worked with outstanding cops in Bransom's Baker District, many of whom we've already mentioned in other stories. One of the best was "Big" Joe Bellar.

Bellar stood 6-foot-4 and played college football before joining the Fort Worth Police Department. He loved to hunt and fish and was lucky to marry the love of his life, Sgt. Lynn Bellar.

One night at roll call, Bransom told us of numerous complaints he'd received about a shoeshine parlor called Lloyds, that featured illegal gambling, drug dealing, prostitution and even a shooting. Bransom wanted something done.

Because of the high crime in our district, we normally rode two officers to a car. But vacations had lowered our numbers and I was alone. I decided to swing by Lloyds and let everyone know we were watching them. Closely.

One guy, known on the street as a regular drug dealer, pimp and troublemaker – decided he had enough cohorts there to take a stand. He started cursing me and being aggressive.

That ended quickly when I choked him out and arrested him.

One of my friends always makes the point that you don't have to kill all the wolves threatening you; you just have to kill one while the other wolves watch.

None of the dealer's friends came to his rescue. He went to jail.

The next day, Bellar was back from vacation during roll call, he heard about Lloyds. Bransom pointed out that I was not given the proper respect we expected at that time. Bellar got mad.

As soon as roll call ended, Bellar headed to Lloyds, with a big stick he carried in his car. That stick could have been a prop in the move "Walking Tall."

He walked in with his handy stick and loudly announced that criminal activity "stops NOW!"

Bellar wrecked the place, upending tables, crushing chairs and breaking anything else his stick could reach. Understandably, everyone inside fled. He never said a word to any of us.

That put a stop to the madness there for several weeks.

Bransom learned of it with all the details and spoke with me about it. "Well, sergeant, you told us to take care of it. Joe obviously took you very seriously," I said.

We laughed, but Bransom learned he needed to be more careful about what he asked us to do.

The sergeant took several of us to work in the notorious Glass Key area and nearby bars. In a month's time, 30 robberies had occurred there, and crime was increasing.

Bransom reserved the police transportation van each night and led the charge against the criminals. After our first month, crime analysts were stunned. We brought those 30 robberies to zero. The analysts called our work incredible, and our tactics should be implemented city wide.

After his promotion to training officer, Bellar stayed with our district.

One of his rookies, who later would rise to captain, showed signs of being overconfident. Bellar said he needed to take that down a notch. We were happy to help.

Bellar took his rookie, who we'll call Alex, to the Trinity River levee that ran behind the police academy. We often practiced our pursuit driving there. Some areas resembled a tunnel at night with trees and brush on each side of the dirt roads. My partner, Mike Miller, and I knew it well.

Alex and I drove in our respective cars.

I took off with Alex chasing us. With the dust and dirt flying, when we had a large lead, I turned off the car lights and slid into a hidden area. Bellar and his rookie drove right by us. We did this several times, losing them each time. Alex had no idea where we were.

Bellar and Miller were in constant contact over the radio during the pursuit.

We showed Alex what we had done and how we had lost him.
If you're not closer, we told him, you will lose in a pursuit.
Now it was Alex's turn to speed away, hoping to lose us. We heard Bellar repeatedly tell the rookie to go faster.

Finally, Alex said he couldn't get away because he didn't know the roads like we did.

"I know," Bellar said loud enough for us to hear. "But they have been chasing with their car in reverse the whole time!"

Bellar died shortly after he retired. I relish these memories.

Sergeant Naymond James

Sacrifice and Change

Told by J.C. Williams Jr.

Naymond James is a legend within the Fort Worth Police Department.

A Fort Worth native raised on the east side, James was a standout athlete in high school – he was a state champion track star.

But being fleet of foot is not his legacy.

James is recognized for his contribution to minority officers who came after him.

When he joined the police department, he was outstanding and the community loved him. But the job didn't pay enough and in the late 1970s, he was forced to leave policing behind to seek out a higher paying job.

Sgt. Dub Bransom was close friends with James. Bransom was active in the police association, constantly fighting with the city over police pay and benefits.

He asked the young ex-officer to give a speech about pay and problems to the city council. James was happy to help.

Naymond made a dynamic presentation and offered recommendations to the council if they were serious about hiring minority officers to represent the community. He made an impression. Police pay increased immediately that year.

While he celebrated the victory, Naymond still missed being an officer, a job he loved. Fortunately, a man he knew, H.F. Hopkins was named as the new Fort Worth police chief. One day, Hopkins saw Naymond downtown and after a short conversation said to Naymond, "We need you to go to the Fort Worth Training Center because they we are hiring you back". Naymond would then make a dramatic impact on recruitment and training. Also as a supervisor in Narcotics leading a team in successful enforcement, arresting numerous street drug dealers.

As a young officer, I worked with Naymond and was impressed with him. He was a sergeant when I assembled my Weed and Seed team and I had to have him on the team for it to be successful.

Naymond headed our neighborhood "seed" initiatives and was directly responsible for many of the programs implemented to help residents – the surveys, safe havens, the neighborhood job bank and transportation to get people to jobs to name a few things.

Naymond was an integral part of the program's success.

Arthur Conway Howerton

The World's Greatest Detective

Told by Kevin Foster

Any discussion of exemplary leadership at the Fort Worth Police Department must include Arthur Conway "A.C." Howerton.

An outstanding homicide detective who chose compassion and reasoning over brute force to gain confessions, he also spent much of his life crusading for the rights of police officers and firefighters.

When he died in 1969, a local newspaper described Howerton as the "World's Greatest Detective." Editors thought so highly of Howerton and his achievements that they suggested removing the quotation marks.

At the time he retired, Howerton was the department's most successful and well-known detective. The Texas native became the first homicide detective in Fort Worth, a job he held for 31 years.

Howerton and his partner, Det. D.S. Harris handled 950 homicide cases during their first eight years. They solved 949 of those cases.

At 6-foot-4 and 245 pounds, Howerton was a large, imposing man. But he chose not to use his size to pressure suspects. Instead, he improvised and developed his own interrogation techniques. He planned his interviews and nearly always gained a confession by talking and sympathizing with suspects.

Howerton moved to Fort Worth in 1929, followed a year later by his brother, Roland Howerton. Roland Howerton became police chief during the 1950s and was credited with breaking the corruption chain between local gangsters and dirty cops.

But A.C. chose not to promote after achieving detective rank. And he was adept working in "the field." At least five different times, the lawman met armed men and succeeded in disarming them, using just his words.

Early in his career, however, Howerton and another officer surprised two men committing a robbery. A shootout ensued and Howerton was struck in his shoulder. He survived, although the bullets remained in his shoulder.

Howerton fought much of his career for pension benefits for police officers and survivor benefits for their spouses. He said in an interview once that had he died after being shot, "his wife would not even have gotten a bouquet."

In the 1940s, Howerton approached his career as a cop in a different way. He saw the need for healthy insurance benefits, pension benefits, improved working conditions and basic rights for police officers.

The creation of the Fort Worth Employees Retirement Fund was due to him. But soon, the City of Fort Worth refused to comply with Texas law to pay pension benefits to the widows of officers W.O. Whatley and V.P. Howell. Howerton threatened to sue the city, and the city relented, paying the benefits owed to the families.

Howerton also founded the Fort Worth Police Officers Association, becoming the first president. He kept that title until he retired 15 years later. He also helped found the Texas Municipal Police Association and remained active in it well into the 1960s..

Howerton also found a new cause. He helped fight for Texas Civil Service laws and saw them passed, protecting police officers and firefighters from political interference.

Throughout his life, Howerton was known for his leadership, scrupulous honesty, hard work, innovative techniques and tremendous skills as a detective and a police officer.

Every active and retired law enforcement officer working in Texas since the 1940s benefits from Howerton's work.

Both houses of the Texas Legislature issued resolutions celebrating the life of Howerton when he died. Today, the Fort Worth Police Officers Association is housed in the "Howerton Building," named in his honor.

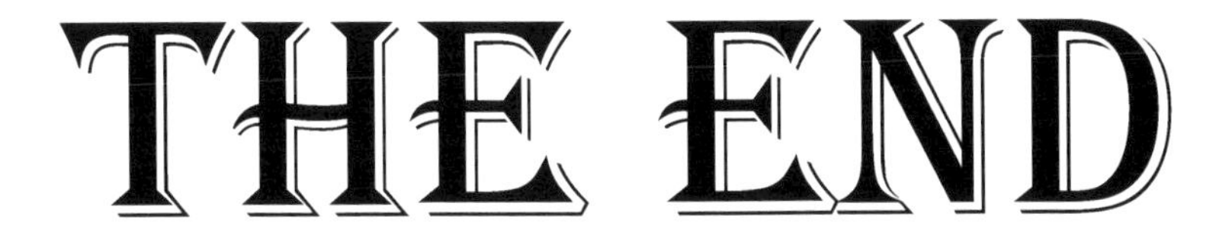

End Notes

[1] [1] Fort Worth Star Telegram, August 1, 1995
Page 1 – "Shooting rampage claims third victim"

[2] [2] Fort Worth Star Telegram, June 14, 2001
Page 1 – "Man executed for killing baby –
he said he regretted firing on family"

[3] Fort Worth Star Telegram June 18, 1995
Page 1, "Scholar's downward spial ends in betrayal, bizarre death"

[4] "Texas Death Index, 1964-1998," ,
Bobby Palomino, Tarrant, Texas, United States December 2014),
Date of death, August 31, 1985

[5] Fort Worth Star-Telegram - January 8, 1982 - page 1
"Dog Brings Home head of woman"

[6] Fort Worth Star-Telegram - January 9, 1982 - page 26
"Tentative identification of body made"

[7]Fort Worth Star-Telegram - April 12, 1982 - page 11
"Police Think Black deaths are related"

[8] Fort Worth Star Telegram March 20, 1990
Page 1 – "At first wine silenced a homeless man's "voices"
But then it took something stronger."

[9] IBID
[10] Fort Worth Star Telegram, April 24, 1982 page 21
"Oklahoman charged in transient slaying."

[11] Fort Worth Star Telegram, April 2, 1990
Page 1 and page 9
"Student playing Russian Roulette shoots himself"

[12] Fort Worth Star Telegram, Feb 12, 1975
Page 6A
"Confessed slayer gets psychiatric exam"

[13] Fort Worth Star Telegram, Feb 28, 1996
Page 1
"Tarrant Man's execution ends 21 Death Row years."

[14] Fort Worth Star Telegram, August 28, 1974 – Page 14-A
"2 FW Officers Fired – Raid Inquiry Grows"

[15] Fort Worth Star Telegram, April 1, 1975 Page 1
"Jury Gives Miller 70-year sentence"

[16] Fort Worth Star Telegram,
June 11, 1986Page 26
"He's not most wanted now"

[17] Los Angeles Times
March 29, 1987
"Cleared after 12 years on the run: Fugitive and
victim both did time for Texas Crime"

[18] Fort Worth Star Telegram September 14,1982
"Bellville escapee nabbed in Fort Worth"

[19] Fort Worth Star Telegram, August 2, 1986
Page A29, "Woman Chooses Poor Business site"

[20] *Outlaw motorcycle gangs – USA overview* Archived 23 January 2022 at the Wayback Machine National Institute of Justice (1991) *"Archived copy" (PDF). Archived from the original on 23 January 2022.*

[21] Fort Worth Star Telegram April 24, 1986
Page 1 – "12 jailed in probe of prostitution ring"

[22] Fort Worth Star Telegram, August 9, 1986
Page 30 – "X-rated films lead to arrests"

[23] Fort Worth Star Telegram
April 5, 1993, page 11
"Suspect in slaying arrested – man apprehended after
chase from Fort Worth to Dallas and south to Waco"

[24] Fort Worth Star Telegram
Feb 18, 1990, Page29
"Man Shot after Auto Accident"

[25] Fort Worth Star Telegram
May 26, 1994, Page 1
"Jury turns tables on felon who sued for $1.7 million"

[26] IBID

[27] Fort Worth Star Telegram
May 17, 1990, Page 1 and 6
"2nd shooting called Dice-game Copycat"

[28] Fort Worth Star Telegram
May 15, 1990, page 1 & 8
"Gunmen Kill Four at Café"

[29] Fort Worth Star Telegram
May 13, 1996, page 1
"Officers trip yields key to solving '90 Slayings"

[30] Dallas Morning News July 8, 1919
"Mutilated Head of man found in pile of rubbish"

[31] 1 Fort Worth Star-Telegram

Family Secrets – Oswald's were questioned for days in Arlington"

November 22, 1993, Page 11

By Mike Cochran

[32] IBID

[33] Fort Worth Star Telegram Aug 16, 1981, P 13 - "Reporters remember Oswald in casket"

[34] Bartlesville Police Department Recovery Report, "Courtesy of Fort Worth History Center, J.D. Roberts Papers".

[35] Fort Worth Star Telegram - January 20, 1981, page 12B - "Marguerite Oswald joins Lee in family burial plot.

[36] Fort Worth Star Telegram
January 19, 2011, Page B01

[37] The Daily Ardmoreite Ardmore, Oklahoma
Thursday, December 22, 1960
"OFFICER KILLED IN GUN FIGHT WITH BURGLAR - FORT WORTH THUG DIES FROM WOUNDS"

[38] Fort Worth Star-Telegram –
February 13, 1962 - page 1
"City man gets life sentence in Oklahoma"

[39] 384 P.2d 54 (1963)
Jerry Milo BROWN, Plaintiff in Error,
v. The STATE of Oklahoma,
Defendant in Error.
No. A-13209.
Court of Criminal Appeals of Oklahoma.

July 17, 1963.

[40] Fort Worth Star-Telegram
November 17, 1982 Fort Worth, Texas Page 23
"Shooting at local club ruled a homicide"

[41] Fort Worth Star Telegram – page 13
February 12, 1923
"Well Aimed Shot makes policeman head lion tamer"

42

FBI Law Enforcement Bulletin (LEB) March 2017
Perspective: Embracing the spiritual dimension of law enforcement

[43] Fort Worth Star Telegram November 18, 1992
Page 19 "Serving Notice – No More Drugs"

[43] Fort Worth Star Telegram, October 20, 1993
Section A Page 26
"Police image depends on who is speaking"

[43] Fort Worth Star Telegram, October 20, 1993
"Ministers, residents tell Fort Worth council they back police"

[43] Fort Worth Star Telegram
November 10, 1994, Page 1
"2 Fort Worth Officers Shot in Drug Raid –
Victims manage to wound suspect"

[43] Fort Worth Star Telegram September 30, 1988
Section 1, page 18
"The Ivory Investigation"

[44] Fort Worth Star Telegram, October 20, 1993
Section A Page 26
"Police image depends on who is speaking"

[45] Fort Worth Star Telegram, October 20, 1993
"Ministers, residents tell Fort Worth council they back police"

[46] Fort Worth Star Telegram
November 10, 1994, Page 1
"2 Fort Worth Officers Shot in Drug Raid –
Victims manage to wound suspect"

[47] Fort Worth Star Telegram September 30, 1988
Section 1, page 18
"The Ivory Investigation"

Oswald Notes:

1 Fort Worth Star-Telegram
Family Secrets – Oswald's were questioned for days in Arlington"
November 22, 1993, Page 11
By Mike Cochran
2 IBID
3 Dallas Morning News
Dec 1, 2017
By Charles Scudder
4 Fort Worth Star Telegram
Aug 16, 1981, P 13
"Reporters remember Oswald in casket"
5 IBID
6 Fort Worth Star Telegram
November 26, 1967
Page 24-A

"Tombstone theft easy, youths say
7 Bartlesville Police Department
Recovery Report,
"Courtesy of Fort Worth History Center,
J .D. Roberts Papers".
8 Fort Worth Star Telegram
November 29, 1967, page 36
"Charges may be filed in marker theft"
9 November 21, 2017, | Fort Worth Star-Telegram (TX)
Author/Byline: Bud Kennedy, Star-Telegram
10 Fort Worth Star Telegram
December 6, 1967, page 17
11 Dallas Morning News
October 5, 1981, Page 3
12 Fort Worth Star Telegram
January 20, 1981, page 12B
"Marguerite Oswald joins Lee in family burial plot.
13 Fort Worth Star Telegram
January 19, 2011, Page B01

14 Fort Worth Star Telegram
January 30, 2015, Page 1

BIBLIOGRAPHY

Publications:

[47]Fort Worth Star Telegram
Feb 18, 1990, Page29
"Man Shot after Auto Accident"

Fort Worth Star Telegram
May 26, 1994, Page 1
"Jury turns tables on felon who sued for $1.7 million"

Fort Worth Star Telegram
May 17, 1990, Page 1 and 6
"2nd shooting called Dice-game Copycat"

Fort Worth Star Telegram
May 15, 1990, page 1 & 8
"Gunmen Kill Four at Café"

Fort Worth Star Telegram
May 13, 1996, page 1
"Officers trip yields key to solving '90 Slayings"

Fort Worth Star Telegram
April 5, 1993, page 11
"Suspect in slaying arrested – man apprehended after chase from Fort Worth to Dallas and south to Waco"

Fort Worth Star Telegram, October 20, 1993
Section A Page 26

"Police image depends on who is speaking"

Fort Worth Star Telegram, October 20, 1993
"Ministers, residents tell Fort Worth council they back police"

Fort Worth Star Telegram
November 10, 1994, Page 1
"2 Fort Worth Officers Shot in Drug Raid –
Victims manage to wound suspect"

Fort Worth Star Telegram September 14,1982
"Bellville escapee nabbed in Fort Worth"

Fort Worth Star Telegram April 24, 1986
Page 1 – "12 jailed in probe of prostitution ring"

Fort Worth Star Telegram, August 2, 1986
Page A29, "Woman Chooses Poor Business site"

Fort Worth Star Telegram, August 9, 1986
Page 30 – "X-rated films lead to arrests"

Fort Worth Star-Telegram –
February 13, 1962 - page 1
"City man gets life sentence in Oklahoma"

Fort Worth Star-Telegram
November 17, 1982 Fort Worth, Texas Page 23
"Shooting at local club ruled a homicide"

Fort Worth Star Telegram – page 13
February 12, 1923

"Well Aimed Shot makes policeman head lion tamer"

Fort Worth Star-Telegram - January 8, 1982 - page 1
"Dog Brings Home head of woman"

Fort Worth Star-Telegram - January 9, 1982 - page 26
"Tentative identification of body made"

Fort Worth Star-Telegram - April 12, 1982 - page 11
"Police Think Black deaths are related"

Fort Worth Star Telegram, August 1, 1995
Page 1 – "Shooting rampage claims third victim"

Fort Worth Star Telegram, June 14, 2001
Page 1 – "Man executed for killing baby –
he said he regretted firing on family"

Fort Worth Star Telegram March 20, 1990
Page 1 – "At first wine silenced a homeless man's "voices"
But then it took something stronger."

Fort Worth Star Telegram, April 24, 1982 page 21
"Oklahoman charged in transient slaying."

Fort Worth Star Telegram, April 2, 1990
Page 1 and page 9
"Student playing Russian Roulette shoots himself"

Fort Worth Star Telegram June 18, 1995
Page 1, "Scholar's downward spial ends in betrayal, bizarre death"

Fort Worth Star Telegram, Feb 12, 1975
Page 6A

"Confessed slayer gets psychiatric exam"

Fort Worth Star Telegram, Feb 28, 1996
Page 1
"Tarrant Man's execution ends 21 Death Row years."

Fort Worth Star Telegram, August 28, 1974 – Page 14-A
"2 FW Officers Fired – Raid Inquiry Grows"

Fort Worth Star Telegram, April 1, 1975 Page 1
"Jury Gives Miller 70-year sentence"

Fort Worth Star Telegram,
June 11, 1986Page 26
"He's not most wanted now"

Fort Worth Star Telegram September 30, 1988
Section 1, page 18
"The Ivory Investigation"

Fort Worth Star Telegram November 18, 1992
Page 19 "Serving Notice – No More Drugs"

Los Angeles Times
March 29, 1987
"Cleared after 12 years on the run: Fugitive and
victim both did time for Texas Crime"

"Texas Death Index, 1964-1998," ,
Bobby Palomino, Tarrant, Texas, United States December 2014),
Date of death, August 31, 1985

The Daily Ardmoreite Ardmore, Oklahoma
Thursday, December 22, 1960

"OFFICER KILLED IN GUN FIGHT WITH BURGLAR - FORT WORTH THUG DIES FROM WOUNDS"

Jerry Milo BROWN, Plaintiff in Error,
v. The STATE of Oklahoma,
Defendant in Error.
No. A-13209.
Court of Criminal Appeals of Oklahoma.
384 P.2d 54 (1963)
July 17, 1963.

Dallas Morning News July 8, 1919
"Mutilated Head of man found in pile of rubbish"

Fort Worth Star Telegram
December 23, 1993, Page 1
"Policeman Struck by DWI Suspect"

Fort Worth Star Telegram
December 24, 1993, Page 13
Test shows man drunk in accident"

Fort Worth Star Telegram
December 23, 1993, Page 1
"Policeman Struck by DWI Suspect"

Fort Worth Star Telegram,
December 28, 1993, Page 1
"Fort Worth officer hit by DWI suspect dies"

Fort Worth Star Telegram
December 28, 1993, Page 1
Police Searching for motorist in officer's death"

Fort Worth Star Telegram
December 29, 1993, Page 1
"Suspect in DWI Surrenders"

[47]Fort Worth Star Telegram
December 22, 1994, Page 35
Wrapped in Grief, opened in hope"

Interviews:

Interviews by Kathy Sanders and J.C. Williams Jr.

Hondo Porter , Retired Narcotics Detective, FWPD
April 11, 2018

Dub Bransom – Retired FWPD Sergeant and US Marshal for the Northern District of Texas
April 11, 2018

Jim Hunter, Retired DEA Agent
May 9, 2018

Paul Kratz & David Thornton (Retired Homicide Sergeants - FWPD)
May 10, 2018

Bob Bentley, Retired Police Lieutenant, FWPD
May 25, 2018

Made in the USA
Columbia, SC
19 October 2024

44561172R00159